The Lost Tribe

A Nick Randall Novel

Robert Rapoza

THE LOST TRIBE
by
Robert Rapoza
Copyright © Robert Rapoza 2017

Robert Rapoza
Rancho Palos Verdes, CA 90275

Website: http://www.robertrapoza.com
Email: bob@robertrapoza.com
Email List: https://robertrapoza.com/contact/

Facebook Author Page:
https://www.facebook.com/profile.php?id=100011748994837

First Printing April 2016
Second Printing May 2018

Printed in the United States of America

ISBN-13: 978-1-7323912-6-0

This novel is dedicated to my first and most important fans, my wife Holly, my daughter Heather and my son Ryan. Thank you for supporting me through the ups and downs of writing my first novel. Without your help and inspiration, I might have never finished this book. Whenever I was ready to quit, I could always count on one of you to gently nudge me back to work. This book was a team effort and I love you all for helping me see this dream through to the end.

Chapter One

Peruvian Jungle
July 5, 5:59 p.m.

Dr. Nicholas Randall felt the noose-like effect of the humidity choking the breath from his body. Perspiration slicked down his back like a sudden waterfall forming after a heavy spring rain. The conditions were unbearable, but he pushed onward and ever deeper into the Amazon. Normally, he would have made the trip in the cooler, drier months, but his benefactor had been specific. The trip had to be made immediately, or he'd lose his funding, so Randall and his small group from the University of Lima found themselves slogging through the lush vegetation during the hottest and wettest time of the year. They traveled without speaking, the dwindling sunlight fading through the foliage.

A former Army Ranger and once considered a gifted archeology student, Randall was now deemed an outcast in the field for his controversial theories. Randall believed that someone or something had intervened in the development of the indigenous population and had propelled their technology forward at a staggering rate. He had first conceived the theory as a graduate student on a field assignment over twenty years ago. It had almost destroyed his career. In fact, had it not been for his longtime friend and colleague, Dr. Francisco Andrade, Randall would have been

1

forced out of the field years ago. Only Francisco's support had made this trip possible, and Randall realized that this excursion was his last chance to redeem his reputation.

Now he found himself deep in the rainforest with only his guide, a linguistics expert from the University of Lima, and his two graduate assistants, Phillip Drew and Mike Gomes, in tow. They needed to find the ruins quickly, or they would be forced to make camp in the middle of the jungle before they were consumed by the encroaching darkness. Making matters worse, they had lost contact with their home base days ago and were running low on supplies.

"Finally, there's the entrance up ahead," Ernesto said. A linguistics specialist from the University, Ernesto was clearly uncomfortable being out in the middle of the jungle during the summer. He made no effort to mask his feelings as he swatted a mosquito and threw his pack to the ground.

Randall stopped next to Ernesto, glad to have a chance to rest his aching muscles. Though he had seen tougher conditions while in the service, he had been a much younger man at the time. He wiped the sweat from his short black hair, straining to see the small opening in an otherwise solid wall of jungle plants, but eventually spotted it. The entrance was carved into the solid rock side of a mountain. After days of searching, they had finally arrived.

Amaro Angara, the local guide who had led them to the site, paused, staring into the dark opening. His body language spoke of his reluctance to enter.

"Ernesto, ask Amaro if he's going in." Randall said, the salty taste of dirt and sweat entering his mouth as he spoke.

After a brief exchange, Ernesto replied. "He says it's forbidden for his people to enter the sacred ruins."

2

"Phil and Mike, come with me. Ernesto, wait here with Amaro. We'll scout inside the ruins, then figure out where to set up camp."

The three ventured through the small opening. The passageway wound its way down a twisting ledge, which had been carefully cut into the stony surface. Randall's pulse quickened as he examined the tunnel. He ran his hand along the rock wall, marveling at how the surface felt as smooth as glass. One thought entered his mind: *This wasn't done with primitive tools.*

He stepped back from the wall and shined his light straight down the passageway. He realized that the opening was a perfect square, the corners fitting together with a precision, unlike any he had seen in past ruins. Next, he trained his light on the floor and traced the pathway from the entrance as far as his beam would illuminate. The floor was etched with a repeating diamond pattern and was clear of any dust and debris. Someone was maintaining the tunnel.

Although the Inca had been skilled artisans, Randall knew that this tunnel and what lay inside the mountain weren't Incan remains. A sense of foreboding mingled with his excitement as he realized the enormity of the ruins and their implications. Whoever had built this entrance possessed advanced machining technology.

"Dr. Randall, take a look at this!" Phil called out.

"What is it? Phil, where are you?"

"I'm around the corner. You have to see this!"

Randall turned the corner then immediately stopped. The path led into a single large room with intricately carved

3

symbols on one wall. Darkness enveloped the room, broken only by the beams of their flashlights.

Phil stood next to the wall, his light trained on the strange symbols. He struggled to decipher the writing. "What language do you think this is?"

"I'm not sure." Randall held up his light for a closer look and studied the writing carefully. He traced a finger along the smooth grooves that formed the shapes. Beads of sweat gathered on his temple, and his mouth went dry.

Phil frowned. "It resembles Cuneiform, but that doesn't make sense. How could one group of Incans use a completely different form of writing from the rest of their empire? Besides, Cuneiform was used in southern Mesopotamia, and that's 8,000 miles away. What's going on here, Professor?"

As Phil spoke, Michael entered the room.

"That's a good question, but it's not Cuneiform. The only other place I've seen this language was in the tablet room of Paititi," Randall reflected, remembering the first time he witnessed the great jungle city of Amaro's tribe.

Randall studied the symbols intently. There was something almost familiar about the way they were arranged. They reminded him of something — something so obvious, and yet so elusive, that the professor couldn't put his finger on it. Each symbol was neatly centered in a carved square, almost like …

A distant cracking noise and a horrific scream echoed from the entrance of the ruins.

"What the hell was that?" Phil asked.

Mike keyed his radio. "Ernesto, are you there? Come in, over."

The only reply was static.

"Ernesto, can you hear me?"

Still no reply.

"I can't reach anyone on the radio."

A sound arose from the entrance—shuffling boots and muffled voices. Someone was coming, and the three of them were trapped inside the chamber. The only path out was the way they had come in.

Randall's mind worked feverishly.

"Do you hear that?" Phil asked, cocking his head. He peered around the corner and shone his light down the tunnel. The rocky wall above his head exploded in a hail of gunfire.

Phil ducked his head back behind the corner. "Holy crap, someone tried to kill me! What do we do?"

"Were those gunshots?" Michael asked. Eyes wide.

"Yes! We need to get out of here!"

Randall's mind raced. Either someone had followed them and wanted the contents of the ruins for themselves, or the keepers of the ruins wanted it to remain a secret. Though armed and well trained to respond to a hostile threat, the fact that Phil and Mike were present and had no background in combat, Randall realized their safety rested on his shoulders.

The footfalls were getting louder—the shooters were almost in the chamber.

Randall heard one gunman giving orders to the others. They would be there at any moment.

"I don't want to die here," Phil whispered.

Randall relied on his Ranger training to quiet his mind, blocking out all feelings of fear. He focused on the task at hand, carefully studying the odd symbols etched into the rock face in front of him. He had found most of these symbols in his research and understood them. Based on this and their arrangement here, he deduced the meaning of the others. Though there was no way to confirm his assumption he had to act now.

Randall reached out and tapped the symbols in the order he believed appropriate. The wall folded away from him, revealing an opening in the solid rock. The sudden movement caused Phil and Mike to jump back. Sensing their hesitation, Randall pushed both student assistants through the entrance.

He turned and shined his light. The section of rock had swung inward like a door. "Help me close this!"

The three men pushed with every ounce of strength they could muster. The rock door swung closed. A moment later they heard heavy boot steps entering the outer chamber.

"Where are they?" a voice said from the other side of the wall.

Randall allowed himself a moment to gather his thoughts. He had bought them some time to determine their next steps.

Phil tapped his shoulder. "What do we do now?"

Randall shone his light around the room. Unlike the outer chamber, there was writing on three of the four walls. Randall gestured to it. Phil nodded. The key to their escape was the writing. They were safe for now, but for how long?

Chapter Two

Randall deciphered the writing. He had started with the far-left wall and worked his way around. The symbols were arranged in neat rows, forming large pictographs, like Egyptian Hieroglyphics. He was amazed by the discovery of this inner chamber, but had no time to enjoy it.

Minutes earlier, all activity and sounds had ceased from the outer chamber. Something had happened that caused their pursuers to stop searching for them. As a result, the inner chamber was cast into an eerie quiet.

The silence was broken by a high-pitched, static-filled whistling noise coming from Mike's belt. His radio was still on.

"The sound came from this direction," a voice called out from the outer chamber. The words were followed by pounding on the wall separating the two rooms. Their pursuers had located them.

Phil pointed to Mike's belt. "Your radio!"

Mike switched it off, but it was too late.

"I can hear them. Get the C-4."

Panic replaced concern as Randall raced to decipher the remaining glyphs. He heard the unmistakable sound of several men jogging from the outer chamber.

"Dr. Randall, hurry!" Mike said.

Randall struggled to interpret the strange writing, finding more unfamiliar symbols here than in the outer chamber. He needed more time. "This symbol, I can't figure it out."

The sound of boot steps flooded the outer chamber. "Place the charge here."

A soft thud reverberated through the wall. "Everyone clear out."

"We have to do something!" Phil said.

"Wait," Randall said calmly. "If I'm right about this, we might have a way out of here."

Randall gently pressed against the symbols on the wall. A faint humming sound emanated from somewhere nearby.

"Did you hear ...?" Phil began to say, but before the words were even out, the students and the professor felt the sensation of weightlessness. In a moment's time, their lights went out, and they were engulfed by total darkness.

Chapter Three

Hampton, Virginia
July 5, 11:27 p.m.

As the head of the engineering division of Gemini Orbital Science, a large aerospace company in Virginia, George Walker was used to late nights. Tonight, however, was late, even for him. He scratched his head and looked at his watch: 11:27 p.m. He was tired, but this was an important night. It was so important, in fact, that the CEO of the company personally asked him to meet with this client. Tonight, George was meeting with the man who had ordered $1.2 billion worth of satellites from Gemini Orbital. According to Mr. Crespi, the CEO of his company, their client was in town on business and was leaving the next morning. Tonight was the only time he could meet, and he had asked for Walker personally. As the saying goes, the customer is always right, especially when he's spending a cool $1.2 billion.

Walker stood up from his desk and walked down the long hall that led to Test Bay 2. The moonlight filtered through the window, casting shadows across the hallway. At the angle of the moonlight, Walker's body cast a hideously elongated shadow on the left side wall. He shivered for a moment and immediately felt foolish that he, a fully grown man, could be afraid of the dark. Especially at work. Finally reaching the door, Walker turned the handle and let himself in. He sat down and waited near the fourth and last satellite of his customer's order.

As a firm that made sophisticated componentry and satellites for military and communications applications, Gemini Orbital had several cleanrooms — enclosed spaces in which airborne particulates, contaminants and pollutants are kept within strict limits. Test Bay 2 was the largest cleanroom at the company. This was the room where a team of engineers assembled and tested the latest satellites built for the company's ever-growing list of clients. It was also the home to the final satellite that Walker's team had built for the man he was meeting tonight. Walker was proud of his work, and it had been a long road getting here. As a small boy, he had been sickly, forced to spend most of his time indoors. He had picked up the space exploration bug during the long days stuck inside, reading books about space, while other kids roamed around the neighborhood. Now, he mused about how he had turned a bad situation into the passion of his life.

"Mr. Walker?"

Walker jumped. "Yes? Hello?"

Three figures moved out from the shadows to face him as he stood by his satellite. Two of them were burly men with short-cropped hair and hard, angular features. The third was physically smaller, but walked with great confidence. The lead man had short, neatly combed yellow hair, framing an oval face with tight, firm skin. His hawk-like, sky-blue eyes conveyed an air of authority, bordering on intimidation. Walker immediately assumed he was the client, but the presence of the other men was odd. They were clearly his bodyguards, but why would he need them for a meeting with an engineer? Uneasiness crept into Walker.

"Mr. Walker, I would like to introduce you to Mr. Dumond. He's the one who arranged for you to lead this project," one of the bodyguards said.

Walker stepped forward, extending his hand to greet his guests. Dumond did the same.

"It's nice to meet you," Walker said. "Thank you for making this possible. I can't tell you how pleased we were when you hired our company to build the satellites. I was also very flattered that you asked for me personally."

"You earned it, Mr. Walker, and I can see by this fine satellite that we chose our team leader well." Dumond spoke with an accent, but Walker couldn't place it. Perhaps French?

"Thank you, Mr. Dumond. As you know, this is the last in the series of your four satellites and it's scheduled to be placed into geosynchronous orbit next month. This will give you some redundancy since you only need the three satellites you currently have in place to cover the entire Earth."

"Have all of the arrangements been made for the launch? Is there anything else you'll need to do?"

"We're all set. The i's have all been dotted and the t's have been crossed. Our logistics team is all set to deliver this beauty to the base for launch. All I have left to do is sit back and watch it fly."

"Will your company need you to be present for the launch, Mr. Walker?"

"No, but I'll be there, anyway. Watching one of these go into the sky is the big payoff for all the hard work we put into them. I haven't missed a launch since I started in this business!"

"Well, there's a first time for everything, isn't there?"

"Huh?"

The two men flanking Dumond grabbed each of Walker's arms.

"What the hell are you doing?"

Dumond approached Walker, a large silver gun-like object in his hand.

"What's that thing? Get it away from me!"

A large, strong hand covered Walker's mouth.

"I can't afford to have my investment endangered. Besides, I need your expertise as an energy engineer to help me utilize my new power source." Dumond raised the device to Walker's neck and pushed the trigger. Walker heard a soft hissing sound like air escaping, and then everything went black.

Chapter Four

Arlington, Virginia
July 6, 1:32 a.m.

In the complete darkness of her bedroom, archeologist Dr. Samantha Randall slept soundly in her bed. The stillness was shattered by the ringing of the telephone.

"What time is it?" Sam said groggily.

Searching for her glasses with one hand, she fumbled for the phone with the other. Sam glanced at the clock. 1:32 a.m.

"Who is this?" She asked in a sleepy voice.

"Samantha, is that you?"

Sam struggled to clear the cobwebs from her mind. The voice sounded familiar, but she couldn't quite place it.

"Sam, are you there? It's Francisco."

"I'm here. Do you realize what time it is in my neck of the woods?"

"Sorry to wake you, but I have urgent news about your father."

Sam's heartbeat quickened. "What's going on? Is Dad alright?"

"He disappeared. He was leading an expedition in Peru and was supposed to arrive at the site today. We've been waiting for him to check in with us but haven't heard from him. In fact, I haven't spoken with him in over a week.

We've tried to contact him several times but haven't had any luck. I'm worried, Sam. Your father normally checks in like clockwork."

The news hit Sam like a hard slap to the face. Sam and her father had barely spoken since her mother's death nearly three years earlier. "What can I do?"

"You understand how your father thinks better than anyone. He left some notes at the base station, but we're having a hard time interpreting them. We need you to fly down here to lead a search team to try to find him. We have his starting point and can put you in contact with someone who can help you retrace his path."

Sam sat in the darkness of her room, contemplating the situation.

"Sam, please."

"I'll see what I can do. I have to pack and find a flight. I should be able to catch a plane by the end of the day."

"I booked you on a flight leaving at 6:35 a.m. Time is of the essence; we need to find them quickly. This jungle is unforgiving."

Chapter Five

Sam sat in the business class section of a Boeing 777 bound for Lima. Her seven-hour flight would provide her with plenty of time to think about the many events that had led to this moment and what was to come.

She vividly remembered the last conversation she had had with her father so long ago. She had blamed him for sending her mother to retrieve an artifact from a colleague, an errand from which she would never return. After learning of her mother's death, she had told her father that she never wanted to speak to him again. He had tried on several occasions to reach her and had even asked friends to try to reason with her on his behalf. She hadn't bought any of it. The realization that she may never speak to him again stung her heart and regret washed over her.

They had been a close family—Sam, her younger brother, John, and her parents—but everything changed on that fateful day. Her father was away on yet another of his expeditions, trying to prove his crazy and controversial theory that someone, or something, had helped push along the development of human technology. While he was gone, a colleague had called with important information about his research. He claimed he had something that Sam's dad urgently needed and convinced her mom, Anne, to pick it up for him. Sam remembered speaking to her on the phone right before she left to get the package. Anne was irritated that her husband had gone on the expedition right before their family trip to Italy, but she graciously agreed to pick up his package.

It was a wet, spring evening as she drove home on Route 51. The rain had fallen for days, the roads were slick, and visibility was terrible as wind gusts carried the rain almost sideways. According to witnesses, a semi had been attempting to merge onto the ramp, and the driver hadn't seen Anne's car. The large truck had pushed her sedan off the side of the road and over an embankment. The car had flipped several times before bursting into flames. By the time the EMTs had arrived, there were little more than charred remains.

Sam had blamed her father for going on the trip and causing her mom to go out in such terrible weather to get his stupid package. The last time they spoke had been shortly after the funeral. Her mother's death devastated Sam, and her father seemed like a good target for her frustrations.

Sam knew deep inside that no one was to blame for her mother's death. It had been an accident. She also knew that it was the pain of losing her mother that had caused her to become angry with her father. But now she might lose him, too. It was too much to take, so Sam did the only thing she could do at a time like this; she put her analytical mind to work planning a course of action to find him.

Since Sam's silence had made it clear that she would not answer her father's phone calls or emails, he had begun writing letters to her to let her know what he was doing. At first, she refused to open them, but with time, she relented and began reading the letters. In a small way, knowing what her father was doing gave her comfort. She had read all his letters except for the most recent one, which had sat unopened on her desk. Now, she was on the plane holding that letter and hoping she could find clues about his disappearance.

February 9, 2012

Hi Sweetheart,

I was really hoping to see you before I left on this trip.

Our donor wants us to get started as soon as possible. He didn't say why he was in such a hurry, but I guess I feel the same way given what we're looking for. The elder from the jungle tribe spoke of an ancient city, Paititi, deep in the rainforest where there is some sort of relic. According to the elder, stories have been passed down through several generations that this relic was a gift from the gods. If what the elder has told me is true, it's the key to proving that something altered the course of human development.

Sam, I don't know if I'm just being paranoid, but something doesn't feel right about this trip. I've had the weirdest feeling that someone is watching us as we get ready to go. I don't even know who this donor is that's funding us. When I asked Francisco about him, he said that the donor wanted to keep his identity a secret, but that he thinks very highly of me and is very interested in my research. I guess I was so flattered that I never really questioned why he was so interested. Now I'm beginning to wonder why he chose me and why he's in such a hurry.

I wanted you to know that I have a small safety box at the bank near the airport in Lima. Most of my notes and research in it. You'll find the key to the safety box in this letter. I haven't shared this information with anyone else, and I don't want you to tell anyone about this, not even Francisco. You're the only person I trust.

17

Well, that's it for now. I guess the next time I see you I'll either be famous or out of work!
Dad

A lump formed in the pit of Sam's stomach. Slowly, she lifted the key out of the envelope. Inscribed on it were the words "Banco de la Nación." That's where her dad's safety box must be. She thought it strange that he hadn't wanted Francisco to know about it. They had always been so close, and her dad had always said that he trusted him with his life. Sam squeezed the key, then tucked it safely into a small zippered pocket on her pants. She looked at her watch: 8:27 a.m. She was exhausted, and the day was just beginning. Closing her eyes, she hoped she might get some sleep on the rest of the flight.

Chapter Six

Inside the ruins, Randall slowly began to move again. He rubbed the back of his head and felt a golf-ball sized lump, which ached terribly. His mind slowly cleared, but he struggled to make out his surroundings in the darkness. The last thing he remembered was being in the chamber examining the symbols before everything went black. The symbols had been buttons, and he had activated some sort of trapdoor in the chamber's floor. Still unable to see in the darkness, he heard moaning from nearby.

"Are you guys alright?" Randall asked.

"I think so. What the heck happened?" Phil asked.

Mike groaned. "I think my leg is broken."

Randall reached for the flashlight he kept in his zippered pants pocket. He clicked the switch, and it lit up the dark chamber like a searchlight. It didn't take long for him to find Phil and Mike. Examining Mike, he noted there were no bones protruding through the skin, but his leg had a nasty black and blue bump. Mike was clearly in pain, and winced as Randall examined his leg.

Randall's heart stopped when he heard footsteps on the ceiling above them, followed by the sound of men talking. One of them seemed to be speaking into a radio, reporting back to someone about losing track of Randall and his assistants. He also heard the clicking of metal. Someone had chambered a round into a weapon. In the glow of his light,

Randall held his finger to his lips, letting Phil and Mike know not to make a sound. Slowly, they heard the footsteps exiting the chamber.

"Come on, we need to get out of here before they find us," Randall whispered, motioning to the chamber above them. He grabbed Mike under one arm and pointed for Phil to do the same on the other side. Mike groaned loudly as they lifted him to his feet.

The sound of the person walking above them stopped immediately. Randall clamped his hand over Mike's mouth. They remained frozen, fearful of alerting their pursuer above. Finally, the footsteps left the upper chamber. The trio moved silently forward, trying to find a way out.

"Can we stop for a minute?" Mike grimaced as he spoke. "I don't think I can keep going."

Randall and Phil gingerly set their friend down on the cold, dusty ground, careful not to jostle his injured leg.

"Phil, stay here with Mike. I'm going to look for help or a way out. Do you have a light?"

Phil fumbled through his clothing without luck. His flashlight must have fallen out when they hit the ground under the trap door. Then he felt a heavy rectangular object in one of his pockets. "I have my phone. Give me a minute, yes, I have the flashlight app on it." With a couple touches of the screen, a glowing light appeared around Phil and Mike's face.

Randall handed Phil his backpack. "There's water and food in here. Mike, I have a jacket in there, too. Put it on to stay warm."

"What about you?" Mike asked in protest.

20

"Don't worry about me, I'll be fine. Phil, take care of Mike. I'll be back as soon as I can." Randall handed Phil his side arm.

Phil glanced at the pistol, then to Randall.

"Do you know how to use this?" Randall asked in a hushed tone.

"Not really," Phil replied.

Randall provided some basic weapon instructions, patiently answering Phil's questions. Satisfied that he could now safely operate the gun, he turned to go.

"I'll find help and come back for you. Stay quiet so they don't hear you," Randall nodded to the ceiling, then left.

Chapter Seven

Lima, Peru
July 6, 1:47 p.m.

It was mid-afternoon, and the bright sun shone through the large windows as Sam exited the plane into the airport. Passengers streamed through the terminal and into the arms of loved ones waiting for them. As she looked around, it took her only a moment to spot the sign with her name.

"Hello, Professor," the man holding the sign said as she approached. "My name is Domingo Sanchez and I will be driving you to the University of Lima to meet Dr. Andrade."

"Thank you, but I need to make a stop before we go to the campus. Can you take me to the Banco de la Nación?"

"Of course, but may I ask why? Dr. Andrade is very anxious to see you."

"I need to exchange money for this trip. In my rush to get here, I forgot to in D.C."

"But they have this service here at the airport. Can you just exchange it here?" Domingo pointed out the obvious to Sam.

"I would feel better doing it at a bank. I know it sounds funny, but my father always taught me to go where the locals conduct their business."

"Of course, Professor, I'm at your service. May I take your bags?"

"Thank you."

The trip to the bank was a short, seven-minute drive, directly along Av Javier Prado Este. They passed through an area that was a mixture of commercial buildings intermingled with open space. Having never been to Lima before, Sam enjoyed the view as they sped past the Parque Pallardelli. Domingo pulled up to the bank and opened the door for her. "Do you need help with translation?"

"No thank you," Sam said. "My Spanish is pretty good, and I'm looking forward to getting more practice."

She exited the car and stepped onto the sidewalk, which was packed with people milling about. The Lima business district was like other major metropolitan areas, with large buildings lining each side of the road. Businessmen and women wearing suits and skirts walked down the sidewalks conversing about the latest office gossip and big deals they were working on.

To the right of the car, she saw the bank from her father's letter. It was concrete and glass, built in a very utilitarian fashion. Sam entered the front door and walked up to the business teller.

"Hola, cómo pueda le ayudo?" The teller asked, inquiring how she could help.

"I need your help with a safety deposit box." Sam held out her father's key.

"You're American, okay." The teller switched to English. "Is this the key to your box?"

"Yes, and I'd like to get it, please." Sam's outward calmness belied her nervousness.

23

The teller typed at her keyboard. Her expression changed to a somber look. "According to our records, this box belongs to Dr. Nicholas Randall. Do you have ID?"

"Of course." Sam retrieved her license from her purse. "Dad asked me to pick it up for him. I'm on my way to meet him at the University." Sam handed the ID to the teller, who looked momentarily confused.

"Is there a problem?"

"No, this is fine," the teller said, handing the card back to Sam. "Come this way." She motioned for Sam to follow her to the back of the bank where the safety deposit boxes were located. The two walked down a long flight of stairs. To Sam, it had the distinct feeling of walking deep into the catacombs of an underground tomb. The lack of windows only fueled the feeling.

At the bottom of the stairs, there was a locked gate. Which the teller unlocked. Both women walked in. The room's walls were comprised of rectangular boxes, some large and some small. The teller stopped in front of a small one. "This is your safety deposit container. Just push the buzzer when you're done."

Sam set the box down on the counter and took a deep breath. "Here goes nothing."

She opened the box, and her eyes immediately caught sight of a hard-bound leather notebook. Her father's journal. She lifted it gingerly from the box and opened it, flipping through the pages. There were notes, diagrams, and maps, all written and drawn in her father's handwriting. She unzipped her backpack and slipped the book into the main compartment.

Thinking that the box was now empty, she began to close it when something else caught her eye — a beautiful necklace. It was on a thick-linked gold chain, which was looped through an intricately carved medallion. She picked it up and looked at it more closely. Her eyes were immediately drawn to the outside of the medallion, which had unevenly spaced notches around its perimeter. She ran her fingers over them, noting their squared ends. She then observed strange writing on its outer edge, circling it in a band much like the writing on a coin. Sam had never seen writing like this before. In the middle of the medallion was a square box with a round jewel in the middle. The box consisted of small rectangles stacked upon each other like a wall. It reminded Sam of the all-seeing eye on the back of a one-dollar bill. The jewel was a beautiful light blue and seemed to be inset into the wall.

She slipped the medallion into her backpack, closed the box, and rang the buzzer.

In a short time, the teller reappeared. "Can I be of further assistance?"

"No, I'm done, thank you."

Back in the University's car, Sam thought about her dad's journal and the strange medallion. Was it a gift? Sam dismissed the notion. Clearly, the medallion played a role in her father's research, but what? Was there a hidden message in the writing? Who had it belonged to and where had he found it? It was like a big puzzle, and not only did Sam not know where the pieces went, she didn't even know what pieces she had, and which were missing.

"Here we are, Dr. Randall." Domingo's voice seemed to be speaking to her from another dimension. "Dr. Andrade is waiting inside for you."

Samantha looked up the steps of the main administration building and was impressed by the structure. It appeared quite old, constructed with neatly carved stone blocks. The design was clearly an example of old Spanish architecture and was unlike anything Sam had seen back home. She walked up the steps and opened the heavy wooden door.

Francisco was standing in the hallway speaking to a young lady wearing glasses when he saw Sam.

"Samantha!" Francisco wrapped her in a big bear hug. He was a huge man, six-foot-four and a bit bigger in the waist than the last time she had seen him. "It's so good to see you!"

"Thanks, Francisco, it's good to see you, too. You haven't changed a bit," Sam lied. Age had clearly paid a visit to her friend. Aside from putting on a few pounds, his hair was gray and thinning. He also had deep wrinkles on his forehead, undoubtedly from years of stress caused by supporting her father's unpopular theories. He had really been good to her dad and had clearly paid a price for supporting him.

"Thank you, dear. You must be tired after your flight. Let's get your bags and sit down to talk. Domingo, please get Dr. Randall's bags and bring them to my office."

"Of course, Dr. Andrade." Domingo smiled kindly.

"My office is this way, Samantha."

Francisco led her down the ornate marble hallway into a spacious office decorated with exotic relics from around the world. Francisco had a beautiful mahogany desk, hand-carved by a master craftsman. It must have been worth a small fortune. Apparently, being the Vice President of Academic Affairs for the University had its privileges.

"How was your flight?" Francisco asked.

"It was good, but a little long. Francisco, what happened to my dad?" Samantha wasn't wasting any time with small talk.

Francisco took a deep breath and sighed. His dark brown eyes looked deeply into Sam's. "Sam, what do you know about your father's research?"

"I know that he was trying to prove his alternate theory of human technological development in this area. I know that he made multiple trips here over several years to study a tribe in the jungle. He had been trying to find some temple in the jungle that he believed held the key to proving his theory and had finally convinced the elders to take him to the temple."

"You have most of the story, but you're missing a few big pieces. Your dad probably didn't go into detail about the tribe, did he?"

Sam drew her head back, confused by Francisco's statement.

"What about the tribe?"

Francisco looked squarely into Sam's eyes.

"A wealthy donor provided funding for your dad to conduct research on a local tribe not far from here. He had made several visits to them and was hoping to learn more about their ancestry."

"Who was the donor and why was he interested in my dad's research?"

"I don't know. He, or she, wanted to remain anonymous, but whoever it was believed in your father."

"Go on."

"There was something special about the tribe. They were unique, physically."

Sam cocked her head to the side; she wasn't sure what was coming next.

"The tribe is known as the Capanhuaco, and your father was the first person to meet them. They are about four feet tall and have abnormally large, close-set eyes. Their noses are very small—almost nothing more than two slits in the front of their faces, and they have larger than average heads. Compared to their bodies, their head size is off the chart. We had a doctor confidentially examine several of the Capanhuaco, and their internal organs are fairly like our own, except their lungs are larger. He wasn't sure why, but believed it allows them to spend large amounts of time underwater or in areas that are not well ventilated."

"What has this got to do with what happened to Dad?"

"The ruins that your father was searching for are sacred to the Capanhuaco. Outsiders are expressly forbidden from entering them. According to legend, their ancestors foretold of a Great Reunification with their brethren living deep within the mountain. When this event occurs, the two tribes will unify and travel back to their ancient homeland."

"What's the name of these ruins?"

"Actually, they're not ruins. The underground city your dad was looking for is Vilcabamba."

"There's an underground city?"

Andrade nodded. "The prophecy also says that the Great Reunification will be announced by the physical upheaval of the land that will grow so enormous, it will eventually destroy Vilcabamba and the Capanhuaco's jungle home, Paititi. About two years ago, earthquakes started occurring near Paititi. They've become more frequent and now occur daily, sometimes happening two or three times a day. Your father believes it's a sign that the Great Reunification is nearly at hand."

Sam listened intently, watching Francisco's eyes for signs he might be lying. He wasn't.

"We're not sure why, but the tribe needs someone's help to make the prophecy come true. Without this help, the Reunification can never take place. That's the reason they agreed to take your father to Vilcabamba."

"Is that where he was going when he disappeared?"

"Yes. And according to the stories the Capanhuaco shared, their ancestors had an exceptionally advanced technological society. Everything about them defies conventional human development theory. They were far too advanced for their time in history, having built a huge underground civilization with roads, large buildings, heating and... even lighting."

"Excuse me?"

Francisco pursed his lips and let out a deep sigh. "Based on discussions with the elders, the underground city has electricity."

Samantha sat back in her chair, blinking her eyes. She felt like a boxer who had just taken a right cross to the jaw. In all his letters, her dad had never mentioned any of these details about this odd tribe. Why? This was one of the most incredible discoveries of their time, and her dad hadn't mentioned a word about it to her.

"So, you're trying to tell me that a civilization that's, what, 1,500 or 2,000 years old, has electricity?" Sam asked, her voice straining.

"We carbon dated the tablets that contained the ancient texts and put their age at 4,000 to 5,500 years," Francisco replied.

Sam was stupefied, unable to respond to what she was being told. Every ounce of her scientific being was unable to grasp her colleague's words. If anyone else would have told her these things, she would have dismissed them as the ramblings of a demented individual. But this was Dr. Francisco Andrade, one of the most distinguished and published archaeologists in the world. He was respected, and even revered, in his field. He was also the best friend her father had ever had and was a man who had defended her father at a time when no one else would even take his calls—including her. He was as close to family as anyone in the world, and he was dead serious.

"Samantha," Francisco was now speaking in a soft, almost apologetic tone, "there's more. Do you remember the night of your mother's accident?"

His words drew Samantha's gaze back to his face.

"The call she received was from someone who had a rare artifact that was critical to your father's discovery. The package she picked up was an item that would have allegedly provided incontrovertible proof to his theory. Unfortunately, it was lost along with your mother on that terrible night."

A cold shiver ran down Sam's spine. Somehow, she knew that the medallion from her father's safe deposit box, the one in her backpack at that very moment, was the artifact.

Somehow, her father had acquired it, and only she and her father knew.

Sam rubbed her eyes, hoping that she might just be dreaming and would awaken from this nightmarish spider web that had ensnared her. Sadly, she wasn't dreaming. This was real. She tilted her head down, sat back in the chair, and began to sigh and shake her head.

Francisco's voice was a whisper now. "I know this is hard, and I'm sorry to have to tell you this under these circumstances, but you're the best hope we have of finding your father. I need your help, Sam. He needs you. You have to lead another team into the jungle to find the ruins. Your father is running out of time. I'm not sure what supplies they have left, but I do know that they can't survive out there for more than a few more days."

Francisco waited patiently, clearly realizing the confusion Sam was experiencing. Finally, she spoke. "When do I leave?"

Chapter Eight

The country of Peru is famous for the many ancient ruins that dot the countryside. Best known is Machu Picchu, preserved on an isolated mountaintop site above the waters of the sacred Urubamba River. Most likely built as an estate for the Inca emperor Pachacuti, the site lies at one end of the Sacred Valley of the Incas. Located on the opposite end is the ancient city of Cuzco, the capital of the former empire. Dotted with countless churches and museums, the former colonial city is famed for its cobbled streets and leafy squares.

These, along with the many other sites, such as Vitcos-Yurak Rumi, an intricately carved granite boulder the size of a city bus, amazed Sam. Despite her father's disappearance, she couldn't help but marvel at these incredible archaeological finds. She mused that one day she would return to Peru and give them the attention they deserved, but not today. Today, she had her sights set on finding her father.

The first part of their journey was an uncomfortable jeep ride over unpaved dirt roads. Francisco had decided to stay at the University in case Randall or his students tried to contact him. He also felt that he could be more helpful serving as cover if anyone asked questions about either of the Randall's' whereabouts. Instead, four University employees accompanied Sam. Their next stop was the tribe to see if they would provide another guide for the last leg of the journey.

Sam was still trying to sort everything out when she realized just how tired she was. She had only gotten a few hours of sleep in the last two days, and it all seemed to be hitting her on this bouncy jeep ride. She tried her best to close her eyes and get some rest, but every time her body began slipping into a restful state, the damn jeep would hit a bump and jar her back awake.

Finally dozing for a while, Sam awoke again just in time to see her new translator staring at her from across the seat. The young graduate student looked away as Sam's eyes caught hers. Monica Solis was not a field researcher, but she was one of the few people at the college who could communicate with the tribe. The language they spoke was not a common dialect, and with Ernesto missing in action, Monica was about the only person left. Sam shifted in her seat. After a few moments of awkward silence, Sam addressed her admirer.

"How long have you been studying at the University?" Sam asked.

"This is my sixth year. I'm almost done with my master's thesis," Monica replied quietly.

"That's wonderful! Congratulations, that's quite an accomplishment!" Sam was genuinely happy for her. She was always proud of anyone who made the sacrifice to earn an advanced degree. "Your parents must be very proud of you."

"I wouldn't know," Monica answered sheepishly, "I've never met them."

"Oh," was all Sam could muster.

"I grew up in foster homes, moving around every few years. When I was 18, I applied to the University and was accepted. I received financial assistance, and between the grants, loans and this job, I have been able to work on my degrees."

Sam nodded her head in understanding.

"Dr. Randall, we're here," the driver said.

Sam looked out the jeep's window and saw that they had reached a clearing on the edge of a river. Francisco had explained that the only access to the tribe was by boat. Sam saw four workers packing supplies into what seemed like two very small boats to carry them and their gear. This was going to be an adventure.

The entire experience caused Sam to reflect on her dad's past as an Army Ranger. He didn't talk much about his deployments, which made sense since they were typically covert operations, but she couldn't help but wonder how he felt before a mission. Did he experience the sense of nervousness she felt at this moment? He always seemed calm in the face of danger, but he had once confided to her that being a Ranger didn't mean he wasn't afraid. He had simply learned to confront and compartmentalize those feelings to complete the task at hand. That thought brought a sense of confidence to Sam now as she prepared to embark on the journey to find her father.

One of the men packing the boats stopped working and turned to Sam.

"Hola, Dr. Randall, I'm Anselmo and I will be piloting one of the boats up the river today," he stretched his hand out to Sam.

"Thank you, Anselmo, and nice to meet you," Sam replied, shaking his hand. "And who else do we have here?"

"This is Jorge, Rodrigo and Daniel. Daniel will be piloting the other boat as we take you to the tribe."

Sam shook each hand in succession, greeting each man warmly. "Thank you all for helping out on such short notice. We really appreciate it!"

"Sí. You're welcome. We only hope we can help you find your father," Daniel replied with a serious look on his face. "We can only imagine what you are going through."

"Thank you, Daniel, you're very kind."

The group finished loading their gear and launched from the shore.

The two boats motored slowly up the river. The views were breathtaking, but Sam couldn't help but feel a sense of nervousness about meeting the tribe. After Francisco's description, she felt very uneasy about the initial encounter. If Francisco was correct, the existence of this tribe, and the ruins her dad was seeking, would change human history. There was also the fact that no one had spoken to the elders since her dad went missing, and there was no guarantee that they would be willing to help again. Sam shook her head and exhaled deeply, as if trying to expel her uneasiness, rationalizing that there was no sense worrying about it now.

It was then that Sam sensed that something wasn't right. She glanced up at the others in the boat, but no one else seemed to be concerned. They were going about their business, steering the boats, and talking about what lay ahead of them. Despite this, Sam couldn't shake the uneasiness. Then it hit her: the noise of life on the river had stopped. The birds and animals had fallen silent for some reason, and an eerie quietness had descended upon them.

Without warning, the earth began to shake violently, as if the devil himself were trying to force his way up to the surface. At first, the boats were steady, unaffected by the shaking of the land all around them. But seconds later, the waves started coming, and the boats began rocking wildly from side to side.

Caught off guard, Jorge, who was in the other boat, lost his balance and fell headfirst into the water. Sam watched in dismay as Rodrigo reached over and tried to pull his friend back in. Another rogue wave crashed into the side of the boat, sending everyone, and all the boat's contents, into the churning water. The earth stopped shaking, but the waves kept coming, pounding Jorge, Anselmo and Rodrigo, who struggled to stay afloat.

Sam looked at Daniel. His face was ashen. "Steer us closer to them—we need to get them out!"

The sound of her voice brought Daniel out of his trance. Fighting the current, he steered the boat toward the three men in the water. They rounded a bend in the river. The sight made Sam's heart stop cold. Ahead lay an area of frothy water that spanned the entire width of the river. From bank to bank, dangerously large rocks jutted out of the churning waves. They were headed for the rapids.

"Hurry! If we don't get them out, they'll be killed!" Sam yelled.

The boat inched its way closer to the three team members in the water. They had all seen what lay ahead. Two swam with all their might, trying desperately to reach the safety of

Sam's boat. The third barely stayed afloat. He screamed desperately for help.

Sam stretched over the side of the boat, trying to pluck Jorge out of the churning water. Her body halfway out of the boat, she grasped at the exhausted man's arm. The added weight caused her to teeter over the side. Monica grabbed Sam's waist to keep her from falling in herself. The two heaved Jorge over the side. The three collapsed in a heap in the center of the boat.

Sam struggled to her feet. The rapids and jagged rocks drew nearer. "Hurry!"

The second person to reach the boat was Anselmo. Physically drained, he clung to side, unable to climb in under his own power. Daniel grasped him by the arm and pulled him halfway out of the water. The boat dipped heavily to one side. Water lapped over the edge. Panicked, Daniel released Anselmo's arm, dropping him back into the churning river. Anselmo sunk like a stone.

"No!" Sam screamed, jumping into the water after him. She dove beneath the waves, searching frantically for Anselmo. Visibility was poor, the roiling water creating a cascade of bubbles. Sam pulled her body through the river using long strokes. She scanned for any sign of the boat pilot. There was no trace of him.

She kicked, turned at a right angle, and investigated the deeper water. Karachi, native Peruvian fish, darted past her, their sleek, muscular bodies cutting through the water with ease.

Sam's muscles ached from fighting the currents. Her lungs burned as she drained the last bits of oxygen from them. A long, dark figure appeared in her peripheral vision.

Sam spun. Her eyes met Anselmo's, which were wide with fear. Sam kicked with her remaining strength, scooped him under his armpit and pushed toward the surface. The pair broke through to daylight, Sam gulping air as they breached the water.

"Grab his arm!" Sam screamed.

Monica and Jorge grabbed Anselmo's limp body and hauled him into the boat like the catch of the day. Sam grasped the side of the boat, which sat dangerously low due to the added weight. She searched for Rodrigo. Unable to see him, she heard a faint cry for help near the capsized boat. It was only a few yards from the rapids.

Sam took a deep breath. She pushed off the boat, but several arms grabbed her, stopping her forward movement. They yanked her out of the water. She tumbled helplessly back into the boat.

Rodrigo's cries for help stopped. Sam struggled to her knees and glanced out at the water. The shattered remains of the second boat drifted down river. A moment later, a badly beaten body floated up to the surface—face down.

"Sam, are you okay?"

In a state of shock, Sam didn't respond. Her mind was foggy, and she felt numb. She stared blankly at her hands, which felt like they belonged to someone else. Reality slowly crept back into her shock-addled mind.

Monica shook Sam. "Sam, you're scaring us! Are you alright?"

Sam slowly nodded in response. "We need to get Rodrigo."

Using the motor on their boat, they steered clear of the worst of the whitewater and finally arrived at a calmer point in the river. They retrieved their friend's body. Their party reduced to five, now.

No one spoke for some time as the crowded boat slowly glided forward. The only perceivable sound was the rhythmic whir of the engine and the soft sobs from Anselmo, who clung to the body of his departed friend.

They rounded another bend in the river and an encampment came into view. From a distance, the village seemed like any other they might encounter on a trip to this region.

Small thatched huts littered the shoreline. Expanses of dirt were interrupted with fire rings made from local stones. Sam saw several people milling about on shore. As they drew closer, she could see the faces of the tribe members more clearly, and she felt a mix of awe and surprise.

Just as Francisco had said, they were diminutive, their bronze-skinned bodies no more than four feet tall. Their heads were unusually large for the size of their bodies, and their eyes were too big for their faces. Their appearance was striking. As the boat inched closer, Sam spotted several tribes-people wearing fine headdresses. They stood in a semi-circle; almost as if they were waiting for Sam and her team to arrive.

The boat ground its way onto the sandy beach. Anselmo and Daniel jumped out and pulled them farther onto the sand. Sam and her team barely had time to climb out of the boat before two of the tribe's people came forward and began to address them.

Still reeling from the loss they had just suffered, Sam was momentarily taken aback. She glanced over at Monica, standing by her side, hoping for an explanation.

Monica seemed to understand the dialect. "He's saying that this young man will be your guide to the temple your father was looking for." The young man knelt in front of Sam.

"Please tell him to get up. Let them know we need help with Rodrigo."

Anselmo tugged at Sam's arm. "Professora, Daniel will take him back in the boat."

Once again, Sam nodded. It was the only thing she could do. Anselmo and Daniel dropped off the remaining supplies, then loaded Rodrigo's body into the boat. The two men shared a somber look, shook hands, then Daniel entered the boat and shoved off.

Sam stood motionless, watching the small craft disappear around another turn in the river.

Monica spoke to the young kneeling man, and he arose to his feet.

"How did they know we were coming?" Once again, Sam was confused by the turn of events.

The elder spoke to Monica at some length, gesturing to the skies with his hands.

"He says the ancestors spoke to him in a dream. They told him that the great protector was in danger and that his daughter was coming to help him. The ancestors instructed him to provide his son as their guide and to tell her that she must hurry to save her father from imminent danger."

Sam shifted uncomfortably. "Ask him if I can see the tablets Francisco referred to — the ones from their ancestors. I need to see if there's anything that might help me find my father."

Before Monica could respond, the elder spoke again, explaining to Monica that they had prepared the tablets for Sam. Without warning, the elder turned and walked toward the jungle. The group followed.

As they walked up the beach, the jungle became dense with vines and trees. Only a narrow, winding walkway offered any relief from the overgrown vegetation. The group walked for what seemed like a mile, then, without warning, the jungle opened and revealed its secrets. A city of stone sat amid a huge clearing. Large, stony structures rose out of the jungle floor, complete with stone walkways and irrigation channels. Sam froze in awe, her eyes surveying the scene in disbelief.

The elder who had met them at the boat did not hesitate. He continued to walk at a brisk pace toward a large structure in the center of the city. Hundreds of people milled about, living their daily lives right in front of the archaeologist.

How in the world hasn't this city been seen by planes or satellites passing overhead?

The questions she had for the tribes-people were numerous, but there would be time for that later. She needed to find her dad.

The elder ascended the temple steps, the University team right behind him. He led them through an arched entryway. Sam felt overwhelmed by the artwork. Perfectly sculpted statues lined the walls, and beautiful frescos adorned the ceilings. She was like a kid in a candy store! So many questions, but no time to ask them.

The elder strode with a purpose, straight to the tablet room. Perched high upon marble columns, looking like sentinels standing guard to some unknown treasure, were large stone tablets. At the very end of the row, the last column was broken, the top sheared off. The elder motioned to them, inviting Sam to look.

Sam walked up to the first tablet. There was strange writing that she didn't recognize. Sam puzzled for a moment, then remembered something. She had seen the writing before, but not in a textbook or library. She opened her backpack and removed her father's notebook. Flipping through the pages, she scanned for something familiar.

It has to be here… yes!

Many of the symbols on the tablet were in her father's book. Better still, he had deciphered them. She compared the symbols on the tablet with the translations in her father's journal. Pieces of the inscription were clear, but she was unable to translate the tablets entirely.

"What do they say?" Monica asked in a small voice.

"The tablets tell the story of the ancient ancestors being visited by the Great One who came from the heavens. The Great One was taken to meet the king of the tribe, who announced that his first daughter would marry him, bringing peace and prosperity to the people. I can't quite make out this next part, but I think it says something about teaching the people skills they didn't previously possess." Sam paused, her eyes narrowing as she tried to decipher the ancient text. She tilted her head as if she was having a hard time grasping what she was reading.

"Well?"

"I'm not sure I'm translating this correctly, but I think it's referring to an underground city named Vilcabamba and something important that's located there." Sam ran a finger over one symbol repeatedly. "That can't be what this means."

Monica inched closer. "What?"

Sam didn't respond. She pondered what she was reading, translating it in her mind. "There are still too many symbols that I don't understand, but it seems to talk about a jungle city and its inhabitants. If I'm reading this correctly, that city is known as Paititi. Then it says something about the Great One returning to his resting place among the stars."

Sam was stupefied. She realized at once that she was standing in the middle of Paititi, but wondered what its connection was to Vilcabamba. Whatever the connection, her father must have gone searching for it when he went missing. But how did he know where to find it? Sam scoured the tablets again, searching for any clue she might have missed, but here was nothing that explained the whereabouts of Vilcabamba. She then checked her father's journal, but found nothing there, either. *So how do I find it?*

"Maybe they didn't leave directions. Maybe they wanted to keep the location of Vilcabamba a secret. If that's the case, then the directions must have been passed down by word of mouth." Sam felt a heavy gaze upon her, and realized, for the first time since she had glanced at the tablets, that the elder was standing beside her. Was she imagining it, or did his face hide the faintest of grins?

They walked back into the entryway, where Anselmo and Jorge waited. "So, what did you find?" Anselmo asked.

"I understand what my father was looking for and where he went. We need to leave immediately. Monica, can you ask the elder how long it will take to get to the underground city?"

"Two days. Our guide told me right before you and the elder came out of the Tablet Room," Monica replied.

It's like they know what we're going to ask before we even ask it. Sam had a strange feeling that there was more to this than she realized. She wondered if her dad already knew.

Chapter Nine

"How are you doing, buddy?" Phil asked.

"Been better." Mike said, Phil's voice awakening him from a dreamlike state. "Do you think Dr. R has found anything yet?"

"He'll come through, he always does."

Mike nodded, his eyes drooping closed. He had the utmost confidence in their mentor which was something he couldn't say about most of the people in his life. Born and raised in one of the rougher sections of South Boston, or Southie, as the locals called it, Mike was used to relying on himself. Many of the kids he had grown up with were either dead or in jail, but not Mike. He was a smart neighborhood kid who understood that education was his ticket to a better life.

When he first met Dr. Randall, he had immediately liked him. The professor had been one of the first people to see something special in Mike and had taken him under his wing. Mike still recalled the day when the professor approached him, a crooked smile on his face. He asked if Mike would be interested in earning a stipend to be one of his paid assistants. Mike had jumped at the chance, but wasn't sure about Dr. Randall's other graduate assistant, though.

Mike initially saw Phil as a spoiled, arrogant, rich kid who wore designer clothes, had the newest cell phone and drove a brand-new Jeep Wrangler. On the surface, Phil was the exact opposite of Mike. Slowly though, the two had gotten to know each other and bonded over fieldwork with the professor. Eventually, Mike realized that Phil was simply a goofy, fun-loving guy who loved working for Dr. Randall as much as he did. Phil didn't have a mean bone in his body, and the two eventually became best friends. In fact, Mike saw Phil as the brother he never had and, aside from Dr. Randall, there was no one in the world he trusted more.

A deafening blast jolted Mike awake, its suddenness taking him by surprise. Rock, dirt and light simultaneously washed over him. Men dressed in military garb rappelled the short distance to the floor of the cavern. They closed in on the two students, who froze in disbelief. Phil responded first, leaping to his feet, bravely positioning himself between his friend and the approaching menace.

He held the gun Randall provided in his outstretched hand. "Don't try anything."

The nearest mercenary slapped the weapon from his shaking hand before Phil realized what happened. A hardened boot heel then landed a blow to his abdomen. Phil buckled over in pain, unable to catch his breath. He stumbled backward against the rock wall.

The mercenary turned his attention to Mike, shining a bright light directly into his eyes. Mike recoiled from the brightness, turning his head, and rotating his body away from the light. He jerked his broken leg to the side. The sudden movement caused pain to radiate throughout his body. Mike rolled into a ball, cursing his broken leg. As he writhed in pain, he heard heavy military boots approaching him and felt the warm breath of a large figure hovering above. Without warning, a huge gloved hand lifted him from the floor by the collar of his shirt. The sudden straightening of his broken leg registered immediately in the pain center of his brain. Mike howled in agony.

"Where is Dr. Randall?" a gruff voice asked angrily.

"I don't know," was all Mike could manage, his body screaming in pain. The large man set him back on the ground, lifted a heavy booted foot, and placed it squarely on the middle of the now protruding broken bone. Mike nearly lost consciousness from the intense pain.

"Where is Dr. Randall?" It was more a growl than a question.

"He's gone. We don't know where he is. He left a few of hours ago, and we haven't seen him since." Phil was on his feet, but was still crouched over, hands on his knees, trying to regain his breath. "We fell through the floor and tried walking, but Mike couldn't make it, so Dr. Randall left us some supplies and went looking for help. I swear that's all we know."

The solider walked over to Phil and pummeled his face with the butt of his gun. Phil's nose splattered in the process. He rolled on the ground unable to defend himself, wondering if he was about to die.

Another voice sounded from the darkness. "What have they told you, Lieutenant Granger?"

"Captain, they said that Dr. Randall left a couple of hours ago searching for help."

The Captain walked over to Phil and bent down over him

"Trust me, it could have been worse." The Captain said, a tinge of sadistic joy in his voice. He barked orders to his men to take the one with the broken leg back to their base camp, but he had other plans for Phil. "You're coming with us," he snarled. "And in case you get any ideas, I want you to know that all I have to do is give the order and the Lieutenant will finish the job he started before I got here."

The Captain stood up to face the Lieutenant. "Contact Colonel Ackers and let him know we have the graduate assistants and are in pursuit of Randall," he ordered.

"Yes sir, Captain Middleton!"

Granger grabbed Phil by the back of his collar and dragged him to his feet while two of the other men hauled Mike back into the upper chamber. Phil watched as his friend disappeared through the opening, wondering if he would ever see him again. A boot in the back interrupted his thoughts. Clearly his captors wanted him to walk in the direction that Dr. Randall had gone.

Chapter Ten

Tagomago Island
July 6, 4:21 p.m.

One by one they arrived. Some by air, others by boat. Their destination was the island of Tagomago, part of the Spanish Balearic Island chain. The small private island, located due east of the Spanish mainland, appeared on the surface to have all the trappings of a wealthy man's paradise. Its steep cliff walls rising out of an azure colored sea were topped with lush green vegetation, creating a breathtaking view for travelers lucky enough to fly over the tiny Eden.

As with most undeveloped islands, a single road running northwest to southeast, connected the far-flung reaches of the isle with the main living area situated almost at the dead center of the tiny speck of land. A single harbor on the east side of the island served those arriving by sea, and a small, but meticulously maintained helicopter pad north of the main compound, allowed for the safe landing of the visitors arriving by air.

The island was home to Frances Dumond, the lead member of the Alliance, an unlikely group of wealthy captains of industry. The names of the members of this secretive cabal sounded like a *Who's Who* list from the Forbes 500. Normally fierce competitors, on this day, they gathered as willing partners on a venture unlike any other. Unlike

49

typical board meetings taking place in the financial and industrial centers of the western world, this group gathered in the sprawling compound overlooking the Mediterranean Ocean to hear an update on their unusual partnership.

As the four arriving members and one guest took their seats at the oval shaped table, a man with tidy yellow hair and piercing blue eyes entered the room from a door concealed in an alcove in the side wall. He strode purposefully to an open spot near the center of one side of the great table, keenly aware that all eyes were upon him. Finally arriving, he took his time straightening his outfit before sitting.

"Nice of you to finally join us Dumond," Johan Kristoph commented. The founder of Heimat Energie was the oldest member of the group and felt that he should be the leader. A fact he frequently reminded his junior partners.

"Good to see you, too, Kristoph," Dumond replied.

The others appeared entertained by the icy exchange between the two men.

"What's the status of the project?" Margaret Seivers, CEO of Composite Materials Corporation, asked pleasantly, redirecting her peers.

"It appears Dr. Randall has disappeared into the ruins. Colonel Ackers reports he and his men are searching for him as we speak," Dumond replied.

Kristoph pounded the table. "You mean they lost them? How is that possible? Ackers is incompetent. We never should have trusted him with this assignment."

"Patience Kristoph. Ackers has never let us down before," Dumond said in a calm voice. "He also intercepted a phone call from Dr. Andrade to Randall's daughter. It appears she recently departed from the University with a small party to try and find her father."

"How do you know this, Dumond?" asked Rheingold Gerhardt, Kristoph's first lieutenant.

"I have eyes everywhere, my friends. In a game such as this, one cannot afford to be outwitted by his adversaries. Information is the key to our success," Dumond replied.

"These eyes you mention, Dumond, where else, may I ask, do you have them?" Alfredo Reynoso, President of Comunicacion Nacional, inquired with a raised eyebrow.

"Gentleman, we need to concentrate on the task at hand," Margaret Seivers interjected once again, trying to break the tension. "Let's remember it was Mr. Dumond who approached us with this idea and he has always provided us with the services we require. I'm sure he will do so once again."

Unsatisfied by Margaret's reassurances, Jianyu Chang, the CEO of shipping giant Shanxi Shipping Lines, continued the direct line of questioning. "Should we have any concerns about these latest developments? Are we sure Randall hasn't escaped and is in contact with the authorities?" Chang's question generated nods of agreement from others around the table.

"We've poured a great deal of resources into this venture, and eventually, we will all need to show a return for our investment. I'm becoming concerned that your plan may not succeed," Alfred Reynoso commented.

Trying to restore order to the meeting, Dumond spoke in a low, calm voice, "My friends, I would remind everyone that each of you entered into this arrangement willingly. Every one of you rose to your status by taking risks that others deemed as unacceptable. Furthermore, you are each poised to reap tremendous rewards once our project is complete."

The room went quiet. Once again, Dumond demonstrated why, in a group of highly successful people, he was chosen as their leader.

Dumond continued his lecture, "As Ms. Seivers pointed out, we have to stay focused on the objective at hand. Aside from a few academics, we are the only people who know about the discovery of Paititi and the ruins which might lead to Vilcabamba. Without hard proof of their existence, those who support the professor would never dare to come forward and claim he has evidence that a highly advanced civilization exits in the rainforest. Aside from this minor setback, we hold all the cards. I feel confident that the professor, his colleagues and even his daughter are no match for Colonel Ackers and his men. Within a few days, we will possess the power source from the ruins and we will dispose of those who could come forward to expose our plans."

All the Alliance members appeared satisfied with Dumond's assessment...except for one. Kristoph locked eyes with the unspoken leader of the group.

"You had better be right, Dumond," Kristoph pushed himself to his feet and strode to the door. His footfalls clicked loudly on the travertine tiles. With that, the industrialists each got up from the table and began to follow him out, leaving Dumond behind. He watched closely as Johan Kristoph and Rheingold Gerhardt walked together to their helicopter. Kristoph was animated, almost flapping his arms to emphasize his point to Gerhardt. For his part, Gerhardt looked on in subdued amusement. Dumond continued to watch until their helicopter carried them deep into the sunlit sky.

Of all the members of The Alliance, Kristoph was the least stable and seemed to be in a constant state of dissatisfaction. Dumond found this odd for a man who possessed such great wealth and power, but then he reasoned that insecurity can do that to a man. Despite his enormous empire, or maybe due to his empire, Kristoph was like a petulant child, angry when he didn't get his way. He had been unhappy with the choice of sending Ackers and his men to handle this assignment, but the rest of the group had agreed that Ackers was the right man for the job. Dumond was certain that the other members of the group would have fallen into line much more easily had it not been for Kristoph's constant grousing.

Dumond turned from the huge pane of glass and walked down the hallway into his office. From there, he checked his computer for an update about Dr. Samantha Randall and her team. It appeared that they were on their way to find her father. "Good," he thought. If Ackers could not find the elder Dr. Randall, his daughter would be a good bargaining chip to lure him out of hiding.

Chapter Eleven

The jungle was an almost impenetrable wall of vegetation. Sam and her group had spent the previous day walking through the maze-like structure of the rainforest, and she had realized that without the elder's son, they would have been doomed to roam the jungle in circles until they collapsed from exhaustion. The heat and humidity were overwhelming, but Sam's desire was stronger than ever to find her father. The guide had been moving at a quick pace, but now he stopped.

"What's going on?" Monica asked.

"I'm not sure. Monica, could you…" Sam was cut off by a sudden rumbling, and the earth beneath their feet began to rock. The group steadied themselves as the earth shook violently. After fifteen seconds, the movement stopped.

"What was that?" Jorge asked nervously.

"It felt like an earthquake, I think that's what hit us when we were on the river. Monica, can you ask the guide if this is common?"

Before she could ask the question, the guide spoke.

"He says that this has been happening more frequently, lately," Monica translated. "According to his people, this is a sign that the great unification is near."

"How often, Monica?" Sam asked

"Every day."

"This is the second one in just a few hours. That's not good. We'd better keep moving, I get the feeling we don't have a lot of time," Sam said.

Just as the words exited Sam's lips, a cracking sound echoed from the distance. Jorge dropped to the ground in front of her, a chunk of his head exploding outward into a million pieces of bloody flesh. Monica screamed as pieces of his brain splashed onto her shirt and pants. A moment later, Anselmo, also fell to his knees, his eyes open wide in disbelief as bullets ripped through his torso. His eyes blinked, and his mouth moved slowly, trying to speak, but the only sounds that came from the dying man were primal gurgling sounds.

Sam grabbed the horror-stricken Monica and pushed her through a small opening in the overgrown vegetation. "Run!"

The two women stumbled through the jungle, nearly tripping over the vines and roots littering the ground. In the distance, they could hear gunfire interspersed with cursing. Sam's heart raced as her thoughts turned toward a simple idea: *I need to survive.*

The thick brush slapped at their face and arms, but they didn't dare slow down. They ran for what felt like miles. Ahead, Sam saw the shapes of two dark-clad figures sweeping through the jungle. She stopped suddenly, dropped to the ground, and pulled Monica down with her. She covered Monica's mouth with her hand suppressing a scream.

They sat motionless as the figures passed, moving in the opposite direction. A gentle whoosh of air passed Sam's cheek. The bark on the tree next to her exploded.

Monica screamed.

Sam lunged forward, pulling the interpreter behind her through the dense vegetation. The sound of heavy footsteps followed closely behind.

Cover, we need cover, somewhere to hide.

Sam heard her heartbeat in her ears. Felt the adrenaline coursing through her body. Her muscles burned. She had to keep moving. Their pursuers were getting closer.

Why are they chasing us? What do they want? Sam's mind searched for answers, but there were none. Just fear and running.

Run or die.

The sound of their pursuers disappeared. Sam dropped to her knees, pulling Monica down by her side again. The two women shimmied under a fallen tree, sheltered at last.

Sam tried to calm her breathing. She looked at Monica, who was catatonic. Sam scanned the area, looking for telltale signs of movement. There was nothing.

She heard a sound behind them. Turning, she found herself looking down the barrel of a military assault rifle. There was no escape. As if to punctuate the thought, the two figures that had passed by them earlier materialized from the brush. They were surrounded.

"Dr. Randall, I presume?" a grinning figure asked, menacingly.

"Who the hell are you and what do you want with us?" Sam responded defiantly.

"That's not important, professor. Someone wants to meet you. Get up and make no sudden movements."

Monica grabbed Sam's arm like a small child afraid to lose her mother.

Sam patted her arm. "It's okay, Monica."

Chapter Twelve

Nick Randall moved forward through the passageway, his halogen flashlight providing ten to twelve feet of light in front of him. He could easily become disoriented in such a dark area with no distinguishing features. Randall recalled numerous stories of cave explorers becoming confused by the darkness and wandering around aimlessly until their light ran out, trapping them forever in a cold, dark tomb. Understanding this, Randall walked close to one wall of the cavern, making an arrow in the dirt floor that pointed back to Phil and Mike about every twenty feet.

Randall rubbed his eyes, suddenly feeling very tired. Though his body was still muscular and lean, he was no longer the young man he was when he had served as a Ranger. His age, coupled with the harsh conditions of this excursion had pushed him to his physical limits. People not familiar with the professor were surprised at his strength and incredible physical endurance, especially for a forty-nine-year-old. The events of the day, however, had worn him down, and he suddenly felt every bit his age. He rubbed his aching muscles and kept walking. The quiet darkness giving him ample opportunity to recall past events from his life.

In high school, Randall had excelled at athletics, playing both varsity football and baseball. A safety in football and a second basemen in baseball, though not the biggest or strongest athlete, his work ethic and drive to excel was unmatched. In fact, his varsity football coach had once commented that if all his players had possessed Randall's mental make-up, the team would be perennial state champions.

Randall carried this same drive into the military, joining the army to serve his country, but also to provide for his new family. He married his high school sweetheart Anne shortly after graduation and it wasn't long before she was pregnant with Sam. Randall excelled during his deployments and was quickly identified as someone who would be a good candidate for special operations. He applied for the 75th Ranger Regiment and rose to the challenge, completing his Ranger Assessment and Selection Program (RASP) at Fort Benning and officially became a Ranger.

Randall served proudly for six more years before leaving the military, his skills finely honed from years of service. Despite his pride at serving, the constant deployments had frequently taken him from his new family, which now included their second child John.

Randall turned his focus to his academic studies in Anthropology and discovered what would become his lifelong love of Archeology. The sense of history and the adventure of discovery was an intoxicating elixir for Randall, and it drove him to pursue his PhD in the field. He still vividly recalled the exact moment when he had developed his seminal theory, sending his career and his life on a new trajectory. It was on a field assignment at an excavation less than 100 miles from his current location. At the time, Randall was a graduate student from Georgetown

University working on a dig near the ancient city of Nazca. While cataloging artifacts, a colleague had asked if he would like to join him on an aerial survey of the land.

During the flight, Randall experienced an event that would shape his future in archeology. From their aerial vantage point, the two archeologists witnessed something unexpected on the landscape, below. Stretched over several miles were enormous shapes carved into the desert landscape. Unrecognizable from the ground, these shapes took clear forms when viewed from an airplane. Among the shapes were a condor, a whale, human hands, a hummingbird, and — strangest of all — a human shape that appeared to have a large, dome-shaped helmet. The human figure carved into the desert landscape bore a striking resemblance to an astronaut. It was also clear that these figures were laid out with geometric precision, with some of the lines running parallel for miles.

Upon landing, an inquisitive Randall conducted his own research on the theories associated with the Nazca Lines. He was exceedingly disappointed and perplexed by the prevailing theory that the lines were pathways for the ancient Nazca people to walk upon for ceremonial purposes. Most amazing of all, no empirical data to support this theory had been presented in any of the literature.

Randall was dumbfounded and questioned the veracity of the theories. Though his actions created some controversy, he didn't stop there. One of the benefits of studying archeology was gaining access to vast amounts of research and data on a variety of subjects. As he dug deeper, Randall discovered holes in other established theories. His research became an obsession, and his graduate thesis about an alternative and controversial new theory about the history of the region caused a stir at the University.

His his new line of thinking didn't sit well with his peers, and nearly cost him his Ph.D. Had it not been for his mentor Francisco Andrade, he wouldn't have earned his degree. As it turned out, Randall now worked for Francisco, who had found the wonderful benefactor who had funded this trip.

Randall then remembered the first time he had visited the Capanhuaco and how they had been reluctant to share their secrets with him. It had taken time and energy to earn their trust, but he finally convinced them to help him. When they showed him their incredible jungle city, Paititi, he realized it was the first piece of the puzzle he needed to prove his controversial theories. It was that fateful day which had propelled him down the road that led to this trip.

Now, many scenarios played through his mind. Were the tablets right? Did Vilcabamba, the underground city, really exist and was it nearby? Would he be able to find it and, more importantly now, would he be able to find help for Mike?

Randall felt a twinge of guilt for bringing Phil and Mike on the trip, even though he had been completely honest with them. They knew that this could be a dangerous trip, but they had been eager to go.

In fact, they had demanded to go. At one point, Randall had planned to make the trip with only a local guide and translator, but when the dynamic duo had found out about the professor's plans, they had insisted that he take them. "What's the point of studying archaeology if you can't be in on the biggest discovery ever?" Mike had commented to

Randall when the two had confronted him in his office. "Besides, we trust you, Dr. R."

I wonder if they still feel that way.

Randall checked his watch. He had been walking for almost two hours, and there was still no sign of anything other than continuing darkness punctuated by occasional tunnels veering off into more darkness.

Can't stop. Must find help for Mike.

It occurred to him that he hadn't slept in over 24 hours. Until this point, the adrenaline had kept him alert and focused, but having been in complete blackness for several hours, his body was beginning to tell him that he needed rest. He stopped, dropped to the ground and closed his eyes for a moment.

Randall took a deep breath and rested for a minute. Opening his eyes, Randall wasn't sure if his imagination was playing tricks on him, but there appeared to be a soft glow of light ahead in the tunnel. He scrambled to his feet, trying to focus on the glow. He switched his flashlight off, closed his eyes for about a minute, and then reopened them. He could see it more clearly, now, a soft glow in the distance. His pace quickened as clicked his light back on. The beam bobbed up and down as he ran. He caught something out of the corner of his eye and pointed his light toward the ground. There in his path was a fissure in the rocky floor. Randall stopped abruptly, his momentum nearly carrying him into the opening.

Catching himself, Randall teetered on the edge. He pulled his body back from the abyss, though not before kicking a small rock into the opening. The rock descended but made no sound. It simply vanished into the emptiness. Randall assessed the opening and estimated the fissure to be about four to five-feet wide. He considered his options. He could go back the way he had come and try another route or try to cross the chasm. Going back meant starting over, which could likely lead to another dead-end.

Randall decided to push forward. Backing up and taking a deep breath, he ran as fast as his fatigued body would allow, his flashlight bouncing crazily. Randall tried his best to keep the fissure illuminated. As he approached the edge, he lunged across the opening to the other side. As he landed, his left ankle buckled under him and he tumbled forward into the cavern. He felt a sharp pain on the back of his head as he hit the ground, losing consciousness for a few moments. When he awoke, Randall winced as he touched the bloody bump which had formed. He picked himself up, dusted the dirt off his shirt and pants and continued walking with a slight limp. His left ankle throbbed with pain from the rough landing.

As he drew closer to the light, the cavern opened into a huge space. The sight that met his eyes shocked him. The small tunnel opened into a gigantic cavern, easily the size of twenty football fields set side by side. The cavern appeared to be hollowed out of solid rock and, just as with the upper chamber, the walls were perfectly smooth. The cave radiated outward in a huge arc that spanned from one end of the opening to the other. Amid the cavern were finely crafted stone temples radiating out in a grid pattern reminiscent of a large modern-day city. Randall realized immediately that he had found Vilcabamba. It looked remarkably like Paititi.

Randall stood in awe of the sheer beauty of the architecture. Large stone columns stood at the entrance of the steps that led down into the city. Slowly, he moved forward, not so much walking of his own cognizance, but more being drawn into the otherworldly sight before him.

The intricacies of the stonework were remarkable. The shapes of snakes, birds, leopards, and other creatures lept from the facades of the buildings. As he walked, the creatures appeared as if alive, their eyes following his every move. It suddenly dawned on him that he could see the detail so clearly because the cavern was so well lit. Randall's eyes darted toward the ceiling. A glowing orb shined so brightly he had to divert his eyes. His mind struggled to comprehend what his senses were experiencing.

Randall shook his head in disbelief. Slowly the sense of disbelief gave way to a feeling of awe and loneliness.

I wish Sam could be with me to experience this moment.

But he was alone in the vastness of this subterranean world. Randall was shocked back to reality by the feeling of a hand touching his lower back. He jumped at the sudden contact and turned, startled, only to find … nothing. "What in the hell…?" As his voice trailed off, his eyes slowly moved toward the floor of the cavern, and then he saw their silhouettes.

Chapter Thirteen

Due to recently increased activity from the El Misti volcano, a small team of scientists had gathered to monitor the situation in anticipation of an impending eruption. Led by Dr. Thomas Reinsdorf of the United States Geological Survey Volcano Hazards Team—part of the Volcano Disaster Assistance Program (VDAP)—the group grimly assessed the situation. An enormous eruption was, at most, only days away.

VDAP had been formed in cooperation with the Office of U.S. Foreign Disaster Assistance (OFDA) of the U.S. Agency of International Development (USAID) following the 1985 eruption of Nevado Del Ruiz volcano in Colombia. Over 23,000 people lost their lives from that eruption, and it was VDAP's job to prevent the huge loss of life in the future.

Toward that end, Dr. Reinsdorf found himself working alongside his Peruvian counterparts, reviewing the data from the seismometers and other monitoring equipment located in, and around, the volcano. A huge, barrel-chested man who stood six-five, most people who met Dr. Reinsdorf said he reminded them more of a football player than a scientist. His associates, not wanting to miss a chance to needle the good-natured volcanologist, had lovingly nicknamed him The Linebacker.

Today, however, Reinsdorf sported a serious look on his face as he reviewed the seismic wave patterns picked up by his sensors. The data was disturbing, and what was taking place under the surface of El Misti was becoming very clear. The underground region he and his team were monitoring was becoming more active. Earthquake activity beneath a volcano almost always increases before an eruption because magma and volcanic gas must first force their way up through shallow underground fractures and passageways. When magma and volcanic gases or fluids move, they cause rocks to break and vibrate. When rocks break, they trigger high frequency earthquakes, which tend to occur in swarms consisting of dozens to hundreds of events.

El Misti was following this pattern. Of course, this wouldn't be the only data he and his team reviewed. Other scientists were also monitoring gas release, ground deformation and satellite imagery to assess if magma was moving toward the surface. Reinsdorf was certain what the total data package would tell them, but he would wait for his team to report back to him before acting.

Making matters worse, El Misti was dangerously close to Arequipa, the second most populous city in Peru, with over 844,000 inhabitants. Given that El Misti was a stratovolcano that had last erupted sometime in the late 1400s, Reinsdorf's concern was well justified.

Stratovolcanoes are sometimes called composite volcanoes due to the layered structure caused by sequential outpourings of eruptive materials. These layers of rock add to the deadly nature of the eruptions as the hardened shell permits the build-up of tremendous pressure. As a result, when stratovolcanoes have erupted in the past, they have historically resulted in thousands of deaths.

Two famous examples were the eruptions of Krakatoa and Vesuvius. Best known for its catastrophic eruption in 1883, Krakatoa resulted in over thirty-six thousand deaths, and the near destruction of its namesake island. In comparison, Vesuvius, famous for its destruction of the towns of Pompeii and Herculaneum in 79 A.D., resulted an estimated sixteen thousand deaths. If El Misti erupted, prior to evacuation, it would make the destruction caused by these two volcanos pale in comparison.

Reinsdorf also realized that atmospheric conditions might carry ash or lahars, a type of debris flow, directly to any nearby city. Under these conditions, the death and destruction could be even more severe. Entire cities could be buried under ash and rock, causing the residents to choke, burn or smother in the deadly cocktail of debris. After checking the latest weather reports, Tom confirmed that the worst-case scenario conditions were developing.

Making matters worse, the ash from El Misti could also wreak havoc on aircraft anywhere in the vicinity. With modern aircraft engines operating at temperatures high enough to melt any ingested ash, tiny blobs of lava would be created inside the engine. These blobs would then be forced back into other parts of the engine where the temperatures are lower. The molten lava would then solidify on the turbine blades, blocking airflow and causing the engine to stall. This likelihood, along with the probability that pyroclastic and lava flows rendering roads unusable, would further complicate rescue efforts.

As all these scenarios swirled in Tom's head, part of him wished that someone else could be the responsible party on this rodeo. But years of experience successfully monitoring other volcanos and coordinating evacuation plans meant he was clearly the best-suited person to lead the VDAP team, hence his appointment to the position.

Reindorf was called back to reality at the voice of his assistant Keith Peterson.

"Tom, the satellite imagery is in."

"Thanks, Keith. Call the team together and let's have a look in the conference room in ten minutes."

"Sounds good. I'll get the crew together."

Reinsdorf walked to the conference room, running down the list of actions they would take, based on the most recent data. If the signs were right, his team would make emergency plan recommendations to protect the citizens in and around Arequipa.

His team would be responsible for the various elements of the plan, including evacuations. It would be a huge undertaking to develop and implement the strategy, but of course a great deal of the responsibility would fall upon local emergency response personnel and local elected leaders.

Tom walked into the conference room and was happy to find his team assembled and ready.

"All right Keith, bring up the feed."

Peterson brought up the satellite imagery on the monitor and began to switch between the various images. "The first image was taken a week ago, and you can see the deformation beginning to take place in the lower quadrant of the frame. The next image was taken yesterday, and you can see that the deformation has increased substantially, which would correspond to magma build-up in, and around, El Misti."

"Theresa, what are the gas monitors telling us?" Tom asked Theresa Gonsalves, a local engineer with the Peruvian government.

"The sensors are showing that the volume of gas is increasing, which corresponds with the other data we're receiving. It looks like the indicators are all there."

"Unfortunately, I agree," Reinsdorf said. "Unless this magma build-up suddenly finds a place to dissipate, it looks like we have a dangerous situation developing here. Theresa, we need you make the arrangements for us to meet with local civil defense authorities, so we can start the emergency planning process. Keith, contact the regional office to get our logistics staff out here as soon as we can. I want a rough outline of a plan put together in the next seventy-two hours. Let's get moving people, we have a lot of work to do."

Chapter Fourteen

The Humvee sped along the dusty road, kicking rocks into the air as it raced toward a destination unknown to Sam who sat wedged between armed mercenaries. As disturbing as it had been seeing her colleagues gunned down in front of her, Sam was equally dismayed at being forced into a military vehicle with weapon toting thugs. None the less, Sam wouldn't allow her captors to see the faintest sign of distress. Her eyes were alert, as she scanned back and forth between the soldiers seated in the Humvee—her mind working on a solution. She glanced over at Monica who wasn't faring as well. She seemed catatonic, clutching Sam's arm as her only lifeline to sanity. Out of the corner of her eye, she could see that the lead abductor, Captain Middleton, couldn't suppress a sickeningly evil grin, as he contemplated their fates.

The Humvee rumbled into a compound, which more resembled a resort than a forward operating base. Although the buildings were only temporary structures, to the untrained eye they seemed as solidly built and as permanent as concrete and steel reinforced buildings found at any commercial park.

The complex was laid out in a semi-circular pattern with the administrative building in the center and the other facets of the compound emanating outward. To the east was the small dock and shipping area with a container ship awaiting its cargo. Near it, was a small loading crane and container truck of the variety found at commercial ports. A small warehouse sat at the western end of the shipping area. To the west of the administration building was a small landing pad with a shiny new Eurocopter EC 135 sitting at its center. The beautiful, luxury copter looked like a large, looming bird sitting with its nose facing the Humvee, rotors sagging under their own weight. To the north of the administration building, were the luxury living quarters, complete with dining facility, staff quarters and command center. Sam mused that it was amazing what could be accomplished when money wasn't an object.

The mercenaries led the academics into the main administration area where their host was waiting. Dumond stood in the doorway, his hands clasped behind his back, a wry smile upon his face. "Welcome to my compound."

"Who are you, what do you want with us, and what have you done with my father?" Sam seethed, her eyes narrowing as she looked into Dumond's.

"Dr. Randall, I'm offended. Is this the way to treat the man who sponsored your father's research?" Dumond replied.

"What do you mean?" Sam asked

"Dr. Randall, Dr. Randall, Dr. Randall," Dumond said, shaking his head. "I'm your father's biggest fan. Why, when he was just a young graduate student giving his lectures and being shouted down by his peers, I'm the one who helped save his job."

"What are you talking about?"

"I heard about your father through some colleagues of mine and decided to pay him a visit. I heard him speak

71

about Dr. Drake's equation for predicting the amount of intelligent life in the universe and found his theories fascinating. In fact, when I paid a visit to Dr. Andrade, it sounded like your father was on his way out of academia. Of course, not by his own choice."

"You know Francisco?" Sam asked.

"Indeed, Dr. Randall. In fact, I made quite a generous donation to the University to keep your father around. You could say that my associates and I are very interested in seeing him complete his research here."

"Your associates?"

"That's right. There's a group of us who feel that your father has discovered something very important here. So you can see, I haven't done anything with you father. In fact, we can't seem to locate him. We were hoping you might help us find him."

Samantha laughed. "Why the hell would I do that?"

Dumond's expression turned to one of a father addressing a disrespectful child. "Because you really don't have a choice now do you? As I've explained, Dr. Randall, I have a great deal of resources invested in finding what your father is looking for, and I'm willing to do anything to protect my investment. Even if that means killing you and your friend, here."

Dumond stepped closer to Sam, grasping her throat between his thumb and index finger. Sam's eyes widened.

"I see you've met Captain Middleton. If you don't do exactly as I say, he will be the one to carry out my orders to dispose of you and your friend, and I promise you, the Captain won't be gentle." From the periphery of her vision, Sam detected a disturbing grin from Middleton.

Dumond released his grip.

"What exactly is my father looking for?" Samantha asked.

"A power source unlike any other, one that could change the face of energy on this planet. Do you realize what the right person could do with such a device?"

Samantha could see that Dumond was excited about the prospect, but she was also sure that he was about as far from being the right person to find this device as she could imagine.

"In the hands of the right person, this device could change the political structure of the world as we know it. All other energy sources would immediately become obsolete, and the man who owned the technology would become a king." Dumond emphasized the last words with a nod of his head. Once again, he moved within inches of Samantha, his face virtually pressed against hers. "So you're going to help me find it. Captain Middleton escort our guests to their quarters."

Middleton gestured for Samantha and Monica to move toward the villas, his finger resting on the trigger guard of his assault rifle. The two complied, walking slowly while surveying the compound.

The living quarters were lavish, featuring polished stone floors and artwork adorning the walls. The room had two overstuffed couches, which looked very cozy to Samantha, especially in her exhausted condition. As nice as it was, it was still a cell, and they were prisoners. Samantha was reminded of this fact as she tried to open the door, only to find it bolted from the outside. Without doubt, guards armed to the teeth, and aching for a reason to use their weapons, were stationed just outside the door. Middleton had explained that they were waiting for someone else to join their group before they returned to the jungle.

Sam wasted no time. She searched the room for anything that might help them escape. There were no windows, or electronics for that matter, other than the lights and a small cooler with water. Sam plopped herself on the couch, tired and frustrated. She closed her eyes and rubbed her head, trying to think, but it was no use, they were stuck until someone opened the door. "If I'm stuck here, I might as well make good use of my time," Sam said absentmindedly as she reached for her backpack. Odd that no one had thought to check it or take it from her. She removed the medallion first and then her father's notebook.

"What's that?" They were the first words Monica had uttered since the jungle.

"My father's notebook and an artifact he found. I think there's some significance to this medallion, but I haven't had a chance to think about it yet." Sam looked at the medallion and felt the weight of it in her hand. It was heavy and still had the same odd glow in the middle.

"It's beautiful." Monica's eyes were fixed on the medallion as she inched closer to Samantha. "Where did he find it?"

"I'm not sure." Samantha handed the medallion to Monica, who handled it carefully, turning it over as she examined it, closely.

"Do you know what this writing means?"

Sam noted Monica's interest in the medallion. There was something different in Monica's tone when she asked, a confidence that hadn't been there before. Maybe she was coming out of her shell.

"I'm not sure, but I think there are clues about it in my dad's journal. He's a very meticulous person when it comes to research, and if he felt this medallion was important, I'm sure it is." Sam flipped through the pages of the journal. There had to be something in there to help explain why the medallion was so important. She was missing something, and if she could just find it, everything would be clearer.

"The detail on this is incredible," Monica said. "Whoever made it was an amazing craftsman." She set the medallion on the table and walked to the other side of the room.

Sam was engrossed in her father's journal. His notes were thorough, and Sam was impressed by the tenacity of his research. A strange sense of warmth flooded her as she read the journal, and memories began to return to her. Her dad had started keeping these notes when she was young. The pages were dated, corresponding to different research trips he had taken over the years. Sam remembered accompanying him on a couple of trips that had turned into "family vacations."

Only an archaeologist's family would consider a trip to the Peruvian jungle a vacation.

The thought made her smile. She shook her head, understanding how small threads of her life wove the tapestry that had become the very essence of who she was today.

At that moment, Samantha Randall realized why she loved archaeology so much. Her job wasn't just a means of employment: it was a part of who she was. A part of her family's foundation. They were a family formed by her father's love for the past and finding the truth. The realization doubled her desire to unravel this mystery and find her father.

There had to be something in the journal, something she had missed when she read it in the temple a couple of days ago. Sam read the journal from cover to cover but could find no mention of the medallion. She threw the journal onto the table in front of her, in frustration. It had to be there somewhere, but her sleep-deprived mind was missing it. She pushed herself up from the couch and walked across the room to Monica, who seemed startled by Sam's sudden appearance.

"Sorry, didn't mean to surprise you," Sam said, sensing Monica's unease. The poor thing was a very nervous person.

"Dr. Randall, what do you think they're going to do with us?"

"I'm not sure, Monica, but as long as they can't find my dad, or this power source they're looking for, we'll be okay. They need us, and as long as they need us, we'll be fine," Sam said, with some trepidation in her voice.

Suddenly, the ground shook beneath them, and the two women were knocked to the ground. "Quick Monica, under the table!"

Sam crawled under the heavy metal table near the wall just in time to see a picture fall from the wall and crash to the ground where she had stood just moments before—the edge of the frame gouging the floor. Sam scanned the room, looking for Monica, who was lying on the floor, exposed. Having been caught off guard by the violent shaking, she had fallen and smashed her head against the stone floor. Sam called to her, but to no avail; Monica had been knocked unconscious.

Sam scrambled from beneath her safe spot and stumbled over to her friend. As she reached Monica, she could see a large, black and blue lump forming on the right side of her forehead. Grabbing her by the arm, Sam dragged her under the desk, just as more debris crashed to the floor. She was breathing heavily, now, partially from the physical exhaustion, partially from the trauma of the earthquake. Sam's hands shook as she tried to catch her breath and calm her nerves. As quickly as it had begun, the shaking subsided, leaving her trembling under the heavy, old desk.

Finally able to relax, Sam checked on Monica, who was still breathing and had a pulse. Sam called her name softly, holding her head on her lap. Slowly, Monica regained consciousness, groaning and moving her head. As she awoke, she frowned, and her hand went to her forehead, finding the lump. Monica let out a quiet, "Ouch," and tried to focus on Sam.

"What happened?"

"We had another earthquake. You must have fallen and hit your head. How are you feeling?"

"Not so great. No offense, Dr. Randall, but this has not been a good trip for me."

"You can call me Sam."

Sam gently eased Monica to the floor and got her a pillow from the couch, placing it under her head. The room was a mess, broken glass and dust littered the ground and furniture. She cleaned the debris and dust from the couch as best as she could and walked back to Monica.

"Can you get up? I think you would be more comfortable on the couch."

"Are you sure the shaking's over?"

"I think so. Here you go." Sam leaned over, reached under Monica's shoulders, and helped her to her feet. Monica was wobbly, as the two walked over to the couch.

"Thanks, Dr. Randall," Monica said, meekly.

"You're welcome. I'm going to see if I can get some ice for your head." Sam walked with determination to the door and banged on it, yelling for her captors to open it. Somewhat to her surprise, the door swung outward and she found herself face to face with two uniformed men, sub-machine guns in hand. It was the second time today that Sam had looked down the barrel of a gun, and it was equally terrifying on both occasions.

"What the hell do you want?" one of the guards snarled.

"My friend is hurt. She banged her head badly, and we need some ice and something for the pain." Sam made eye contact with the angry guard, never letting her eyes leave his.

"Who gives a damn about your friend?"

"Look, if your boss wants to drag us through the jungle in this heat, he's not going to want us moving slowly because we're hurt. All I'm asking for is some ice and aspirin."

"Back up." It was the other guard, who was now taking the lead. "Move over to that corner." He motioned with the end of his gun. Sam obeyed, putting her hands up and moving to the far corner of the room. "Check out the one on the couch."

The angry guard grunted his disapproval, lowered his weapon, and walked over to Monica, who was still rubbing the lump and groaning in pain. "She's telling the truth, this one doesn't look so good." The angry guard shot a menacing glance in Sam's direction and walked back over to his comrade.

"We'll see what we can get you," he barked, abruptly slamming the door. The heavy lock clicked back into place.

Sam could hear the two men speaking briefly, followed by the sound of their heavy footsteps walking away. She thought about how appearances could be misleading. Even though she gave the outward appearance of being calm and brave, on the inside she was an absolute wreck.

Scratching her head, she walked back over to Monica and noticed something odd on the floor. There, by the table near the couch, Sam noticed that her father's book had been knocked to the floor by the earthquake. Squatting to pick it up, she realized for the first time that the cover seemed to have a tear in it. Looking more closely, Sam realized that it wasn't a tear, but rather, a seam in the leather. Picking up the book with her left hand, Sam examined the seam more closely. She gently lifted the fold and reached inside, discovering a piece of paper tucked away in a hidden compartment. The paper was folded into quarters and was worn. Unfolding the paper, she realized it was part of the clue she had been searching for, earlier.

"What is it, Dr. Randall?"

"Excuse me, Monica?"

"You just said, 'Oh my God!' Is everything all right?"

Sam hadn't realized that she had spoken. She turned the paper over to look at the back, but the it was blank. She rotated it once more in her hand, to better see the writing. Her father had written this information and, apparently, hadn't wanted it to be discovered. The note explained the missing tablet from the jungle temple and translated some of the symbols that Sam had been unable to decipher. According to her father's research, the markings on the medallion were the inverse of the markings on the wall of the tablet room in Vilcabamba. The words on the edge of the medallion were also translated on the sheet. Written on the sheet under the medallion writing, in large print was, "THE KEYSTONE."

"What can this mean?"

"Dr. Randall?"

Sam strode across the room to her backpack. Unzipping the main compartment in a single motion, she reached in and gingerly removed the medallion. She looked at it more closely this time, with the trained, objective eye of a seasoned scientist. Around its outer edge, were unevenly spaced notches reminiscent of those found on a large gear. The strange writing on the medallion was the same as the phrase written by her father on the sheet of paper. Sam studied the paper more closely. At the center of the medallion picture, there was a square made of small rectangles stacked upon each other with a round jewel in the middle—a jewel that resembled the one in the middle of the medallion.

"Oh my God."

"Dr. Randall, you're worrying me. What's the matter?" Now Monica's voice sounded a bit more demanding. As Sam turned to face her, she noticed that Monica was sitting up on the couch, hands on the edge of the cushion, her feet flat on the floor. Her arms were stiff, and her leg muscles were flexing. She looked like a coiled spring ready to snap.

"I think this medallion is a key to something, but what?" Sam held it by the chain with the inscription facing Monica.

"See the serrations around the outer edge?" Monica nodded. "I had originally thought that this was simply an ornamental design, but now I think they serve the purpose of fitting into a precisely carved opening. I also hadn't noticed the importance of this raised ridge around the jewel in the center. If you look closely, the ridge has tiny grooves all around it. Almost like the grooves are meant to help you get a grip on the ridge."

Monica looked confused.

"The writing is also a clue. If my father is right, and he usually is, the inscription reads 'THE KEYSTONE.' My father was away on research when he got a call that someone had retrieved a significant relic for him. Since he wasn't home, my mom called him, and he asked her to get it. He said it was very important and told her to get it as soon as she could. She left to pick it up but crashed her car and died before she could retrieve it for him. Somehow, my father must have gotten the medallion later."

Monica was wide-eyed with confusion, and Sam realized that Monica had not read the tablets, so she didn't understand the history of the jungle tribe. Sam carefully explained the entire story to Monica: the phone call from Francisco, her mother's untimely death, the history of the tribe as explained on the tablets. Slowly, the veil of confusion surrounding Monica began to lift. Just as Sam was finishing her explanation, the women were startled by the sound of the locked door opening. The first face they saw was the guard who had told them they would see if they could get help for Monica.

"Come with us, we have someone who can take a look at your friend's head."

Sam and Monica looked at each other for a moment, then got to their feet and walked toward the door. As they approached the entryway, they noticed that the friendly guard wasn't alone. His associate, along with three other men, armed with MP5 machine guns, flanked him. The nice guard led the group, while two guards walked on the sides of Sam and Monica, and the two other guards flanked them. They exited the building and walked across the compound to another structure.

Sam heard a loud cracking sound, followed by the two trailing guards falling to the ground. Before anyone could respond, Sam watched as the guard on her right was struck on the rear-right side of his head, his right eye exploded outward in a spray of red. The guard on her left fared no better than his partner, as a .223 round blew his neck forward, exploding it onto Sam and Monica. Sam recoiled at the sight, stepping away from the corpses. Next came a series of small explosions around the compound, causing complete chaos. The compound was under attack by an unseen enemy.

Dumond's men were caught entirely off guard. The front guard spun toward the two women he was supposed to be escorting to the medical staff, only to see them sprinting toward the jungle at the edge of the compound.

"Command, this is Sergeant Wall, the prisoners are escaping, we're under attack!" The Sergeant's pursuit was brutally interrupted by several rounds of small arms fire that forced him to dive to the ground for cover.

The two women raced through the jungle, trying to put as much distance between themselves and their captors. The faster of the two, Monica, dashed several yards ahead of Sam.

"Where are we going, Monica?" Sam yelled.

"Keep running!" Monica barked in response.

They ran for some time, the dense foliage slapping at their bodies, as they pushed forward. Sam's lungs burned with oxygen deprivation.

"Monica, stop for God's sake!"

Monica stopped, bent over at the waist, and braced her hands against her knees. Sam did the same, entirely out of breath.

"What the hell happened back there?" Sam asked. She didn't expect the response she was about to get.

"The plan worked," Monica said under her breath.

"What plan, Monica? What are you talking about?"

Monica stood and faced Sam, holding a pistol in her hand. "My plan Dr. Randall. I called the soldiers who attacked Dumond's base when we were in the room. I contacted them after you showed me the medallion and explained what it meant."

"Who Monica? Who did you call?"

"Mr. Kristoph. He hired me to find out what Dumond was doing. Now, I know, and now, I have to kill you," Monica said, tears forming in her eyes.

"Monica, I don't understand."

"That's right, Dr. Randall, you don't understand. There's no way you could understand what I have been through. You couldn't possibly understand what it was like to be a small child, treated like a piece of luggage, being moved from home to home, for no reason at all. You can't imagine the horror of the things I saw, heard ... and felt, as a helpless innocent girl, having to live with strangers who didn't give a damn about me."

"Monica, I ..."

"Stay back!" Monica cocked the hammer of the gun. "You probably had everything you ever wanted when you were a little girl, maybe a nice princess room, a comfortable bed, pretty clothes ... and most of all, a loving mother and father who doted on you." The tears were cascading down her cheeks, now. "Well now I have a chance to set things right for myself. Mr. Kristoph promised me enough money to take care of myself for the rest of my life. Isn't it fair that I get a chance to be happy and taken care of? Isn't it?"

"Monica, you don't have to do this, I can help you."

Monica snorted, her voice quivering. "I don't need your help." She lifted the Ruger P95, and while looking down the barrel with one eye, aimed the handgun directly at Sam's chest. Sam closed her eyes, anticipating the sound of the gun going off and the impact of the round in her chest. Then came the terrible moment when she heard the shot that would end her life.

Standing breathless, Sam realized that she was still alive. Opening her eyes, she saw Monica lying face down on the ground. The impact of the round had catapulted her body several feet forward, and she lay there, eyes wide open, her dead fingers still clutching the pistol. Sam blinked in disbelief, then looked up and saw a huge soldier towering over her holding an assault rifle.

"Where do you think you were going?" Colonel Frank Ackers had found her.

Chapter Fifteen

Randall was surrounded. He was deep within the bowels of the Earth, hopelessly cut off from any help, as he stood facing a group of strange looking beings. He took a quick count in his mind but stopped when he reached twenty. Despite being so badly outnumbered, he didn't feel afraid. There was something about the creatures that seemed to be … calming. Randall mentally reassessed the term "creature." Is that really what they were?

They seemed humanoid in form but didn't resemble any group of humans he had ever seen or read about in his thirty years as a scientist. Physically, they were approximately the size of the Capanhuaco, but there was something about their appearance that was otherworldly. Unlike their jungle counterparts, these creatures possessed no body hair, whatsoever, and their skin was milky white, probably an adaptation to life underground, the professor thought. But there was something else. It took Randall a moment to calibrate his scientific mind, but he finally realized that these creatures possessed no discernible mouths. If that was the case, how did they communicate or eat?

Your daughter and your friends are in danger. The thought seemed to appear in his mind. *There are people holding them hostage, and they intend to force your daughter to decipher your research notes and find you, along with our city.* Again, the thoughts just appeared in Randall's mind.

"Are you communicating with me?" Randall inquired to none of the creatures in particular. Suddenly, one of them came forward and stood directly in front of the professor.

We are. Your daughter and your friends are in great danger, and you must go and help them. You must also bring the medallion to us; the time of reunification is upon us. Our people must be reunited before the great journey can begin.

"What great journey, where are you going?"

Our time here is at an end, and we must return home.

"Where is home for you? Where did you come from? How long have you been here?" The professor's mind raced.

We realize that you have many questions, Dr. Randall, but there is no time for this now. The lead creature reached out an arm. Randall involuntarily bent at the waist and brought his head to rest at the creature's arm level. The creature placed its hand on his head and closed its eyes. What Randall felt next was unlike anything he had experienced in his life. He felt as light as a feather, floating into the air inside the great cavern. At the same time, he felt that his body was still in the same spot. He felt his mind go higher until suddenly he could no longer see his body, the creatures, or the cavern at all.

As Randall floated off into the dreamlike state, his mind wandered through different scenes. At first, he was entombed in an inky blackness that enveloped him like the great whale from the tale of "Jonah." Yet, he could tell that he was moving forward slowly, at first, but building speed.

Ahead, he could see the twinkling of tiny buttons of light way off in the distance. Before he knew it, he was flying by them at such blazing speeds that they appeared as long streaks of whiteness trailing off into the distance. He felt like

86

he was traveling down the tube of a kaleidoscope, with streaks of different colored lights with odd shapes traveling by him so close that he felt he could touch them. Suddenly he awoke in a field with a blinding sun beating down on him so brightly that he had to turn away. Randall buried his face in his lap as the brightness burned his eyes. He heard voices and realized that he wasn't alone. He blinked quickly, trying to adjust his eyes to the bright light. The voices sounded strange, speaking a language he had never heard before, yet he could understand them. More oddly still, the voices sounded familiar.

Slowly, the world came into view, as the blurry images came into focus. Randall was in the middle of a grassy meadow; the stalks of grass chest high and swaying rhythmically with the breeze. The rich smell of fresh grass tickled his nose, and his other senses came alive.

He noticed three people standing near him, but something was drawing their attention away. They were dressed in animal hides and pointing and speaking excitedly at something he couldn't quite make out. Finally, he was able to see clearly and was amazed when he realized what was happening. His friends were pointing at a shiny metal craft, spitting fire from its large rocket motors, settling down gently in the field. Randall stood and discovered that, like his comrades, he was also wearing nothing more than an animal hide and rudimentary foot coverings.

The craft gleamed in the bright midday sun, the reflection glinting off the metal skin. A soft hum emanated from the ship, and a small opening appeared on its underbelly. Slowly, several small shapes appeared from the craft and approached Randall and his new friends. The group huddled closely, unsure of what to do. Then, one of the creatures spoke to them, and Randall understood. The crewmembers of the spacecraft were from another planet and had come to learn about this new world and its inhabitants.

In his dreamlike state, Randall slowly came to grasp that he was not on Earth, but on another world. Vaguely, he remembered being in Vilcabamba and meeting its inhabitants, and then he was suddenly in this new world. It slowly dawned on Randall that he was not actually experiencing these events, but was merely watching them, like a movie seen through the eyes of someone else. IMAX had nothing on this!

Randall blinked his eyes, and the scene changed. It was now a much more modern setting and he found himself looking at a high-tech lab inside a very neat and tidy building. People in suits and lab coats were speaking to each other about something very important. Randall could tell by the serious tone of their voices and the grave looks on their faces. Some of the men seemed to be dressed in some sort of military garb. Strangely enough, in this current setting, Randall noted that these new creatures looked very similar to humans, except that they seemed a little taller, and their features were correspondingly larger. Randall fleetingly thought that these strangers, properly trained and coached, would dominate a team of human basketball players.

That thought passed quickly; however, when Randall saw "him." Or was it a "her?" Standing amid the circle of the lab staff, was an even taller creature standing eight to nine feet in height, its body clad in some sort of shiny metallic fabric. The slender creature had long, gangly arms that nearly reached to the floor. It's hairless, oval shaped head sat perched upon a long, cylindrical neck that rose from narrow, sloping shoulders.

Randall realized that it wasn't the creature's odd appearance that was the cause for concern. Instead, it was the creature's message. The creature explained that the star this small world orbited was becoming unstable and would soon expand, swallowing the planet in its fiery grip. The creature explained that this planet faced imminent doom. The only solution was to build an underground shelter and move as many of the native inhabitants into it, as soon as possible. The alien was carrying a familiar medallion and was explaining to the others that he could help them. He couldn't stop the star from exploding, but he could help them build an underground city. Unfortunately, there would only be room for a very limited number of survivors.

Randall blinked, and the picture changed again. He was now in an underground city, which looked very similar to Vilcabamba. Once again, he was amid several inhabitants, but they looked very different from the ones he had just seen in the lab. These creatures were much smaller, and their heads and eyes were much bigger than the rest of their bodies. Their skin was milky white. He, immediately, recognized them as the creatures he had seen in Vilcabamba. Sadly, Randall realized that these were the survivors of the doomed world and were, in fact, ancestors of the inhabitants of Vilcabamba.

They were studying something, intently, but he couldn't make out what. He moved closer and saw that they were examining something in space. On a large, recessed section of wall was something akin to a computer monitor, only much larger. Filling the screen was a portion of space resplendent with stars, nebula and various other items.

The creatures were focused on one, small, section of the sky, where there appeared to be a spiral galaxy. They had significantly enlarged the image of one of the outer arms of the galaxy, where their ultimate target appeared to reside. On the outer edge of the screen, small characters of a type that matched what Randall had found in his research about Vilcabamba, zoomed by. Finally, the screen slowed to a crawl on a planetary system circling a yellow-tinged star. Randall could see smaller pinpoints of light circling the star, moving in large uneven ovals.

The screen continued its slow enlargement of the planetary system, passing the outer rocky rings. Soon, it had passed the outer planetary bodies, and its zoom-like effect slowed down even more until a small, pale blue world started coming into focus. The planet became larger, until it nearly filled the screen, its large oceans interrupted by irregular outcroppings of land. It rotated slowly on the large screen, and it dawned on Randall that Italy really did look like a boot, when seen from space.

Discussions were taking place among the occupants of the room, though no one spoke. Once again, Randall hypothesized that these creatures had developed the capacity to communicate telepathically, and he was listening to their conversation. The discussion had to do with sending a contingency to the planet to study its primitive inhabitants. Apparently, the species on this distant, alien world were in the infant stages of developing their societies and technology, having reached a critical juncture in their development. The creatures decided to send an exploratory team to the planet to study the inhabitants until they could determine if the inhabitants had the capacity for space travel and if they warranted direct interaction with more advanced species.

Next, Randall found himself floating above Earth, from the vantage point of a satellite. The Earth rotated slowly beneath him, and he was overcome with its grandeur. He began descending through the atmosphere, at first slowly, then picking up speed. Following a long arcing pattern, Randall traced the curvature of the Earth in his mind's eye. The sky was a blinding blue, punctuated by the occasional wispy white cloud. As he drew nearer to the surface, the complex design of modern cities came into view, and Randall realized he had returned to the present and was viewing occurrences in real time. The blue-green hue of the ocean fell off to the left, as he made landfall in South America — on Peru, to be exact.

The jungles were lush and green, and he could feel the humidity thick in the air as he descended. A small encampment in the middle of the jungle came into view. There were signs of an armed conflict, with structures damaged by explosions and gunfire. Dead men lay on the ground, while soldiers with guns stood guard over others who were unarmed. The view continued to become clearer, and Randall focused on the unarmed persons. One was a woman, who appeared to be about twenty-nine years old. "Sam," the professor said, involuntarily.

Chapter Sixteen

Colonel Frank Ackers wasn't a man you wanted to anger. His six-foot, three-inch frame sported 227 pounds of solid muscle. His face held a pencil-thin mustache that curved up slightly at the edges when he was amused, which was rarely. His reflective sunglasses hid the deep-blue eyes of a remorseless killer. The title of Colonel was one held in a previous life as an officer in the British Special Forces—a previous life that he'd been forced to leave in dishonor.

"What were you and your friend doing, Professor?" Ackers asked coolly, walking up to Samantha, his gun pointed directly at her face. "You weren't trying to get away, were you?" the Colonel's smile belied the anger he felt at the assault upon his men. "Do you know who these people are working for?"

Sam remained silent, her eyes alternating between the barrel of the gun and the recently deceased interpreter lying in a pool of her own blood.

"Cat's got your tongue, Professor? That's okay." Ackers sneered as he swung the butt of his assault rifle in a single, swift arc, catching Samantha on the cheekbone. Caught off guard, Samantha tumbled backward onto the ground. Ackers could see she was in pain as she moved her hand to her cheek and felt a large welt forming where the gun had struck. From the look on her face, Ackers could see that Sam was weighing her options, perhaps even contemplating striking him in retaliation. After a moment, the flash of anger left her eyes, and she instead began rubbing her cheek, no doubt despising him.

"Get up." Ackers grabbed her under her right armpit, and roughly pulled her to her feet. Sam recoiled at his touch. "Start walking, Professor." Ackers poked the end of his gun into her side, giving Sam no choice but to walk in the direction of the compound.

As they approached the compound, another person slowly came into view. Sam recognized the familiar face. One that she had grown to hate.

Dumond sneered. "I see you found our guest, Ackers."

"Yes, she was with the translator, who was working for Kristoph. My men and I neutralized their strike team, but there'll be another. They know your objective, Mr. Dumond, and they'll follow us to the ruins."

"So Kristoph is behind this? How did you find out?"

"We captured one of his men alive. I was able to convince him to disclose who he worked for."

"Where is Kristoph's man now?" Dumond asked.

"Sadly, he met a tragic death."

"How many men does Kristoph have working for him?"

"If his man was telling the truth, he started with a mercenary force of forty soldiers."

"Do you have sufficient men to handle the situation?"

"Yes, experience has taught me to always be prepared for counterinsurgencies in situations such as these. We'll plan accordingly."

Ackers shoved Sam forward with one last rough push of his assault rifle. "What do you want me to do with her?"

"Put her back in her cell, we'll be leaving shortly."

Ackers escorted Sam to her cell and returned to the command center to assess the damage that Kristoph's men had caused. Ackers had lost a total of six men, leaving him with 18 remaining soldiers to repel further attacks upon their group. Good fortune had smiled upon Ackers and his men. They had been able to catch the strike team off guard as his group returned from the jungle ruins. In return for killing six of his men, Ackers had dealt the other team a serious blow, killing twelve of them in the firefight.

While a two-to-one kill advantage over his opponent was a good ratio, Ackers knew he had to plan carefully to minimize future casualties to his team. It was hard to gauge how many men Kristoph would utilize in an attack. However, Ackers and his men had the advantage of knowing the jungle and the ruins area, while his opponents had lost their greatest advantage: surprise. Kristoph's men were undoubtedly licking their wounds right now and would not gamble another attack on the compound. The next attack would likely be in the jungle or near the ruins.

ෂ෯

Kristoph pounded the ship's bridge with a clenched fist. His veins popped from his forehead in anger. Somehow, Dumond had outdone him again. "How could this have happened? You told me we had the element of surprise!"

Captain Sauder stood stone-faced. Absorbing the verbal abuse from his employer. "Sir, we successfully attacked the compound and caught them by surprise. The woman you had implanted into their group had relayed the location and size of their force at the compound but made no mention of the strike team in the jungle. They caught us on our rear flank. Before we knew they were even there, they cut my men to pieces. We were fortunate to get out alive."

"Fortunate? That's a poor choice of words! Dumond still has Randall's daughter and his research notes while we have nothing!"

"Sir, we killed six of their men, and their force has been reduced to eighteen. My team is double that size, and we know where they are going. We will follow them to the ruins and take possession of the girl and the research book. This is only a minor setback, I promise you that."

"You had better be right, Captain. Your life depends on it."

Chapter Seventeen

When Randall awoke, he was lying on the ground, the lump on his head throbbing. He ran his hand across the bump and discovered dried blood trailing down the back of his neck. Disoriented, the professor was unsure of where he was. Slowly, his eyes began to focus in the darkness, and he reached for the flashlight in his zippered pocket. He shined it to one side and found only sheer rock. As he turned the beam in the other direction, he was startled to see the chasm he had jumped across, earlier.

Randall stood and shook his head from side to side, trying to clear the cobwebs from his mind. As he rubbed his aching skull, he walked over to the sheer rock face where the path to Vilcabamba had been earlier. He pressed his hand against the stony surface. It was as solid as the ground he stood upon. Confused, he sat back down to assess his situation.

Had he dreamt the entire episode with the creatures? In his groggy state, Randall was unsure of what to make of recent events. His encounter had seemed real, but it was entirely possible his experience was simply a manifestation of his deepest desire to prove his theories. There was no way to be certain, but Randall was sure of one thing. He needed to get back to Phil and Mike and get them some help. He also needed to find out if Sam was in danger.

Suddenly, all his years of research and even the discovery of Paititi were secondary. Three people he cared deeply about were in trouble, and he needed to help them. Strangely enough, even if his vision of Sam had been the byproduct of a blow to the head, Randall could sense that his daughter needed him. Call it father's intuition, but his little girl was in trouble, and he was going to be there for her. The real question was how to get back to Phil and Mike? When he had jumped across the chasm the first time, he had been able to get a good running start. This time, he only had a few feet to get enough speed to jump. Randall searched for anything that might help him get across, but there was nothing except solid rock walls all around him. He only had one choice, and he needed to get moving.

Randall backed up as close to the rock face as he could. He estimated that he had about six to seven feet to get up to speed for his jump across the large opening. If he couldn't get enough speed to clear the chasm, he had a long trip straight down waiting for him.

Taking a deep breath, he sprinted for the edge of the opening and jumped. Randall felt as if he was moving in slow motion. A split second into the jump, he realized that his arc wasn't high enough to clear the chasm. As he moved closer to the other side, he could feel that his body was dropping too quickly. He wasn't going to make it.

Dropping his flashlight, he reached out his arms as far as they could stretch, feeling for the ledge of the other side. The rock outcropping hit him with such force that all the air in his lungs was immediately expelled from his body. His face didn't fare much better as it hit the sheer edge of the chasm.

Somehow though, Randall managed to get his hands high enough to grip the rock ledge.

He dangled in midair, trying to catch his breath while hanging from the side of the rock face. Amid his situation, the only thought that crossed his mind was Sam. She needed him, and he wasn't going to let her down this time. Summoning all the strength in his body, Randall pulled his torso up the rock face until his head and shoulders were above the ledge. Straining with gravity against his own weight, he struggled to keep his positioning, thinking to himself that if he could only get a foothold, he could push his body over the ledge.

Randall searched for a foothold on the rock face with the toe of his boot. First, he tried with the right foot, but it bounced off the rock. He could sense the strength leaving his body. His arms were shaking under the strain of holding up his weight. Randall kicked in the air, trying to direct his left boot to the stony wall in the darkness. He managed to move it close enough to the rock to feel his left boot bounce off, in futility.

His arms, now weak from holding his body up, could no longer support him. He was slowly dropping lower as his grip on the rock face weakened. Randall realized that he was not going to make it.

Dangling over the edge of the chasm, he thought about never again seeing the people he cared about. He had wasted his life pursuing this damn discovery, and now it would end like this, falling to his death in some godforsaken cavern. Without his help, Phil and Mike would probably never make it out. They would eventually die of thirst in this underground tomb. Then there were Sam and John. If Sam was really in trouble, there would be no one to rescue her. As for John, he didn't even know that he and Sam were in Peru. John would lose his father and his sister without ever even knowing what had happened.

"Goddamn it!" Randall yelled.

His grip growing weaker, Randall knew that the end was coming quickly. His discipline born training had allowed him to hold on for longer than most men his age and even younger, but he could only will himself to hold out for so long. As his fingers slowly slid closer to the edge, he suddenly felt something gripping his forearms. A mixture of relief and concern filled him. He looked directly up into the darkness, unable to see what was holding him. A sudden bright light peered over the edge, temporarily blinding him. Soon he found himself being hauled over the ledge. Randall lay on the ground, trying to catch his breath, unable to speak for a moment. Finally, he was able to manage, "Who are you?"

"Are you Randall?"

"Yes, thanks for pulling me up, but can you shine that light in another direction?"

Randall felt two hands grab him, one from each side. They lifted him to his feet. His eyes still not readjusted to the darkness he sensed there was more than one person in the cavern with him.

"What's going on?"

"We work for someone who has an interest in your research. You need to come with us."

"I can't leave now, my two graduate students are stuck in this cavern. One of them has a broken leg and needs medical attention."

"That's not our concern."

The two men who had helped Randall were now pushing him forward. He could feel the barrel of a gun poking into his back.

"Where are you taking me?"

"Our employer wants a word with you."

Chapter Eighteen

The sleek, 472-foot-long luxury liner floated on a glassy sea. Custom built by German yacht manufacturer Peters Schiffbau, the six-level ship cruised along at 14 knots, driven by its 13,400 horsepower engines. Its owner, Johan Kristoph, frantically paced the length of the meeting room aboard his ship while Rheingold Gerhardt, his assistant, watched in quiet amusement.

A wealthy industrialist, who had amassed his great fortune in the energy business, Kristoph was a man accustomed to getting his way. The German energy mogul, and founder of Heimat Energie, had built his empire on his ability to always stay one step ahead of his competition. This ability had allowed him to become one of the wealthiest and most powerful men in the world. With this wealth and power, also came influence. Many was the time when Heimat Energie, facing stiff competition from another large firm bidding for the same project, benefited from Kristoph's ability to wield his influence to guide the transaction in his own favor. Blackmail, extortion, bribery were all terms Kristoph's competitors had used in describing his tactics, but he simply dismissed the slings as sour grapes from lesser foes. It had been many years since he had lost a business transaction to another man, but that had all changed the day he met Francis Dumond.

The two men's companies were competing on a large government energy contract to supply power in Finland. Nuclear power accounted for almost 26 percent of Finland's electricity generation and lacking the natural resources that most of the world uses to generate electricity, the country would either have to build a new reactor or import resources.

Kristoph had used his contacts to discover the details of most of the competing proposals and felt very confident that his company would win the contract to build a new nuclear power plant. The only proposal he hadn't been able to view, was from a large French firm, Areva, which had also submitted a proposal to build a reactor in southwest Finland.

Much to his embarrassment, the public power consortium Teollisuuden Voima (TVO) awarded the contract to Areva. Stunned and angry, Kristoph demanded to know why the consortium had chosen Areva over his own firm. He would never forget the reply. Dumond, speaking instead of the consortium members, simply stated, "My offer was better than yours." It was the way he had said it and the grin that slowly spread over his face. He was clearly mocking Kristoph, and no one mocked Kristoph.

On that day, he had sworn his revenge on Dumond. Revenge at all costs. Kristoph's thirst for retribution consumed him, but he realized that getting his vengeance would be difficult. A series of events had to align in just the right manner to allow him the opportunity to extract his retribution on the Frenchman.

Finally, after years of waiting, the perfect opportunity had arisen. When Dumond had brought Dr. Randall's discovery to their secretive group, The Alliance, Kristoph knew at once that he would finally have his chance. Per Dumond, Randall had discovered an ancient power source that would transform the landscape of energy for generations. Seeing this as both a threat and an opportunity for The Alliance, Dumond devised a plan to provide funding for the professor and keep tabs on his progress. He had brought the concept to the group, having put the plan into play prior to their approval.

The planning and early stages of executing the plan were unbearable. The Frenchman was just so damn smug about everything. It didn't help that the rest of the group—titans of industry, but not energy people—followed Dumond's lead like a bunch of lapdogs. Not once did anyone else in the group consider Kristoph's opinions or dissentions, even though he had many more years of experience in the energy field then his counterpart. Thankfully for Kristoph, he had the benefit of his associate, Gerhardt, and Gerhardt's reminders that he needed to stay focused on the prize. His plan was simple. Kristoph had found an informant inside of Dumond's team, who would keep a watchful eye on Dr. Randall's progress. When the time was right, the informant would notify Kristoph, who would swoop in and steal the power source for himself.

Keeping quiet had not been easy. Kristoph had been forced to bite his tongue on many occasions, just to keep the plan moving forward. He had to remind himself that there were two prizes to be gained from his plan. First, of course, was revenge. That went without saying. Second, was the possibility of possessing a new, endless power supply, one that no one else possessed or could ever rival. Anyone who controlled this technology would wield unlimited power.

It wasn't until the group had met on several occasions, and Kristoph had learned more details, that he had been able to develop his own scheme and put it into action. While the rest of the group was satisfied to follow the French pig, and take whatever scraps he threw their way, Kristoph had decided that he could control the power source on his own and deal a crippling blow to Dumond in the process.

Dumond had tried his best to conceal certain pieces of his plan from the group, but Kristoph was a resourceful businessman and had learned details about the second expedition to the temple: the one led by Randall's daughter. He saw the opportunity at once and wasted no time in acting. He had been able to convince a young interpreter to serve as his informant. Kristoph was amazed at how little he had to promise to gain the girl's allegiance. What he had agreed to pay her was less than he spent on brandy and cigars in a year. Not that he had intended to pay her—why spend money on a frail, useless woman, when he could dispose of her with a single bullet?

Of course, this would no longer be necessary because of that damn Dumond! How could he have gotten the upper hand again? Kristoph had held the element of surprise, and his plan had been working flawlessly until that asshole, Ackers, came along and ruined it. He would make sure to repay Ackers for the grief he was suffering when this was over. Kristoph pounded the table in anger.

"We have Dr. Randall. The men are bringing him to us as we speak," Gerhardt said.

"Well, where in the hell are they, then?"

"Patience, Kristoph. Captain Sauder updated us a few minutes ago. Their ETA is seven minutes."

"Until Randall is standing here, in this room, right in front of me," Kristoph said, pointing to the ground at his feet, "I will not be patient or satisfied!"

Gerhardt sighed and nodded, quietly.

Shortly, the two men heard the familiar *whoosh, whoosh, whoosh* of the helicopter's blades. Randall had finally arrived. Kristoph stood at the sound of the helicopter, and began to pace impatiently again, stopping to check his watch every few seconds. This would be the turning point in his relationship with Dumond. Without fanfare, the doors to the deck opened and Captain Sauder and his men brought the prize to his feet.

Kristoph studied Randall. He was medium height and lean and appeared to be in his late forties or early fifties. So, this was the man whose research would change the destiny of the world?

"Who are you and what have you done with my daughter?" Randall demanded.

"I don't have your daughter," Kristoph responded.

"Then, where is she?"

As he spoke, Randall moved closer to Kristoph as if trying to menace him. A quick jerk on his handcuffs from Captain Sauder checked him, the steel of the cuffs biting into his skin. The Captain also struck him with the butt of his Colt AR15, causing Randall to stagger and fall to his knees. Kristoph motioned for his prisoner to be lifted to his feet again.

"Let me explain something to you. I will ask the questions, and you will do exactly as I say, or I will personally see to it that you meet a slow and painful death.

Maybe I will even let the good Captain and his men have some enjoyment with you before we kill you."

Randall turned to see a smile creep over the face of the Captain at this comment. It wasn't the first time he'd heard such threats. Though it had been twenty years since his service, he still felt his chances were good of surviving. He just needed to wait for an opportunity to present itself.

"How far was the underground city from the location where Captain Sauder and his men found you?"

"I'm not sure."

"What do you mean, you're not sure?"

"I haven't actually found the city."

Kristoph let out a long sigh. He was losing his patience. "Professor, perhaps you need something to help jog your memory." The Captain dealt Randall another blow to the head. Randall fell to his knees once more and was again jerked to his feet.

"I hope we have an understanding now," Kristoph sneered.

Randall scanned the room before turning his attention to Kristoph. He remained calm, his training kicking in. Unfortunately there was nothing in the immediately vicinity to help him out of the situation, which meant he needed to keep the dialog going.

"I was in the underground cavern, jumped across a chasm, hit my head and blacked out. I woke up some time later with this lump on my head." Randall pointed to the bloody bump for emphasis. "When I tried to jump back across, I didn't make it. I was hanging over the ledge, and about to drop, when your men found me."

Kristoph shifted his gaze to his Captain, who was nodding his head in agreement.

Kristoph was stupefied. "Captain." He gestured to the soldier, who replied by pushing the gun harder against their captive's head. Randall felt the cold, hard, steel barrel press into the back of his neck. "You'll have to do better than that Professor."

"You may not like the answer, but it's the truth."

Kristoph brought his face within inches of Randall's.

"You are going to take us back to the cavern and show us what you found. If you try to escape, I will kill you and then hunt down your daughter and your associates and kill them as well. Do you understand me?"

All Randall could do was nod to his captor.

"But first, we need to make another stop. Captain, prepare your men, you're leaving shortly."

Chapter Nineteen

The sleek, dark helicopter raced over the glassy, blue ocean, heading straight for the jungle lined coast. Through his window, Randall watched as they passed from the water onto the land. The aquamarine ocean gave way to dense green brush and trees. Despite his predicament, Randall couldn't help but appreciate the beauty of the Peruvian countryside. The scenery beneath him was the stuff of travel brochures. Lush, green jungle teaming with life as El Misti poked through the foliage, it's weathered and pockmarked face standing in stark contrast to the dense vegetation below.

Randall's mood soured quickly as he remembered Sam and her predicament. Had he truly seen his daughter in danger or was his imagination simply running wild? There was no way to be sure. He couldn't allow his mind to take that dark turn. He needed to focus on the situation at hand and hope that while they were in the jungle, an opportunity to escape would present itself.

"We're approaching the landing zone. Everyone make sure you're strapped in," the pilot announced.

Randall's inquisitive mind got the better of him as he wondered where they were going and why. Kristoph had ignored his questions and had his minions escort Randall to the waiting chopper, which had been sitting on a landing pad situated on the aft deck of the vessel. Randall had watched Kristoph as he stood at the bridge of ship, monitoring the chopper as it had taken off and flown low, skimming across the water like a rock skipped by a small child on a day at the beach. During the flight, Randall had tried to engage his captors in conversation, but they had simply sat quietly, faces etched as if in stone. It was a familiar experience to Randall who harkened back to his days as a Ranger. They were all large, burly men with serious expressions. All except for one man, who was tucked away in the far corner of the craft. Looking conspicuously out of place, he stood out amongst the former soldiers like a weed in a prize English garden.

He was a mousy looking man with bushy eyebrows hidden beneath heavy black rimmed glasses. He wore a denim shirt and brown trousers with brand new heavy hiking boots that looked like they had just come out of the box. Randall was certain that if he had seen the man in his natural habitat, he would have been wearing a sport coat with patches on the elbows sitting amidst a large stack of ancient books. Academics tend to have a certain stereotypical look, and although Randall didn't fit the part, this other man surely did. He made a mental note to strike up a conversation once they landed. If he could get close enough to speak.

The pilot eased the Bell helicopter onto a soft patch of grassy earth and landed with a soft thud. The wind from the blades brushed the tall grass away from the chopper, causing it to sway rhythmically as they landed. A mercenary slid the side hatch open and hopped to the ground, crouching to avoid the still rotating blades of the copter. One by one they disembarked from the craft and gathered at the edge of the clearing.

109

"Professor Richter, you'll lead the way. Keller, you escort him and keep him safe. Ochoa, you and Dodd will guard Randall. Make sure he doesn't get any ideas of disappearing into the jungle," Captain Sauder said to his men, glaring at Randall to emphasize his point.

Randall smiled. "Wouldn't dream of it Captain."

"Move out!" Sauder growled.

The small group moved quietly through the underbrush on a path that looked like it had been recently traveled upon. Covered by dense foliage draped above, the path was concealed by the jungle, invisible to prying eyes peering from above. Randall watched as Professor Richter led the group, stopping occasionally to stare at a piece of paper he clutched in his left hand, while wiping his brow with a cloth in his right hand. Richter was clearly out of his element and reeked of self-doubt and worry.

Randall strode up next to Richter. "Is there a problem?"

"No, there's no problem. It's just this damn humidity," Richter answered, once again mopping his brow.

"It's the time of year. This is the most humid period in the rainforest. Normally we wait to do our fieldwork in the cooler months," Randall said reassuringly.

"You've been in the jungle before?"

"Yes, many times. My research has taken me to Peru on multiple occasions over the years. It's beautiful but the weather can be tough. How about you?"

"I've only been to these jungles once before. I'm not an outdoorsy person. I enjoy the comforts of my study or the library. This isn't my cup of tea. As you can see, this heat is really getting to me."

110

"Don't feel too badly, it's hard on everyone, even these guys," Randall said, jerking his thumb in the direction of Kristoph's men. "They may do a better job of hiding it, but they're struggling with the humidity just as much as you and I."

Richter cast an eye at Captain Sauder who simply glared back at him. Richter quickly turned away.

"If you say so Dr. Randall."

"Call me Nick."

"Nick, I'm Kraus," Richter said, extending his hand. The two men shook hands, Randall smiling broadly at Richter.

"Break up the meeting and keep moving!" Sauder growled.

Richter jumped at the sound of the Captain's deep voice. He scrambled further up the path. Unperturbed, Randall turned and stared at Sauder and shook his head. He jogged back to Richter's side.

"This path looks well worn. I'm surprised to find such an open path through this jungle. I've never seen anything like this before," Randall observed.

"It traverses several miles of the rainforest. In fact, it connects to another compound I saw on my earlier trip," Richter replied.

"A compound? In this jungle? Do you mean ruins?"

"No, a modern compound with several buildings, a helicopter and even a small port. I'm not sure who built it. Must be a pharmaceutical company or some such thing. Whoever constructed it, certainly had a lot of money."

Randall nodded.

The two men continued walking along the jungle path with Richter occasionally dabbing his forehead with his handkerchief.

"If you don't mind me asking, how did you end up working with our friends back there?" Randall asked.

"You know how tenuous funding can be. I was working at a small school in Maine called Bates College. Perhaps you've heard of it?"

"Of course, it's a great school."

"My department head had notified me our funding had been cut, and I was the professor with the least tenure, so I was the odd man out. I've been in academics my entire adult life and didn't know what I would do if I couldn't teach. That's when I was approached by a woman named Catherine who worked for Mr. Kristoph. She told me that he was interested in my work and was willing to make a large donation to the college if I would help him with a project. I asked about the nature of the project, but Catherine reassured me it would be simple for a man with my expertise. She was quite convincing," Richter said, blushing.

"I'm sure she was."

"Anyway, I jumped at the chance to save my job, and now I find myself here in this jungle."

"What exactly is this project you were hired for?"

"My specialty is the ancient civilizations of the Sacred Valley. There's a legend about Ayar Cachi and the hidden civilization that resides in the mountains not far from here. Have you heard about it?

"I've heard some things, but please go on."

"As the story goes, the tribe that lived outside of the mountain were descendants of a group expelled from the underground city of Vilcabamba. One of them was a woman who allegedly had supernatural powers. According to the legend, she was able to sneak back to Vilcabamba and steal the top of Ayar Cachi's staff. When her tribe found out what she had done, they buried her alive with the relic she stole. They placed the top of the staff on a heavy gold chain and hung it around her neck in the belief that its weight would hold her spirit down and trap her in her underground tomb for eternity. Most people believe the story is just a fable to teach young members of the tribe the evils of stealing, but I know the story is real."

"How are you so sure?"

"My thesis was on this legend and during my research, I found this," Richter removed a small item from his jacket and handed it to Randall who continued walking as he examined it. The item was wrapped in oilcloth to protect it. Randall gingerly removed the cloth to reveal a small leather book. The cover was worn, but the pages within the book were surprisingly well preserved. He flipped it open and immediately recognized the writing. The characters were the same symbols he had seen at Paititi in the tablet room.

"What is this book?" Randall asked.

"It's an ancient text discovered by an archeologist near the Sacred Valley. He found it inside a cave near the remains of several humans. He believed they were outcasts who suffered from some sort of genetic mutation."

"What sort of mutation?"

"They were very short, only four feet tall, and their skulls were huge in relation to their body size. Here, take a look at this," Richter said excitedly flipping the book to a page marked by a deep red ribbon.

Randall stopped walking, his eyes fixed on the page which showed a carefully drawn golden medallion.

"Isn't it beautiful? I think I know where it is, and that's why Mr. Kristoph hired me. We're going there right now!" Richter said.

"Keep moving!" Sauder shouted.

Randall didn't look back, but resumed walking. "You say you've been on this path before. Did you find where the medallion was buried?" he asked.

"No, not yet. That's what makes this so exciting! We're going to discover a previously unknown tomb and be the first humans to see its contents since she was buried!"

Randall stole a surreptitious glance at the mercenaries. They lagged him by several yards, just outside of hearing range.

"Kraus, do you know why Mr. Kristoph brought me here?" Randall whispered.

A look passed over Richter's face as if he had just tasted a lemon for the first time. "Of course, you're the language expert who can help us translate any writing on the tomb. Although, I can read most Incan languages, I can't read this one. That's why we need you."

Randall glanced over his shoulder again at Sauder who was still several paces back.

"I don't think you understand what's happening here. Kristoph didn't hire me to help you. I'm being held captive. My research team and I were exploring ruins nearby when someone tried to kill us. These men are hired mercenaries who are looking for the medallion and Vilcabamba. If we don't find the medallion, we're not leaving this jungle alive," he whispered.

Richter stopped in his tracks and glared at Randall.

"What? No, you're wrong. I know they're not the friendliest people, but Mr. Kristoph hired them to protect us, not kill us!" Richter shouted.

"What are you two talking about?" Sauder snarled, jogging up directly behind Randall. "I told Kristoph we couldn't trust you," he said, knocking Randall to the ground with the butt of his gun.

Richter's face went ashen, and his eyes widened in fear.

"As for you, do your job and find the goddamn tomb," Sauder said, grabbing Richter by the collar. All the academic could do was nod vigorously in agreement.

"Why don't you leave him alone," Randall said, rising to his feet and brushing himself off.

"Shut the hell up! I'm tired of babysitting both of you. All I need is one good reason to end this here and now!"

Richter scrambled up the trail like a frightened jackrabbit, glancing back over his shoulder as he went. Randall remained silent. He glared at Sauder then moved past him and jogged to catch up with Richter.

"Kraus, slow down."

Randall could see his counterpart was in a state of panic. His breathing was fast and shallow, and he was perspiring far worse than even the humidity dictated. Randall grasped his arm and pulled him to a stop.

"Look, I understand how you feel. You just had the rug pulled out from under you, but you have to remember, they need our help to find the medallion. As long as they need us, we're safe," Randall said as Sauder pulled up alongside them.

"I don't know where you two think you're going but..."

"We weren't going anywhere except to find the tomb. You have your expertise and we have ours. Let us do our jobs, otherwise your boss will never get what he wants. Think about that for a minute. Do you really want to disappoint Kristoph? Somehow, I don't think that would be a wise career move," Randall said.

The two men faced each other, silently staring each other down. Sauder scowled at Randall, his breathing hard and throaty. Randall's face, on the other hand, remained expressionless.

Sauder blinked first. "Find the damn tomb."

The group resumed their trek along the path, rounded a turn and found a small opening on the north side of the trail. Randall was the first to enter, followed closely by Richter and then the mercenaries. Unlike the arched pathway they had been following, the clearing was round, and the overhead vegetation had been pruned back higher than the path itself. Over time, the jungle had slowly reclaimed the once open clearing, but remnants of the opening were still visible.

"Spread out and look for the entrance. It will look like a large stone set into the side of a hill," Randall said, scanning the area.

The team dispersed and searched the clearing. After a short time, Randall heard the distinct voice of his fellow scientist.

"I think I found it!" Richter shouted.

Randall located him in front of a large mound on the east side of the clearing. Framed in logs taken from nearby trees, a large stone rested to the left of the open entrance. Someone

116

had already been there. Randall and Richter exchanged glances, the latter man's hands trembling with fear.

"What are you waiting for," Sauder said, pushing his way past them as he entered the earthen mound. Randall was the next to enter followed by Richter.

The tomb was dark, except for a shaft of light coming from the entrance and from the beam of Sauder's gun mounted flashlight. Despite being open, the air inside was stale and musty. Randall clicked on his own light and surveyed the interior. The shaft fed into a main chamber approximately six to eight feet from the entrance. Large ceremonial jars, used for washing, flanked the entrance to the main chamber that was adorned with a small altar in the center. The altar was constructed of rock and was completely bare. To the rear of the chamber, another entrance led deeper into the mountain.

Randall entered the passage with Richter close behind. The tunnel ended and opened into another chamber, smaller than the first. Directly in the back, cut into the dirt, was a large rectangular opening with a stone sarcophagus. Randall and Richter moved toward it and immediately realized it was open. The heavy stone cover lay on the dirt floor, propped against the side of the coffin.

Richter approached slowly with Randall by his side. They peered into the stony tomb and found the remains of the old woman from the legend. Long bony fragments of what were once her arms were neatly folded, hands clasped near her waist. Her rib cage lay exposed and appeared to have a roughly circular indentation near the sternum, but the medallion was missing.

"It's not here," Richter said.

Randall shined his light into the coffin, searching for additional contents. He spied a small rectangular item wrapped in cloth laying near the skeleton's feet. He reached for it.

"What did you find?" Sauder said, shining his light at the Professors.

Randall snapped his hand back out, just as Sauder arrived by his side. The captain's sudden appearance kept him from retrieving the article.

"Just skeletal remains. Someone else must have gotten here before us," Richter replied.

Sauder shoved him aside roughly and walked up to the sarcophagus. Shining his light into the stone coffin, he confirmed that the medallion was missing. He turned to face Richter.

"You said it would be here. Where the hell is it?"

"It was here...someone must have found it before us," Richter stammered.

Without fanfare, Sauder raised his weapon and shot Richter directly in the chest.

"No!" Randall yelled, catching Richter as he fell backward. He gently set him on the ground.

"Let's go," Sauder said, swinging his weapon in front of him and walking out into the main chamber.

Randall shone his light into Richter's face which was contorted in pain. Tears rolled from the dying man's eyes as he looked at Randall.

"All I wanted was to keep my job," Richter whispered.

"It's okay, we'll get you out of here. Just hang in there."

Richter's eyes drooped close, and he stopped breathing. Randall felt for a pulse but found none. He sat on the floor holding him, his mind refusing to believe what had just happened.

Sauder reappeared in the doorway. "Come on, we need to get back to the ship," he said coldly.

"You son of a bitch! You didn't have to kill him!" Randall yelled. He set Richter's body on the ground and strode toward Sauder's figure, which was outlined by the light on his gun. He heard a loud clicking noise as the light raised, pointing directly at his head. Sauder had chambered a round.

"Better think twice Randall or you're next."

Randall was furious at the sudden turn of events. He considered rushing Sauder, knowing he had a reasonable chance of catching him off guard and seizing his weapon. Slowly, sanity crept back into his consciousness and he realized the other mercenaries would simply wait him out. They also likely had flash-bang grenades and would toss them into the tomb and then use overwhelming force to either kill or recapture him. He had no choice but to wait for a better opportunity to escape. He turned away from Sauder and knelt beside Richter's body.

"What the hell are you doing?"

"I'm sure he has family that might want his belongings," Randall said, finding Richter's wallet and removing a ring he had on his right hand. "Unlike you psychopaths, most of us have loved ones who would want to have something to remember us by. The very least I can do is try to give them that."

Sauder snorted, "You're wasting your time. If I were you, I would be more worried about my own future."

"Yeah, well maybe I know something you don't," Randall said, rising to his feet. He walked directly toward Sauder. "I know Kristoph doesn't have a goddam thing except for me. If he wants to beat Dumond, he needs my help. That means you and your men can't do shit to me until Kristoph finds the medallion."

Randall saw the light swing up just before felt something hard came down on his head then everything went black. When he awoke, he was back on Kristoph's ship, lying on a bunk in a cell.

Randall sat up, rubbing his head, which ached terribly. He quickly searched for Richter's possessions, but they were gone. He was alone in the empty cell. Randall tried to make sense of the surreal turn of events that had ended with Richter's death, then realized there was no sense to be made. These were ruthless killers who only cared about getting the medallion and nothing more. He was jarred back to attention by the sound of the door unlocking.

"Get ready, we're leaving again," a soldier said, walking over to Randall and jerking him to his feet.

"Where are we going now?"

There was no reply.

Chapter Twenty

The two Aerospatiale SA 341 Gazelle helicopters flew in formation, carrying the 12 members of Dumond's party to a landing zone near the ruins. Sam had been happily surprised to see Phil, again, when she arrived back at the compound. Phil had explained to her how he, Mike and her father had found the chamber room and fallen through the trap door. He also told her how Mike had broken his leg, and how her father had left them with all his supplies while he looked for help. Not surprisingly, Ackers had found him with Mike and had taken Mike somewhere, but Phil hadn't seen Mike, since he was lifted from the cavern.

The odd part of the story was the way Phil and Ackers had followed Dr. Randall's footprints until they had come to a chasm deep within the mountain. The footprints had ended near a sheer rock face on the other side of the chasm, but they couldn't find Dr. Randall. Sam's heart sank into her chest when she heard this news. It seemed that her father must have fallen into the chasm. It was hard to tell who had taken the news worse, Phil or Sam. Sam realized that her dad was a father figure to both Phil and Mike, and the pain she felt at his loss was reciprocated by both of his favorite graduate students. With the elder Dr. Randall now gone, all hopes of finding Vilcabamba rested with Sam.

"Do you think we'll find the city, Sam?"

"I'm not sure. If dad couldn't find it, I don't see why I would have any better luck. He'd been researching this for years and knew where to look, better than anyone."

"It's okay, we'll be fine," Phil said with feigned confidence.

"We will be fine, and we'll find Mike, I promise." Sam looked straight into Phil's eyes, and he immediately saw the same look of determination he had so frequently seen in her father's eyes. It was hard not to get emotional thinking of the Professor.

The two helicopters landed, and three mercenaries disembarked. The fourth pointed his gun at Sam and Phil and motioned for them to exit the helicopter.

"Watch the props!" came the warning from one of the soldiers on the ground.

Ackers and Dumond had been on the lead helicopter and were already on the ground waiting for them. The group of twelve waited as the helicopters shut down their engines.

Ackers signaled to two of his men to stay and guard the helicopters. "I want radio silence, unless there are signs of Kristoph's men," he barked.

"Who's Kristoph?" Phil asked.

"Apparently he and Dumond are in some secret organization. From what I can gather, they're the ones who funded my dad's research and this expedition to find the temple."

"If they're working together, then why are they fighting?"

"It sounds like Kristoph is trying to steal the power source from Dumond."

"Great, so we have two groups of psychopaths trying to find this thing. That's comforting."

Sam couldn't help but smile at Phil's honesty. "We'd better stay focused; things could turn nasty in a hurry."

"What do you mean, Sam?"

"Something tells me that Kristoph and his men aren't giving up so easily."

Phil sighed. "They really don't prepare you for this type of stuff in grad school."

The group pushed on through the jungle.

The Amazon Rainforest contains an incredible diversity of both plant and animal life, and it seemed like they had encountered every variety of the former and many of the latter. From her perspective, the jungle was a nearly impenetrable wall of vines, plants and trees. Sam wasn't entirely sure if her captors really knew where they were going, a thought that was reinforced when the group stopped near yet another solid wall of vegetation.

"Why are we stopping?" Samantha asked.

"We've arrived at our destination," Dumond replied.

Sam stared at Dumond, who was at the front of the group conversing with Ackers. At first, she didn't see it, but as she shifted slightly and continued to look, the entrance to the ruins came into view.

"That's amazing," she said.

"Indeed it is, Professor. Now, I need the two of you to stay close by as we go in." Dumond motioned to Ackers's men to bring them forward.

As Sam walked through the entrance into the ruins, she was amazed at the incredible sight that befell her eyes. Looking at the passageway head on, it was a nearly perfect square. As she walked through it, she ran her hand along the smooth wall.

"How did they build this with the crude tools they had?"

"That's what your dad asked," Phil replied, grinning at yet another similarity between daughter and father.

The group walked on and finally arrived at the chamber room. Sam immediately noted the bluish glow of the wall and the way it curved away from the center. The glowing color of the wall seemed to match the glowing color of the jewel in the medallion. Sam wondered if there was a correlation. When she saw the carvings on the wall, she recognized immediately that it matched the writing in the tablet room at Paititi. Then she saw the hole in the floor of the room where Ackers and his men had blasted their way into the underground cavern. As an archaeologist, the blatant disregard that Dumond and his men showed for this antiquity angered her to no end. She could feel hatred rising inside of her.

"We'll rappel in," Ackers said, pushing Sam aside. "Set up the equipment here," he barked to his men, who quickly responded by opening their equipment bags and removing the nylon ripcord used by mountain climbers. In a quick, fluid movement, one of Ackers's men disappeared into the blackness, while another belayed his line.

"Ladies first." Ackers held the line out to Sam.

"Clip in your carabineer here, walk to the edge, and let your weight carry you over," another mercenary instructed Sam.

Without hesitation, Sam followed the instructions perfectly and soon found herself being lowered into complete darkness, except for the light from the halogen headlamp of the soldier who had gone before her. As she touched the ground, Sam realized that the vertical descent was fifteen to twenty feet. Now she understood how Mike had broken his leg. The rest of the members of the team followed suit with one soldier remaining in the chamber room.

Ackers shined his light in the direction that he and Phil had previously traveled, and Sam immediately saw the footprints. Her father had been down here a day ago and now she was literally following in his footsteps. The irony of the situation wasn't lost on her.

"This way."

There was an eeriness to the cavern, the only sound being that of shuffling boots, and the only light came from the headlamps worn by the mercenaries. Sam thought that it would be very easy to become disoriented in this environment.

"Stay in formation," Ackers barked.

Almost as if to confirm her thinking, Sam occasionally saw an arrow drawn in the dirt floor, pointing back toward the opening in the floor of the chamber room. Her father, never one to leave something to chance, must have drawn them, in case he became confused and needed directions back to Mike and Phil. She smiled at the connection she felt with her father at that moment. The group continued in silence, occasionally passing a tunnel, which crossed their path and veered off into the darkness.

Suddenly, they came to a stop.

"Why are we stopping?" Sam whispered to Phil.

"It's the chasm," Phil replied.

The thought of her father falling into this dark, seemingly endless pit was almost too much to bear. Sam had to fight back the tears and control her breathing. Now wasn't the time or place to show emotions.

"Dr. Randall, where should we go from here?" Dumond asked in a sickeningly sweet tone.

"I don't know. There's nothing from my father's research that explains how to find the city."

"That's not the answer I want to hear, Professor." Dumond walked over to one of Ackers's men, snatched the HK MP5 sub-machine gun from his hand and chambered a round as he walked over to Sam. "If you want your friend to live, you had better start coming up with some better ideas." Dumond stopped next to Phil and pointed the barrel of the gun at the side of his head. "The next move is yours, Professor."

Sam's heart raced, and her stomach churned. "My father found these ruins, so I know the city must be here, we just need to look more to find it."

Dumond pushed the gun into Phil's cheek. "I could search the caverns without you and your friend here. You need to give me a good reason to keep you both alive."

"Wait, there is something." Sam had hesitated at first, but she had no choice now. "My father found this." She unbuttoned the top two buttons of her shirt and removed the medallion from around her neck. In the darkness, she could clearly see the deep blue glow of the jewel in its center. It grew brighter. Almost like a beacon, letting her know that their destination was much closer than before.

Dumond walked over and snatched it from her. "What is this?"

"It's a medallion that was taken from the underground city. I'm not sure what it's for, but I believe it may be some kind of key."

"A key? For what?"

"I don't know."

"Dr. Randall, you disappoint me. You expect me to believe that your father didn't tell you what this medallion is for?" Dumond walked back over to Phil. "Unfortunately, you leave me no choice." He raised the gun and took aim.

As he did, a single bullet grazed his cheek. Dumond spun on his heel in the direction of the gunfire. The shot had come from the tunnel veering to the left of the chasm.

"Put your guns down!" barked a deep male voice from the darkness.

Kristoph's men had fanned out in the darkness and cut off Ackers and his men from the main shaft of the cavern.

"Kristoph?"

"Yes, Dumond, and you had better put your dogs on a leash now, or I'll have you all killed."

"So Kristoph, decided you didn't want to share the spoils with the rest of us? Well, not to worry, one less person means more for the remaining members."

Unseen in the darkness, Ackers and two of his men had turned off their headlamps and taken offensive positions to lay cover fire for their group. The cavern burst into a cacophony of sound, light flashes, and dust, as Ackers and his men unleashed full automatic fire on Kristoph and his team.

Instinctively, Sam grabbed Phil by the arm and dragged him to the ground. Without headlamps, the two were concealed in the darkness of the cavern. Sam could hear the whizzing of bullets passing near her and Phil, as she shimmied to the side of the cavern, taking cover behind a large protruding boulder. Phil followed closely behind and arrived by Sam's side, out of breath and terrified.

"Are you okay? What are we going to do? These guys are trying to kill each other, and we're caught in the middle."

Peering out from their rocky protection, Sam viewed the unbridled chaos taking place in the cavern. The utter darkness of the cavern served as a backdrop to the mayhem, punctuated by bursts of flames emanating from the various weapons discharged by both groups and from the flailing headlamps and gun-mounted flashlights. The near deafening echo of the gunshots and the waves of dust and dirt kicked up by bullet impacts further muddied the situation. Shrieks of pain and cursing dotted the chaos, creating a perfect storm of anarchy. Trying to focus on finding a way out, Sam realized that she was able to locate the mercenaries by the burst of flames from their guns, and suddenly she was struck by a thought.

"Phil, when I give you the word, follow me."

"What?"

"Ready ... go!"

Sam popped up from their hiding place and sprinted toward the gunfire on the far end of the cavern. Phil, bewildered, followed as closely as he could.

Bullets whizzed by them as they ran. Sam felt a small searing heat near her right shoulder blade but didn't pause to investigate. Stopping meant certain death, and she wasn't ready to give up yet.

They ran for what seemed like an eternity, the combination of fear, exertion and dust draining their lungs of air. Sam's chest felt like it was caught in a vise, squeezing the oxygen out of her. She didn't break stride. *Run or die* were the words that kept flashing through her mind.

She sensed a bullet whiz behind her.

"Sam!"

Sam stopped suddenly, almost tripping over her feet. She turned, sensing that something was wrong. "Phil, where are you?"

Phil writhed on the floor of the cavern. He was clearly in pain and could barely speak. Sam nearly stumbled over him in the darkness. Without speaking another word, she reached out and yanked him to his feet. She threw his left arm behind her neck and carried him to the safety of the side tunnel. Upon turning the corner, the two archaeologists slumped their backs against the cold, hard wall.

Phil's breathing was labored. Sam reached into her pocket and found her keychain with a single LED light fastened to the loop. "Where are you hit, Phil?"

"Right ... side ... chest."

Sam saw the entry wound and unbuttoned Phil's shirt, revealing a jagged, circular, bloody indentation below his right breast. Phil wasn't bleeding badly, but he couldn't breathe. The bullet had pierced his right lung, leaving him virtually unable to walk.

"Sam ... go without me."

Tears welling in her eyes, Sam replied through gritted teeth, "I'm not leaving you."

Her body was beaten and exhausted from a lack of sleep, and the physical punishment dealt by her captors, but she refused to leave Phil there to die. Summoning strength from somewhere deep in the recesses of her soul, she lifted Phil onto her shoulder again and the two trudged forward into the bowels of dark cavern.

☙❧

In another tunnel, Randall sat quietly, waiting. Having been brought along by Kristoph and his men, Randall had been instructed to sit quietly while Kristoph's mercenaries dealt with Dumond. Now, waiting in the darkness while the gun battle raged, Randall swore he heard his daughter's voice. Seeing the two shadowy figures running for the side tunnel made his heart jump at the thought that Sam might be alive.

Randall estimated that the tunnel was about 50 yards to his right and down the main shaft of the tunnel. Right where the most brutal part of the battle was raging. The chaos of the gun battle was the perfect distraction. Except for the one guard, nearby, no one was paying attention to him. If he was going to make his move, now was the time.

Randall shuffled his feet on the ground around him, until he finally found what he was looking for. He would have to time this perfectly for his plan to work. After a couple of minutes, the opportunity presented itself. A stray bullet ricocheted several feet above their heads, close enough that Randall dropped to the floor as if dodging it in fear. The guard, sensing his drop, reached down and grabbed him by the back of his collar, hauling him back up to his feet. Randall had just enough time to grab the fist-sized rock.

Feigning a loss of balance, Randall successfully goaded the guard into reaching over to catch him as he fell. Now with the side of his head exposed, Randall swung the rock as hard as he could. The guard, sensing the impending blow, reached up with his left hand just in time to deflect Randall's hand enough to make it a glancing blow.

Still, the hit was strong enough to cause the guard to stagger backward. Randall, realizing that he had stunned the guard, but not enough to make a break for it, launched himself at the mercenary. Like a linebacker punching through an offensive line, he hit the guard squarely in his chest with his shoulder blade, driving him back. The guard's arms flailed wildly, striking blows on the top of Randall's head in a vain attempt to defend himself from his attacker.

Catching himself, the guard managed to regain his balance, stopping his rearward progression. Now, in a much stronger position to defend himself, the guard, hands clasped together above his head, whipped a crippling blow down upon Randall's forehead. Randall heard the snapping sound of his nose breaking. Although he was in excruciating pain, Randall flung both forearms upward, under the chin of his captor, driving his head backward until he felt and heard the sound he hoped for — the mercenary's head hitting solid rock. The sickening noise resembled the cracking sound of an egg shattering as it impacted the floor. The mercenary fell to the ground limply as Randall staggered back. Seeing the man go down, Randall grabbed his gun then made a break for the tunnel on the right.

Although he pumped his legs as quickly as he could, it felt like he was running in slow motion. Just like in a dream, the harder he ran, the slower he seemed to moved. His intended destination seemed impossibly out of reach. Randall felt every heartbeat in his chest and tasted the blood, sweat, and dust coating the inside of his mouth.

Putting his head down, he trudged forward, dodging bullets and bits of rocky debris as he ran. But his attempt to escape didn't go unnoticed. Out of the corner of his eye, illuminated by the bursts of fire from the automatic weapons, Randall saw a solitary figure drop to one knee and raise his weapon directly at him. Somehow, he knew it was Middleton. Through the muzzle flashes, he could see him estimating his speed. He aimed his weapon so that his shot would lead the Professor just enough for the bullet to hit him squarely in his body.

The wall above Randall's head exploded with a force that sent him sprawling down onto the ground. Randall regained his focus just in time to see a shoebox-sized rock tumbling directly toward him. Quickly, he rolled to his right as the boulder smashed into the ground where his torso had been just seconds earlier.

Rising to his feet, he aimed his gun and fired a volley directly at where Middleton's gun had flashed moments earlier. Through the illumination of the running gun battle, he saw Middleton hit the ground to avoid being hit. It wasn't much, but it had bought him some time and Randall resumed his dash for the tunnel. He calculated the time it would take Middleton to get into a prone position and return fire, which is what he had done in similar situations in the past. He could sense Middleton looking through the sight of his assault rifle and doubted he would miss again.

Randall heard a gun blast from Middleton's direction and ducked reflexively as he continued to run. Nothing happened. Somehow, Middleton had missed.

A moment later he reached the entrance to the tunnel, rounded a corner and dropped into a crouched position. His oxygen-deprived lungs burned with such intensity that he felt like they had burst into flames. Slowly, his breathing became normal and he rose to his feet again. He had to find out if it was Sam running in this direction only minutes earlier.

೮ঽ৪৩

It was slow going for Sam, as she tried to carry Phil down the dark tunnel. Phil's breathing had become more labored and his body was limper than it had been at the tunnel entrance. Sam realized that if she didn't find medical help soon, he wouldn't make it. She was also exhausted and knew that she had to stop and take a short rest.

Sam leaned over and gently set Phil on the cold floor of the cavern, struggling to keep her balance. She then lowered herself to the floor next to Phil and held his head while she tried to regain her strength. The two were engulfed by the silence and the enormity of the darkness that surrounded them. Aside from the small LED light Sam held, the tunnel was pitch black and the only audible sound was the sound of their breathing.

For a moment, Sam allowed the darkness and quiet to wash over her as she tried to relax. But she heard more than the sound of their breathing. There was something else, but what?

Sam closed her eyes tightly and listened. There was another sound so faint that she could barely detect it. Like a small child playing hide-n-go seek, Sam held her breath, so she could listen with greater sensitivity. Then she heard a sound that immediately filled her with dread. Someone was coming. Sam could hear the repetitive and unrelenting cadence of boot steps hitting the ground. Her eyes popped open and she wrestled Phil to his feet. She wasn't going to come this far just to let one of those bastards get them.

Sam stumbled forward with Phil, dragging the nearly incoherent graduate student another ten yards, but the footfalls getting closer. She scanned the area with her feeble little light, looking for anything that might help defend them. As she rounded a bend in the tunnel, she spied a small opening in the wall. She willed the two of them forward. The opening was only large enough to fit one of them. Sam gently set Phil into the crevice.

Their pursuer was getting closer. Sam didn't have much time. She needed a weapon. Anything. She dropped to her hands and knees, hoping to find something. At last, she settled on a large rock and sprinted to the wall opposite Phil. Her strategy was simple. She would wait for her attacker to round the curve, hoping that he would see the opening and go to investigate. She would only have a split second to drive the rock into the back of his head and hopefully knock him unconscious. Turning off her light Sam waited in the darkness. She could hear the footsteps getting louder and then begin to slow. She raised the rock, prepared to strike.

Cʒঠᴖɔ

In the beam of his gun-mounted light, Randall spotted a small fissure in the side of the tunnel in front of him. It looked like something was inside. He slowed as he approached, shining his light directly into the opening. It looked like a person inside the crevice, but he or she wasn't moving. Randall drew closer, moving slowly and carefully, unsure if it was a trap. Moving within several feet of the opening, Randall swung his gun light toward the wall opposite the opening just as a figure leapt at him, swinging a large rock with deadly menace. He nearly fired, but had time to utter one word. "Sam?"

Sam froze, recognizing the voice instantly. "Dad?"

Randall lowered his gun. "It's me, sweetheart, I found you!"

The two embraced, Randall's arms engulfing his daughter in a hug. "I thought you were dead. Is it really you?" Sam said, tears welling in her eyes.

"It's me Sam, thank God you're alright. I thought for sure I would never see you again, but then I heard you call Phil's name in the cavern, and I knew it was you. Are you hurt?"

"I'm fine, but Phil was shot in the chest. He's dying, Dad. We need to get him help."

Randall leaned his gun against the rocky then quickly turned his flashlight toward the opening and pulled Phil out. Laying him on the floor of the tunnel, he examined Phil's condition, using the medical skills he had learned in the Special Forces. The weak, rapid pulse, and cold, clammy skin painted a grim picture. Randall shined the light near Phil's face. He was very pale, his breathing shallow and rapid. Phil was showing all the signs of acute hemorrhagic shock, and Randall knew that if they didn't get him medical attention soon, his cardiovascular system would be irreparably damaged and deteriorate to the point of death.

"You're right, we need to get Phil out of here."

Chapter Twenty-One

The firefight had been brutal. Both sides suffered severe casualties. But it wasn't over, yet. Like two vicious dogs locked in mortal combat, both sides took defensive positions, trying to assess damage as bullets continued to fly. Dumond's team had taken the worst of the battle, cut in half by the surprise attack and losing Captain Middleton, who took a round to the side of his head while trying to shoot Randall who was escaping. Ackers and his men had to use the bodies of their fallen comrades as shields against the withering attack. Kristoph's team also suffered casualties, but worse, they had lost Randall.

"Captain, send men to follow Randall and his daughter! Find them and bring them back to me!" Kristoph ordered.

"Yes, sir," Captain Sauder dispatched four men to search of Randall and Sam.

Kristoph finally had Dumond where he wanted him. He and his team of mercenaries were pinned down across the chasm. They had little cover for protection and no chance of escaping unharmed.

Having seen the tunnel to the right of them, two of Kristoph's men now had that route covered. They also had a clear view and control of the tunnel to the left. Any of Dumond's men attempting to make a break for either exit would have to traverse a 20-yard-wide open span with Kristoph's men's guns trained on them. It would be suicide, and Kristoph would be happy to grant them their wish. In his near euphoric state, Kristoph hadn't noticed that Gerhardt had moved next to him, gun in hand. When he heard the pistol cock, Kristoph turned his head to see that his friend had a 9 mm pistol pointed at his nose.

Kristoph frowned "What are you doing, Gerhardt?"

"Tell your men to lower their weapons," Gerhardt replied.

"I don't understand."

"Tell them now, Kristoph!"

"Captain, tell your men to lower their weapons," Kristoph ordered.

"But, sir!" Sauder replied.

"Now!"

"Men, lower your weapons," Sauder ordered.

Dumond slowly and carefully made his way over to Kristoph, flanked by Ackers and his men, who had already begun disarming Kristoph's people.

The look on Kristoph's face was utter bewilderment as he struggled to understand the turn of events unfolding before him. Once again, Dumond wore the same expression he'd had on his face many years ago in Finland. But this time, Kristoph realized he would never again see that look. Slowly, he turned to face the man who had been his closest confidant for so many years. Many thoughts raced through his mind as he looked upon his own personal Judas, but only one word truly described his feelings: betrayal.

"How could you do this to me, after all the years we've worked together?"

"You mean after years of listening to you ranting and raving about idiotic nonsense? Years of being ordered about like a small child or a dullard?" Gerhardt replied.

Kristoph sneered. "You were always well compensated for your work."

"Don't take it personally, Kristoph, it's simply business. My offer was better than yours," Dumond said, raising a pistol to Kristoph's head and firing at point blank range. "Dispose of the others."

"Your orders, Mr. Dumond?" asked Ackers.

"Follow Randall and his daughter into the tunnel," Dumond replied, reaching down to take the medallion from Kristoph's dead hands. "Pity, it seems he didn't want to let this go.

❦

Randall carried Phil through the dark, winding tunnels. He could plainly see that his daughter was exhausted, but, as had always been the case with Sam, she wouldn't dare show outward signs of weakness. They moved with a quickness that bordered on franticness, realizing that both groups of mercenaries were only a short distance away and, therefore, death followed closely.

As they moved along the path in tomblike silence, other passageways crisscrossed their tunnel at semi-regular intervals. The underground caverns were a web-like collection of tunnels, presenting an almost infinite number of possibilities. This fact was at once comforting and disturbing at the same time. It meant it would be more difficult for Dumond, Kristoph and their men to follow them, but also

138

that Randall, Samantha and Phil could become hopelessly lost. This possibility meant almost certain death for Phil in his condition, so they had decided that they would travel along the same path and hope that it led to … what exactly? This was the unspoken question on Randall's mind. Was he hoping that he had actually found the underground city and that his vision had not been a hallucination?

"I need to take a quick breather," Randall said, gently setting Phil down. He then took his light and set it on a rock, illuminating a patch of ground for them to sit on.

Sam sat down next to him and, judging by the way she was fiddling with her hair, she was thinking about something, but wasn't sure if she wanted to share it with him.

"What's on your mind, sweetheart?"

Sam took a deep breath and let out a long sigh. "I'm sorry, Dad. Sorry I've pushed you away for so long. Losing Mom was hard on me, and I couldn't help but blame you. There were so many times I wanted to pick up the phone and call you. It's just that you were so focused on this theory, and I felt like you were choosing your research over us."

"I'm the one that owes you an apology. You're right about my research taking over my life. I just couldn't let it go. I was so damned angry at the way some of my colleagues treated me that I let it consume me. People who I thought were my friends turned on me, and I felt like I had to prove to them and myself, that I wasn't crazy. Looking back, it just wasn't worth it. If I had known what it was going to do to our family, I would have dropped it."

Sam leaned into her dad and sobbed, softly.

"Losing your mother nearly killed me and knowing that I hurt you was almost more than I could take. You and your brother are the two most important people in my life, and I want you to know that I will never let anything come between us again."

Randall pulled his daughter closer and held her as she cried.

"It's okay, we're together, again, and that's all that matters now."

After a short while, she looked up at him, wiping her eyes.

"The lost city, Dad ... Francisco told me what you're looking for. He told me about the advanced culture that's supposed to live there. It's simply not possible that there's been an undiscovered civilization living for thousands of years underground. At some point they would have come into contact with the outside world."

Randall nodded. It wasn't the first time he had heard this line of reasoning.

Sam furrowed her brow. "Francisco also told me about their advanced technology. They have electricity? Really?"

Randall smiled. "I know it sounds crazy, kiddo, but I've found too much proof to think that this is just a legend. To tell you the truth, I wasn't entirely convinced until we found the medallion."

"Okay, I'll give you that. The medallion is an amazing artifact, and the tablets seem to confirm what you're saying. I can understand how you could believe this—to a point, but Dad, we're scientists. The idea that there's an underground city with advanced technology that is somehow related to the tribe in the jungle ... that's a bit hard to swallow. If it's true, why don't the jungle people possess the same technology?"

"How much did Francisco tell you?"

"Pretty much what I've told you. Why?"

"There's more to the story. Are you familiar with the creation story of the tribe?"

"No."

"Yupanqui is the descendent of Ayar Manco, a figure most historians believe is only a legend. He's the last great leader of a tribe that's waiting for the great reunification with the people of the underground city, Vilcabamba. The thing is, the historians got the story wrong. Backwards actually."

"What do you mean?"

"Their theory talks about the way Ayar Manco tricked his brother Ayar Cachi into returning to the sacred cave to retrieve an important artifact. In the process, Ayar Cachi was trapped inside the cave, while Ayar Manco and his siblings founded the civilization in the valley. But that's not the true story. What actually happened was that Ayar Manco and his supporters were kicked out of the Vilcabamba for rebelling against Ayar Cachi."

Randall went on to explain, in detail, the legend that Yupanqui had shared with him including how the ancient ancestors of the tribe were, in fact, descendants of humans who had interbred with visitors from the sky. He explained that these ancient travelers had landed in Peru thousands of years ago, as part of an interstellar research project. They were sent to earth because of the relative similarities in our anatomies and trajectory of our history. Due to the distance and time taken to travel to Earth, the alien civilization had sent visitors who stayed on the planet semi-permanently, creating a hidden civilization as a base to monitor human development.

Sam listened with rapt attention. A few days earlier, her father's story would have seemed like a child's fantasy run amok, but now, she wasn't so sure. "What about the tribe in the jungle? Why don't they have the same technology as the underground dwellers?"

"Remember the legend I just told you? The group you met in the jungle are the ancestors of the group that was kicked out of Vilcabamba. Since they were related, the leaders of Vilcabamba still protected them and even helped them build their city."

"But they didn't share all of their knowledge," Sam said.

"Right. Over time, the jungle dwellers encountered more humans, and there was more interbreeding as the tribe continued to grow. Fast forward to modern times, and now these two groups are waiting to be reunited, but they're missing something they need."

"The medallion!" Sam said.

"Yep, the medallion. I had planned to travel to Vilcabamba, speak to the inhabitants, and then bring the medallion back to them, later."

"Why didn't you just bring the medallion with you on this trip?"

Randall shrugged. "Self-preservation, I guess. I figured that if these legends were all true, and I ran into trouble with the residents of Vilcabamba, having the medallion stored somewhere else would give me a bargaining chip."

Sam sat back and shook her head. Although it was too much for her to process, some of the missing information on the tablets made sense.

After a moment of silence, Randall spoke. "I've seen it, Sam. I think."

"Seen what?"

"Vilcabamba."

"What? How?"

"After Phil, Mike and I fell into the chamber, I decided to look for help or a way out. I walked for hours and felt like I was just moving in circles."

"And?"

"I walked into a gigantic cavern. I mean, this was an enormous opening. Remember Paititi, where you saw the temple with the tablets?"

"Yeah."

"Vilcabamba is twice as large."

"That's impossible."

Randall was looking directly at her now. "And there was some sort of artificial sun illuminating the cavern. I walked down a long staircase that led me straight into the heart of the city, but I didn't see anyone there. I felt like I was in a dream. I kept walking and looking, but the city was empty."

A shiver ran down Sam's spine. "What happened?"

"I had the weirdest feeling that I was being watched, and I turned around to look back at the tunnel I had come from, and then it happened."

"What?"

"I met them. I met some of the inhabitants of Vilcabamba. They were … different, I guess you'd say. They didn't look like Yupanqui's people."

143

"What did they look like?"

"Long narrow faces with large eyes. Barely a hint of a nose and no mouths I could see. And their skin seemed to be almost translucent, but milky in color, and it seemed like they glowed. They didn't have any body hair, either. They were completely smooth. They were about the same size as Yupanqui's tribesman, but I guess the interbreeding of the jungle tribe caused Paititi's residents to take on more human characteristics."

"Did you talk to them?"

"We didn't speak, but they could read my thoughts, and I could read theirs. Telepathy, I guess. They told me that you were in trouble. Then, one of them put their hand on my cheek, and I fell into a dreamlike state. It was like my mind was free of my body, floating above the Earth. I saw a compound in the jungle. It was under attack by men in uniform. I saw you and knew you needed my help."

Sam watched her father's face carefully, looking for signs that he might be joking or misremembering the events that had transpired. She saw no signs of either. "What happened after that?"

"I woke up. I was lying on the ground across the chasm where we were when that firefight broke out. I had a pretty bad cut on my face and a big bump on the back of my head."

"So, you didn't actually find Vilcabamba. You landed on your head, were knocked unconscious, and your subconscious mind dreamt about these creatures and the underground city because you've been pre-occupied with this theory for years."

"Maybe, but it seemed real, and the memories are so clear and followed a logical sequence. I think it really happened.

144

Besides, how do you explain that I knew about you being in trouble?"

"Well, you might have logically theorized that once you were lost, Francisco would contact me and ask me to go looking for you. Given what you went through in the chamber room, it wouldn't be a stretch for you to have believed that the same people who were after you would also pose a threat to me."

"Your logic is sound, Dr. Randall, but I know what I saw, and I feel like the experience was far too vivid to have been a dream or hallucination." Randall stood, grinned and dusted himself off.

With a suddenness that took them both by surprise, the cavern began violently shaking. Dust and rock began crumbling from the walls and ceiling. A boulder jarred loose from the wall above, and Randall instinctively moved to protect his daughter, knocking her to the ground and out of the way of the falling rock. In a moment's time, the shaking stopped, and the two professors huddled on the floor of the cavern, heads covered in a protective stance.

"Are you okay?"

"Yeah, no damage."

"Phil ..."

The elder Randall searched the dust-filled tunnel, looking in vain for his assistant. The cavern resembled a burning building, dust choking the air and reducing visibility to a few feet. "I can't find him, he was right here."

"Dad, where are you?" Sam moved carefully through the smoke-filled cavern, following the light from her father's flashlight. Appearing at her father's side, in the area where he had set Phil down, Sam saw nothing but open floor.

"He's gone Sam. Phil's gone."

Chapter Twenty-Two

Ackers stood next to Dumond in the tunnel system, clearly perplexed at the turn of events.

"There's no sign of them, Mr. Dumond."

"This is most disappointing. Once again, two professors and a student have eluded you and your men. I'm beginning to wonder if it was a mistake to hire you for this job."

"Mr. Dumond, we've completed a sweep of the tunnels in such a fashion that if Randall, his daughter and his helper were here, we would have found them. They are not in this tunnel complex."

"You sound so sure. Have your men discovered the underground city then?"

"No."

"I'm beginning to wonder if Kristoph was right in his assessment of you and your team. Fortunately for me, I have something that Randall is looking for," Dumond said, grasping the medallion. "Sooner or later, they will need this item. Tell your men we are returning to our base. I need time to plan my next move."

The flight back to the base was short, but exceptionally tense, with Ackers emoting the mood of an angry teenager who had just been scolded by his father. When the helicopter finally touched down at the base, Ackers's fury was evident as he grabbed his Sargent's collar.

"Post a man on the perimeter and have the others assemble for debriefing in five minutes!" Ackers screamed into his ear.

"Affirmative, Colonel."

Dumond exited the chopper and made a beeline for his office, closing and locking the door as he entered. To say he was confounded by Randall's ability to once again elude Ackers and his men, was an understatement. Not accustomed to facing the sort of difficulties Randall had dealt him, Dumond needed to focus and regain his edge. He sat down at his desk and removed a small photo he kept hidden there for moments such as this. The photo was of a small, sad boy standing in front of a dilapidated shack. Looking at the picture of himself as a young child immediately took him back to the chapter in his life which served as the very nexus of this project.

As a boy of eleven, Francis Dumond had been abducted, and the experience forever changed him. He was a skinny, painfully shy boy, the result of years of physical abuse at the hands of his alcoholic father. His family was also poor, living in the shantytowns in Villeurbanne, northeast of Lyon, France. The neighborhood was rough, and young Francis was the frequent recipient of beatings at the hands of local bullies. These beatings were mild, however, compared to the punishment meted out by his father.

He still recalled being very small and hearing his mother and father arguing loudly in the adjacent room. The small, fragile child popped his head out of his room just in time to see his father strike his mother in anger, knocking her to the ground. Francis, a child of seven at the time, ran to his mother's side, trying to comfort her as she lay sobbing on the floor, a large welt forming on her left eye. His compassion for his mother was met with a brutal beating from his enraged father, who struck him with such ferocity that Francis thought he would surely die.

He didn't, and sadly this would be the first of repeated beatings Francis would receive at the cruel hands of his father. Beatings that continued until that fateful night so many years ago. He could still remember the details with such incredible clarity that the events of that September evening seemed like yesterday. It was very late in the evening. Francis was in his bed, the cool night air drifting over his body, as he lay there unable to sleep. It was a rare moment of quiet for the young boy, and he was nearly in tears, contemplating the shabby condition of his life. The stillness of that evening was almost tomblike, the sounds of the world outside quiet at that late hour. Francis remembered feeling like he was the only person alive.

It was 2:07 a.m. when the low humming sound started. At first, he wasn't sure if he was imagining it. After all, the mind of an eleven-year-old can certainly create flights of fancy, especially at night. The sound persisted, however, and grew stronger. As he lay there, young Francis realized that the cool breeze had stopped, and the air was suddenly and completely still. The humming noise stopped, too, and there was complete silence, again, but Francis felt that he was not alone in his darkened room. The young boy was suddenly filled with such terror that he lay in his bed motionless, unable to open his eyes. He could sense the entity there in his shanty room, standing over him, watching him. His heart beat furiously, and tiny beads of sweat formed all over his body. Finally, the anticipation became too much, and Francis opened his eyes to see ...nothing. He was alone in his room.

Or was he? Out of the corner of his right eye, Francis detected very faint movement. The young boy, his heart pounding in his chest, slowly turned his head in the direction of the movement. A sight that would forever change him met his glance. The face of the creature was slender and long, its skin a strange bluish-gray hue that almost seemed to make it glow. Its face lacked normal human features, its nose simply small slits in the front of its head. The creature stared at him with dead, black eyes that seemed to pierce right through the eleven-year-old boy. Mixed with a combination of terror and awe, Francis realized that he couldn't move. He felt drugged, as if heavy lead weights were attached to his extremities.

The creature lifted its hand into view. The long slender fingers reached out of the darkness toward him. Francis wanted to scream, but he could only manage a muffled cry reminiscent of the all too familiar nightmare known to everyone. But this was no nightmare. This was real, and he lay there unable to defend himself. The long slender finger reached out for him, slowly coming to rest between his eyes. The boy immediately fell into a deep trance.

When his eyes opened again, his vision was blurred as if he were viewing the world through a gauzy veil. He heard the muffled sounds of talking but couldn't make out what was being said. Blurry shadows danced at the periphery of his vision; Francis felt completely and utterly vulnerable. Trying with all his might, he struggled against the unseen shackles holding down his body, but he still couldn't move.

He let out a weak whimpering sound and felt absolute and complete terror.

He would most likely die here, disappearing forever from the squalid hellhole he called home. Would anyone even notice he was gone? Surely his mother would, and she would shed a tear for him. Or maybe she would think that he finally had enough of his father's abuse and had run away. Aside from her, no one gave a damn about him and, most likely, any memory that anyone had of Francis Dumond would fade away amongst the backdrop of the noisy, brutal neighborhood in which he lived.

This thought of the total futility of his life, the complete lack of importance of his existence, strangely gave Francis a previously unknown sense of strength. Lying on that table in that distant, dreamy place, Francis Dumond decided that, if he survived this ordeal, his life would be very different going forward. The next few hours were horrific. His unknown captors poked and prodded him in all manner imaginable. Francis lay there naked to these cold and heartless creatures that didn't care how terribly small and afraid he was. They simply carried out their studies until at last, mercifully, Francis once again saw a long slender finger touch him between his eyes, and he fell back to sleep.

Upon waking back in his bed, Francis was a changed person. After the terrifying experience, Francis no longer feared any earthly person or situation. He decided that dealing with his father was the first order of business. On most mornings, his father, still in a half-drunken stupor, would come into his room for a morning session of cursing and hitting. Concealing a pipe he found at an abandoned lot near his house, Francis waited for his father who came in as he normally did. This time, however, was different. Francis beat the abuser to a bloody pulp, leaving him dead on the floor of his room.

His mother, having heard the commotion coming from her son's room, approached the door slowly and opened it in fear of angering her husband. She found her son sitting on the floor next to his father's body, lying in a crimson pool of blood. The boy held his face in his hands, the bloody murder weapon lying next to him on the floor. She walked over to Francis and put her arm around her son. He immediately turned to her and melted into her arms, softly sobbing.

They disposed of the body in a nearby field under the cover of night. The next day, the gendarme arrived at their front door with news of the fate of Mr. Dumond. Asking to come in, one of the two officers couldn't help but notice the reticent young boy, thinking it must be difficult for him to learn that his father was brutally murdered. However, this neighborhood was known for its violence, and Mr. Dumond was known for his terrible temper. The list of people who wanted to see him dead was as long as the day. The gendarme made no promise of finding the killer, but the widow Dumond seemed appreciative of their attempts.

From that day forward, Francis was a changed boy. Upon returning to school, he no longer ran from the bullies, but stood up to them. After one such encounter, the he came home with his shirt torn, his lip bloodied, but with a big smile on his face. "What happened to you Francis?" his mother asked.

"I got into a fight, Mom, but you should have seen the other boy!" Francis announced, proudly. Such would be the future for Francis Dumond, who gained a reputation as a tough kid that you didn't want to fight. However, his newfound bravery didn't help his social awkwardness, and he remained a loner and grew to distrust people.

Winning at all costs became his primary passion, a passion that would serve him well in the business world. Dumond quickly learned that intimidation was the quickest route to success in business. But to intimidate others, you needed power and money. Dumond made it his professional and personal goal to become as powerful as he could, no matter whom he stepped on in the process.

This newfound passion was troublesome to his mother, who still saw a lonely and scared child. Dumond ignored her warnings and focused his laser-like attention on his goals. The culmination of the transformation of Francis Dumond was on a business trip in Spain. He was negotiating the terms of a contract, favorable to his company, of course, when he learned from a close relative that his mother had passed away. When asked if he would be home in time for the funeral, Dumond's response was that he had important business to attend to, and since his mother was dead, it wouldn't really matter if he was there, anyway.

Aside from his drive to succeed in business, Dumond was obsessed with the night that had changed his life. Specifically, he wanted to know more about the creatures that abducted him. He conducted research, spending every free moment trying to discover the truth about them. His pursuit led him down a dark and mysterious path, crossed frequently by crackpots and charlatans trying to make a quick buck at the expense of gullible victims. These individuals quickly discovered, frequently to their dismay, that Dumond was not a man to be trifled with. Several shallow graves in indistinct locations of the world attested to this fact.

It wasn't until a trip back to the east coast that Dumond finally discovered a possible lead to follow. He was on a business trip to Washington, D.C., when he heard about a controversial young professorial candidate who was offering a late afternoon lecture. His name was Nicholas Randall, a doctoral student at Georgetown University. Apparently, the young Ph.D. candidate caused quite a stir during a lecture he was offering to archaeology students at the college. His demonstrations of the evidence of past civilizations describing contact with what appeared to be extraterrestrial beings piqued Dumond's curiosity. Dumond decided to sit in on one of his lectures.

Randall was impressive. Prior to launching into his theories, he laid the scientific groundwork for his hypothesis. Citing the work of the Harvard trained astronomer, Dr. Frank Drake, Randall explained to the class the meaning of the now famous Drake Equation, which estimated the number of intelligent civilizations in the galaxy.

Dr. Drake had developed and proposed this formula while working as a radio astronomer at the National Radio Astronomy Observatory in Green Bank, West Virginia. Even assuming very conservative estimates for the variables in question, there was a high probability that more than a dozen such civilizations existed in the Milky Way Galaxy, alone. Applying these same assumptions over the vastness of the universe itself, it was very clear that, mathematically speaking, the universe was teeming with intelligent life.

When further considering that many of these intelligent species could be thousands, if not millions of years older, than our own, Randall was able to successfully lay the foundation that space-faring civilizations were almost a certainty. From there, it wasn't much of a stretch to assume that a pale blue dot in the vast cosmos, teaming with its own life forms, had potentially drawn the attention of at least a handful of these cosmic explorers.

Randall went on to mesmerize the students—and Dumond—with alternative theories of archaeological discoveries. Amazingly, he was able to do so while always providing some form of evidence to support his ideas. He began with maps belonging to the fifteenth century Turkish Admiral Piri Reis, discovered in Topkapi Palace. Much to the delight of his students, Randall explained how the maps, once transferred from a flat grid and projected onto a round globe, accurately displayed the areas of Mediterranean landforms along with the coasts of North and South America.

Next, he spoke of ancient petroglyphs from exotic locales such as Val Camonica in Italy and Tassili in the Sahara. In both cases, the images portrayed humanoid figures sporting unusual headgear reminiscent of Apollo-era astronaut helmets. Randall tantalizingly questioned how people from such ancient civilizations, separated by thousands of miles, could produce such similar drawings.

He continued, showing the class images of an elaborate stone drawing found at the temple at Copan. He then showed another image side by side with the Copan drawing. Gasps emerged from the audience as the figure in the Copan drawing bore a strikingly eerily resemblance to the image of an astronaut sitting in a space capsule. Murmuring arose from the students as Randall pointed out what appeared to be flames and exhaust coming from the bottom of the "spacecraft" in the Copan drawing. How could this be the case when Copan was an ancient Mayan ruin?

Randall clearly enjoyed presenting his ideas, and his enthusiasm only served to draw his students and his special guest ever deeper into his theories. Next, he described the Moai of Easter Island, huge humanoid statues with grotesquely enormous heads, measuring 13-feet tall and weighing over 14 tons each. He explained how the inhabitants of this remote island had fashioned 887 of these huge statues, some even larger and heavier than the others. How had they done so and then moved them into place with only rudimentary tools?

Randall paced the floor, arms moving in rhythm to the elaborate explanations he gave to support his theories. Dumond was impressed with the young academic. He had clearly done his homework, and his theories were well supported.

At that moment, Dumond decided he would keep a close eye on this young Professor. He searched out the Dean of the Archaeology Department and decided to pay him a visit. The office of Dr. Francisco Andrade appeared just as Dumond had imagined. Pictures of exotic lands hung on the walls and strange odds and ends from various archaeological sites adorned his desktop and file cabinets. At first, Dr. Andrade seemed wary of the meeting with Dumond, which seemed odd to him. Soon enough, he discovered why. Apparently, Mr. Randall's theories were not popular with the mainstream faculty, who viewed

Randall with disdain. His ideas, Dumond learned, were considered ludicrous and even scandalous. In fact, there was a petition to have the young doctoral student removed from teaching.

A fellow graduate student named Charles Young led the drive to expel Randall from the school entirely. Dr. Andrade explained that he greatly appreciated Randall's enthusiasm and didn't agree with the other faculty. But the pressure to dismiss him was mounting. In fact, the Academic Senate formally requested that the University President remove Randall under the guise that he posed a threat to the school's academic reputation. Andrade's hands were tied; the young doctoral student's days at the college were numbered.

"Thank you for the information, Dr. Andrade. I hope things change, it would be a shame for the University to lose such a bright, young mind."

"I agree, Mr. Dumond, but short a miracle, I fear Mr. Randall will never earn his doctoral degree or be able to teach again."

"Well, don't lose hope. Miracles happen."

Later in the week, a strange event unfolded. A rather large endowment was offered to the University. Specifically, the donor wanted to fund archaeological and anthropological research, but there was one stipulation for the endowment: the college was to allow Nicholas Randall to pursue his field studies, and work toward his doctorate. The school also was to keep the terms of the endowment a secret from the rest of the campus.

Dumond smiled as he recounted these events, and it served as a reminder of the need for patience and fortitude in the face of defeat. Now, he was close to realizing his goals.

157

His reverie was interrupted by the sound of his intercom. "Mr. Dumond, Ms. Seivers is on the line for you."

"Thank you, tell her I'll be right with her," Dumond said, summoning his willpower. He steeled himself for the conversation he did not want to have, knowing that it was simply one more hurdle to overcome before attaining the ultimate prize.

Chapter Twenty-Three

In the cavern, Randall thought about their options. Sadly, there appeared to be only one. "Since we can't find Phil, I need to find the guys that took us hostage and get the medallion back."

"I was thinking the same thing, but I'm going with you."

Randall shook his head. "I just got you back, there's no way I'm going to put you in harm's way again. I already put Phil and Mike in danger, I couldn't stand the thought of losing you, too."

"Dad, I'm already hip deep into this adventure, there's no way I'm going to bail out now. Besides, where else am I going to go? We don't know where they are or how to get out of here. If something is going to happen to us, I'd rather be with you."

Randall had seen the same determined look in his daughter's eyes before, and he knew there would be no convincing her. She had a sizable stubborn streak—one that she had inherited from her father, as his wife used to point out. "Okay, Sam, we'll go together. I think our best bet is to backtrack the way we came. I don't want us to get lost in this tunnel system. Let's keep the light to a minimum and move quietly to try and sneak up on them."

Sam smiled at her father, grabbed his arm and said, "Okay, let's go!"

Their approach was straightforward. In stretches of the tunnels with no bends or turns, they would use their light to search ahead for signs of Dumond or Kristoph's men. When they approached a turn, they turned off their lights, and the elder Randall would slowly scout around the bend, gun first, looking for headlamps and listening for the sounds of shuffling boots or the clicking of metal. After searching the tunnels for some time, they still had found no sign of the soldiers.

"This is where the fight started. It's the main cavern I walked down and where we escaped." Randall shined his light toward the far end of the tunnel. "There's the chasm I jumped across to get to Vilcabamba."

"Where could they have gone?"

"I'm not sure, but it looks like there aren't as many as before." Randall was now shining his light on several lifeless corpses lying on the cold, damp ground. Sam turned away in disgust. "You stay here, I'm going in for a closer look."

Randall moved closer to the bodies and immediately recognized one of them as the man who had brought him back to the cavern. Kristoph's now lifeless form lay sprawled on its side, a pool of crimson liquid puddled under his head. Even in the poorly lit cavern, Randall realized what had happened to the once proud and angry man. The large caliber weapon that had been fired at point-blank range, had removed a portion of the left side of his upper temple. He moved his light to see that the others in this killing zone had met similar fates. A shiver ran down his spine as he realized that this could have easily happened to Sam and Phil as well. Once again, he felt a twinge of guilt for involving them in this deadly adventure. Returning to Sam, he relayed the news that his former captor was now deceased.

"What do we do now?"

"We should get out of this underground cavern system and get you back to civilization where you'll be safe," Randall replied, the thought of the dead men down the tunnel still fresh in his mind.

"Or, we could go after the medallion, get it back, and return it to the rightful owners," Sam responded.

Randall sighed. "Sam, be reasonable. These guys are heavily armed, and they're not afraid to use their weapons. This isn't a game, and there's no guarantee we'll survive another encounter. I'm sorry, but you're going home, and I'm going to look for Phil and Mike. I got them into this mess, and I'm sure as hell going to do everything I can to make sure they get back safe."

Randall's apprehension was apparent, and the tone in his speech was his serious-dad voice; the one he used when he wanted to make it clear that he was the father, and she was the daughter. It also meant that his word was final. It was the same tone he had used when he told Sam that she would go into a different field than archaeology, so that she could have a stable family life, in one place. It was the same speech he gave her shortly before she had applied to the Anthropology Department at Georgetown University. Both times, his admonitions had fallen on deaf ears, and he was doubtful there would be a different outcome this time.

"Dad, I know you're worried about me, but I'm not a little girl, anymore. I've had my share of dangerous run-ins with sketchy characters. I've also survived some scary near-misses in the field, and I have the scars to prove it. If

Dumond and his men aren't here, that means they likely went back to their jungle base. You have no idea where it is or how to get there. On the other hand, I know where it is, and more importantly, I've been inside the facility. I know my way around and what to expect. You need my help. You can't finish this alone."

Randall stared into the now serious eyes of his daughter, knowing not only that she was right, but that once she set her mind to something, there was no convincing her otherwise. He shifted uncomfortably.

"Well?"

"Okay, we'll go together. But at the first sign of trouble, I want you to leave."

"Deal!"

Chapter Twenty-Four

It was a short trek back out of the cavern and into the chamber room for Randall and Sam. Fortunately, one of the ropes that Ackers's men had used to rappel down, was still hanging into the cavern. After climbing back up and out of the temple complex, the feel of the warm sunlight on their skin was a welcome sensation. They enjoyed it only for a moment, as time was short, and they both knew that they had to move quickly.

Removing her GPS-equipped phone from her backpack, Sam proudly said, "We need to go this way."

"How do you know?"

"When they were holding Monica and me, I marked the camp as a waypoint on my GPS," Sam said, smiling proudly.

Randall shook his head, smiling at his daughter.

The trip to Dumond's base was a difficult march through dense undergrowth. Had circumstances been different, the two scientists would have undoubtedly been impressed enough to realize that they were trekking across ground unseen by human eyes for centuries. The biodiversity in this part of the rainforest was amazing. Everything was alive. But there was no time for enjoying the scenery. They were on a mission, and time was of the essence.

Finally, after several hours of rough hiking, they reached the base. Randall marveled at the sprawling compound that arced across an enormous clearing in the rainforest. Multiple

163

buildings dotted the complex, which stretched east, ending on the coast. Several of the structures were badly burned, no doubt from Kristoph's attack, and others were riddled with bullet holes. The similarity between the sight before them and the vision that Randall had when he was in the dream-like state with the visitors, was eerie. Once again, Randall was overcome with awe at the realization that he had likely not dreamed that event.

"What do we do now?" Sam asked.

"Now we wait and keep an eye on things. We need to see if there's anyone on guard. I'm sure our friends wouldn't just let anyone who happens by to just stroll into the camp," Randall replied

"That's true, but they also eliminated their competition."

"Good point, but I still think we need to watch for a guard."

The two sat crouched for some time, hidden by the dense underbrush. Their patience was rewarded as a uniformed man appeared from the distance and walked in their direction. As he moved, he scanned the perimeter of the encampment, looking for signs of intruders.

Slowly, the figure grew larger and larger until he was about 20 yards away. As the guard drew near, Randall began to wonder if their decision to get so close to the clearing had been a wise one, but the soldier abruptly turned, walking at a near right angle to where they lay hidden in the heavy foliage. He had not seen them and continued his assignment guarding the perimeter. Sam and her father sat motionless as the soldier disappeared into the distance.

"Okay, we were here for 27 minutes before we saw him, so we should have at least that much time to make it over to the buildings. When you were here last time, where did they keep you?"

"I was in that building over there," Sam said, pointing to the center building in the semi-circular encampment.

"We'll have to move quickly. Are you ready?"

"As ready as I'll ever be."

Hunched over, the two ran to the side of the administration building, carefully watching for signs of others exiting the structures. Much to their surprise, no one came out, and they arrived undetected at the eastern side of the building.

As Sam pressed herself into the exterior wall, Randall peered through the small glass window of the exterior door. Through it, he spotted an empty hallway with doors interspersed at semi-regular intervals. The lack of activity both in and around the complex was unnerving, but Randall rationalized that his captors no longer sensed a threat from the other group of mercenaries. He motioned to his daughter that he was entering.

Randall slowly pressed the wooden door inward, extending his arm as he opened the door in case someone suddenly appeared in the hallway. After a moment's time, it appeared that the hallway would remain clear. He slipped inside, leading with his assault rifle, with Sam following closely. The two hugged the wall as they crept down the passageway to the first door. As they approached it, Randall used the same technique he had used on the exterior door, peering through the glass window. The room was empty and appeared to be some sort of break room with vending machines and a big screen. They moved further down the hall to a windowless door.

"That's where they held Monica and me," Sam whispered to her father, who nodded in acknowledgement.

They continued forward. With a suddenness that caught them both off guard, a door down the hall and to the left opened inward. Quickly, Randall pushed Samantha through the door to her former cell. Closing the door behind them, the two huddled against the side wall. Randall crouched, aiming his gun at the door, ready in case he needed to engage the enemy. They waited to see if Ackers's men had noticed them, but with each passing second, it appeared that they had narrowly escaped being caught.

Finally, after what seemed like an eternity, Randall whispered, "That was close. Let's see if the coast is clear." He moved to the far side of the door, grasped the handle, and opened it very slowly, peering out through the crack. As before, there was no sign of life in the hallway. They had not been detected. Randall motioned for his daughter to follow him, and the two resumed their search for the medallion.

After passing an additional room, the two discovered a promising sign. Peering through the window, Randall viewed what appeared to be a study. Books and maps were strewn about tables, and a computer sat idly on a desk. He pushed the door open, slowly. In a moment, they were both inside the room.

It became quickly apparent that this was Dumond's command and research center. Maps of the jungle area were pinned to the wall with colorful directional arrows drawn in careful arcs, representing the movement of people. After a quick study, Sam realized that the different colors represented different groups. Upon closer examination, Sam noticed date and time stamps on the arcs. Clearly, Dumond had been aware of their comings and goings, knowing where and when she and her father's groups were approaching the ruins.

"Sam!"

Samantha glanced over and saw her father motioning her to his side. When she reached him, Sam's heart dropped into the pit of her stomach. On the wall in front of her father was an aerial photo of a complex the size of a small city. The photo was dated March 11, 2016, and from the look of the facility, it was nearly complete. In the middle of the complex was an elaborate containment facility with a web of concrete-reinforced conduit emanating from the center. The conduit fed into an elaborate complex of buildings. Sam immediately recognized that this was an energy generating facility of a size and scale that she had never seen. At the bottom of the image was a simple text line and date that read, "Construction Complete, November 30, 2016."

Even more troubling than this were the images that surrounded the energy facility. On the edge of the aerial photo of the energy plant, were pictures and names arranged in a pinwheel fashion, encircling the facility. The individuals appeared to be professional business people, dressed in suits and ties. Sam did not recognize any of them, except for one, Johan Kristoph. Under his name was written, "Accidental cave-in on April 16, 2016," and his name was crossed out.

Sam scanned the other pictures and realized that each had another short description and date attached to it. Each date was in the future; yet, they were all before the scheduled completion of the power plant. The descriptions were curious: "Industrial Accident, Diving Tank Failure, and Skiing Accident."

"Oh my God, he's going to kill them all and make it look like accidents." There was only one woman in the group, Margaret Seivers. Sam pulled her cell phone from her backpack and took several pictures with the camera, then immediately sent them to a personal email account.

"What are you doing?"

"I don't know what this Dumond character is up to, but I want to have some way of documenting what we've seen."

"Good idea, but I think we need to get going."

"Okay, just one minute."

Sam took a close-up photo of Margaret Seivers, whose planned demise would occur on August 21, 2016 from a "Gasoline Leak aboard Yacht."

"Let's get going, Sam."

"We need to find the medallion first."

Smiling, Randall held out a small box containing the medallion and its chain. "Found it in the safe in the corner," Randall said, pointing to a wall safe across the room.

"How did you know the combination?"

"I tried various combinations of eleven, sixteen, twenty and thirty until I found the right one."

Sam looked puzzled, and Randall realized that she had not seen the connection.

"The completion date the power plant." Randall grinned at his daughter's expression when she realized how her father had solved the riddle. "The old man still has a few tricks up his sleeve, kiddo."

Sam gave her father a sideways glance with a fake stern look and then broke into a quiet chuckle. "Let's blow this pop stand."

The two quietly made their way back to the door and resumed their skulking positions pressed against the wall. Randall slowly moved his head upward, peering through the small window and checking both ends of the hallway. He looked at Sam and nodded. Slowly, he turned the handle of the door and opened it, slightly.

Just as he did, another door down the hall, and to the left, opened outward, and he could see a uniformed arm on the door handle. In a quick, jerking motion, Randall pulled his own door closed and scooted quickly back into the room, nearly knocking Sam over in the process. She stumbled backward but caught herself before falling to the floor. Randall turned in one motion, grabbed her arm, and pulled both of them against the wall and out of the line of sight of the window.

From the hallway, they could hear boot steps marching in their direction. Each step grew louder as the soldier approached their room. Sam's breathing was fast and shallow, and she seemed to be searching for a possible hiding spot. Her eyes grew wide when she realized that there was nowhere to hide. Grabbing her father's hand, she could feel his heartbeat as the two pressed themselves into the wall, willing the soldier to walk by their hiding spot.

The boot steps stopped right outside their door. The door handle began to turn slowly. They were trapped. Randall positioned himself off to the side of the door, ready to grab the mercenary who entered. He would have to muffle him to keep him from yelling for help and then neutralize him. It had been years since he had done this, but the process had been drilled into him.

As the door opened, it seemed to suck all of the air out of the room. They could hear a conversation taking place in the hallway.

"Sergeant, the Colonel wants a word with you."

"Just a moment, I need to get a map of the temple area for our recon plans."

"Immediately, Sergeant!"

The door closed, and Randall heard the boot steps once again, but this time they were walking away. He looked to Sam whose face was ashen. "Are you okay?"

She nodded,

"We need to get out of here now."

Randall once again assumed his position near the small window and, seeing that the hallway was clear, quickly opened the door and headed out as Sam followed close behind. In a matter of minutes, they were out of the building and checking for the guards watching the perimeter. Seeing none, they wasted little time making it back to the safety of the jungle.

Chapter Twenty-Five

The ancestors had spoken to Chief Yupanqui in his sleep, again, last night. Their visits were becoming more frequent, and their communication with him more specific. The main message from the ancestors was that time was quickly running out for the chief and his people.

Yupanqui gripped his staff tightly as he surveyed his peoples' land. This valley had been their home for generations and had provided for them for so long. He felt an attachment to this land that words could not describe. He remembered playing in the nearby forests and fishing in the river with his friends as a young boy. He recalled the ceremony and challenges he'd had to endure in his quest to be recognized as a warrior by his people. This ground was much more than just his home; it was a part of him.

The visions had started shortly after the white-haired scientist named Randall first visited Yupanqui and his people. Initially, the Chief had thought they were nothing more than dreams, but he soon realized there was much more to his nocturnal visits than random visions of past and current events. The ancestors had foretold of a prophecy in which a beautiful young woman would help Yupanqui's people reunite with their brethren in Vilcabamba. They had also instructed Yupanqui to accept Randall and his helpers and to allow them to learn about the tribe's history. At the time the Chief hadn't understood why his forefathers would

171

want outsiders to learn about the tribe's secret, but now their guidance was clearly understood.

Through his dream conversations, Yupanqui had determined that Samantha Randall was the young woman from the prophecy. Although the ancestors had not specifically told him so, he had sensed a strong feeling in his dream that she was the one. The ancestors had also warned that forces were at work, seeking to prevent the reunification. When Amaro, the guide Yupanqui had sent to help Randall, returned to the tribe and told the Chief about the attack on Randall and his people outside of the sacred temple, the Chief knew the ancestors were speaking of these attackers.

This angered the chief on many levels. First, for these so-called warriors to attack unarmed, peaceful people who posed no threat to them was unthinkable. Second, their utter disregard for the most sacred place of his people told the chief all he needed to know about these men. They were his enemies and needed to be stopped.

The Chief was thankful that Amaro had evaded detection and returned to his tribe to warn them. Now Yupanqui would have to rely on him, again, to lead his people against the attackers to help Randall and his daughter.

Yupanqui decided that it was time for his tribe to return to the sacred underground city and help Randall face these savages, even though entering the mountain was forbidden. He prayed for the forgiveness of his ancestors for breaking the most sacred of rules and in his defense, he uttered the words spoken to him by Randall years ago. "Desperate times call for desperate measures." Surely these were desperate times for his people.

Chapter Twenty-Six

Randall and Sam finally stopped sprinting as they made their way back into the safety of the jungle. Sam felt a great sense of relief, but when she looked at her father, she could see that he was hesitant.

"What's wrong?"

"I need to go back to the compound."

"Are you serious? We were lucky to get out alive."

"Mike might be there. I can't just leave him."

Sam cocked her head to one side and looked into her father's eyes. They were filled with a sad but resolved resignation. During the excitement of getting the medallion back, she had forgotten about Mike. Her father, true to form, had not.

With a twinge of selfish guilt, Sam said, "There's nothing I can say to convince you not to go is there?"

"Nope."

"Then I'm going with you."

Randall pursed his lips, and a thin smile returned to his face for a moment. Then the serious look returned. "I have to go alone, Sam. One of us needs to return that medallion to Yupanqui and his people. If I don't make it back, I want you to high-tail it out of here and get back to Paititi and give it to the chief. He'll know what to do with it. Did you save the coordinates, so you can get back to the village?"

Sam knew it was futile to argue the point with her father—he was a stubborn man, and in this case, he was right. "Yes, but by now my phone might be dead. I haven't charged it for several days. I turned it off after I took the pictures in the compound. How will I know if you make it out of the compound, again?"

"Wait here for 60 minutes. If you don't see me by then, I've probably been caught. If that's the case, I want you to find the chief and give him the medallion. Then head back to the University and let Francisco know what happened. I'm sure the chief can help you get there. Maybe if we let the world know what's going on, we can still stop Dumond."

"That's a pretty thin plan."

"We don't have much to work with, kiddo. Take this too," Randall handed Sam the gun. If he was leaving her in the jungle alone, he was going to give her a way to protect herself. She knew how to use it, he had made sure of that when she was growing up.

Sam accepted the assault rifle, then grabbed her father and gave him a big hug. He hugged her back and chuckled, remembering that this was how she hugged him when she was a child.

"Good luck, Dad."

With a final parting smile, Randall turned and headed back toward the compound. Once again, the thick underbrush provided shelter from potential peering eyes, but also made his progress slow. After a few minutes of trudging through the heavy growth, he once again found himself at the edge of the clearing, staring at the compound.

As before, there was no sign of activity, and once again Randall sat patiently waiting for the guard to make his rounds. It didn't take long. The guard came into view and then disappeared to the far side of the compound. Not wasting time, Randall made the, now familiar, run from the safe cover of the jungle to the central building of the complex, stopping outside the external door and pressing his body up against the wall. Slowly he peered through the small glass window, and not seeing any signs of movement, entered the building for a second time.

Randall knew that he was pushing his luck by sneaking into the building again, but his conscience wouldn't let him leave without at least checking to see if Mike was alive. Even though Phil and Mike were technically his graduate assistants, Randall thought of them as his sons — a fact his biological son, John, had picked up on years ago.

Randall eased down the long corridor, staying close to the far-right wall, prepared to move quickly if someone exited from one of the rooms. Having made this excursion once already, Randall had the advantage of knowing that Mike wouldn't be in the rooms he had visited earlier. This helped to narrow his focus and, statistically, made the task of finding Mike easier. This line of reasoning made the professor grin despite himself. Once analytical, always analytical, even when your life was in grave danger. He approached the first new door and slowly peered through the open window. Again, he was astonished to find that the room appeared to be empty. From all appearances, it seemed to be a storage room.

Randall continued his stealthy glide down the corridor to the next room. This was the fifth room of six in the building and, aside from the one room that the soldiers had exited from earlier, the other four rooms had been empty.

Unlike the other rooms, this door was solid metal, with a cylindrical lock on the outside. He grasped the knob and slowly turned it, trying with all his might to be quiet and inconspicuous. The door was locked and would not open. Randall rotated the deadbolt, which made a loud click when it disengaged from the doorframe. Randall scanned the hallway to make sure no one was coming. He stood at the metal door, unsure what he would find on the other side. He steadied himself, then pulled the door open.

Inside, he saw what appeared to be a living quarter with a couch and table. As he craned his neck to get a better look, the door across the hall and to his right, opened. He was forced to scramble into the living quarters, hoping no one had seen him. Randall took a defensive position, crouching to the side of the door, ready to spring on anyone who entered.

"Dr. Randall?"

Randall turned to face the voice that had spoken to him and caught the sight of a familiar face.

"It is you! Thank God!" Mike blurted out.

Randall quickly brought a finger to his lips, signaling for Mike to be quiet. He heard boot steps stop outside the door. Next came the unmistakable sound of someone racking a round in a gun.

Randall knew the mercenary outside was coming in and suspected someone else was in the room with Mike. Unarmed, Randall's only chance was to surprise him. The soldier would be expecting Randall to attack him from the side as he opened the door, so he needed a different strategy. He searched the room for a hiding place. There was a closet six feet behind Mike. Not enough time to get there. Where else? Under Mike's bed. He dove under the hospital bed.

The door to the room burst open. A black-clad soldier stepped in, assault rifle drawn. He made a visual sweep of the room, his weapon pointed outward like a dragon ready to spit fire.

Randall recoiled under the bed He pressed his body as far back from the edge as possible. Slowly the soldier moved forward, making his way around the room. His finger on the gun's trigger.

"Where is he," the soldier growled.

"What are you talking about? By the way, when am I getting some lunch? The room service here is terrible," Mike joked.

The guard wasn't amused.

From his spot under the bed, Randall could only see the black combat boots and lower ankles of the mercenary. They headed straight to the hospital bed. Randall forced himself to focus on the boots. He only had one chance and he had to stay alert.

In one swooping motion, the soldier lowered his head and weapon under the bed. He pointed the barrel directly at Randall's legs. Without hesitation, Randall let loose a brutal kick directly into the gun barrel. The weapon recoiled back into the unsuspecting mercenary's face, hitting him in the nose. The suddenness of the blow sent the soldier sprawling onto his backside. The weapon flopped uselessly to the floor.

Randall scrambled from under the bed and lunged for the weapon. Just inches from grasping it, he felt a sudden jerk backward. The mercenary had grabbed him by his boot. The next sensation Randall felt was a jabbing pain in his back as the soldier dealt repeated blows to his spine with his elbow. The pain was excruciating.

Randall rolled, striking with his elbow which caught the soldier on the side of his face, once again knocking him off balance. Randall scrambled to his feet, while the mercenary did the same. The two men faced each other, the mercenary unsheathed a large serrated knife.

"Get ready to die, asshole."

The two men circled each other, the soldier making a low growling noise. Randall kept his cool and searched for something to parry a knife blow. He grabbed a table light, tearing off the shade.

The soldier let out a sick laugh. "Is that the best you can do?"

The mercenary lunged at Randall, who deftly moved to one side, batting away the knife-wielding hand with the lamp base. Randall took two steps back. The circling ensued.

The mercenary grunted, rushing Randall at full force, knocking him to the ground. Randall lost the lamp base. The two men tumbled and rolled, coming to a stop with the mercenary straddling Randall.

The mercenary swung his knife down at Randall. Randall deflected it just enough to avoid injury. The blade impacted the floor inches from his head. Randall could smell the soldier's stinking breath as his face drew near.

"After I take care of you, I'm going to make sure that little bitch daughter of yours gets it, too. I'm going to enjoy that one. Going to take my time and have a little fun first."

Suddenly the soldier's head jerked up.

"Take that, asshole!" Mike threw his boot at the mercenary's head. He was standing now, balancing against the bed with his good leg.

It was just enough of a distraction. Randall struck the mercenary on the side of his head then rolled to the side, grabbing the soldier's leg and pulling him down. Caught off balance, the mercenary tumbled off Randall, losing his knife in the process.

Both men caught sight of the gun at the same time and lunged for it. The mercenary grabbed it first, but Randall was on him in a moment. The two stood, struggling for control of the weapon.

"Not this time, cocksucker. No prisoners," the mercenary got his finger into the trigger, trying to wrench the weapon from Randall's grip. The assault rifle fired in Mike's direction.

"No!" Randall planted his feet and rammed the mercenary into the wall, driving his head up and back. The mercenary's head violently smashed into the wall then his body fell limp to the floor, blood trickling freely from a gash on his head.

Randall raced to Mike's side. The graduate student lay helpless on the bed, his shirt crimson with blood, two gaping holes in the middle of his chest. His eyes rolled helplessly to Randall as he gasped for breath.

"Hold on Mike, you're going to be okay. You're going to be okay," Randall repeated, tears streaming from his eyes.

Mike grasped his mentor's hand, squeezed once, and then went limp. Sobbing, Randall dropped his face onto the bed next to Mike's body. "No, no, no!"

He cradled Mike's head in his hands, gently closing his open eyes. For a moment, Randall forgot about everything else, his heart consumed with grief. He continued rocking back and forth, holding Mike's lifeless body.

"Excuse me."

Randall spun, ready to fight again. There was someone else in the room.

"Who are you?"

"My name is George...these guys kidnapped me from my company."

Randall just stared blankly.

"We built four satellites for Dumond but had no idea what he would use them for. He lied to us. He's been holding me prisoner here with Mike and wants me to help him finish his plan. He's crazy, and I can't help him do what he wants to do. Please, you have to help me."

Randall's mind spun between grief, anger and disbelief. Still clutching Mike's body, he wiped the tears from his eyes with his free hand.

"Why didn't you say or do anything during the fight? You could have helped us!"

George looked down, averting his eyes from Randall. "I was afraid."

Randall's tone softened. "How do I know that you're telling me the truth?"

"Your name is Nick Randall, right? You have a daughter, Sam, who's also an archaeologist, and you have a son, John. Your wife was killed in a car accident. Mike told me all about you. He looked up to you, Dr. Randall. He said you would come for him and that you would help me. Please, I don't want to die here..."

Glancing again at Mike and realizing that there was nothing he could do, Randall gently set him down on the bed. "Good-bye, Mike."

He glanced over at George. "Come on."

Randall went to the door, opened it and ran for the exit. George followed closely behind. Avoiding contact with Dumond's men, he made the safety of the jungle. Randall dropped to his knees. Consumed with grief, he vomited, repeatedly into the dense foliage.

He wiped his mouth. "First Phil and now Mike. My God, what have I done?" He rubbed his eyes as if he were having a terrible dream and doing so would wake him from his nightmare. No such relief was coming.

He collapsed on the ground and lay there sobbing for several minutes. George looked on, helpless to assist in any way. Finally, Randall forced himself to his feet and shuffled deeper into the safety of the jungle. George followed him, not saying a word.

CB₰

Sam looked at her watch. Her father had been gone for 67 minutes, but she refused to accept that he might not be returning. Finally, she saw movement in the distance. She squatted low behind a large plant and craned her neck to look around the large leaves obstructing her view. She saw a figure moving in her direction. It was her father, but something wasn't right. He was moving slowly, methodically, as if something was wrong with him. Sam's initial reaction was to call out to see if he was okay, but she fought the urge, choosing to watch him instead. Another figure appeared behind him. Sam's heart beat faster.

After several minutes passed, it was clear that the man following her father posed no threat. At one point, the other man came to Randall's side and held his head as Randall doubled over. She couldn't be sure, but it looked like her father was throwing up. Sam strained to make out the other face, but despite her deepest hopes, it wasn't Mike. Confused, she wondered aloud what was going on.

Sam decided it was safe to approach them, and as she got closer, she was thankful to see that her father didn't appear physically injured. She closed within a few yards and could see that he'd been crying. Her dad seemed oblivious to the world around him. The other man slowed his approach and stayed a short distance from Sam and her father.

"Dad, are you okay? What happened," she said softly.

Randall looked up absentmindedly, "He's gone, Sam."

"What do you mean?"

"They shot him. He's gone. First Phil, now Mike." Randall slumped to the ground, his hands folded across his knees.

"Oh my God, I'm so sorry. Mike was a wonderful guy. I'm just so sorry." Sam put her arm around his shoulders, unsure of what else to say or do.

"They were like sons to me. They trusted me and looked up to me, and I got them both killed." Randall lowered his head and wrapped his hands around it, shaking from side to side. Sam held him, trying to comfort him.

After a few moments, she spoke softly. "They loved you, Dad. Whenever I talked to either of them, they always said how much you meant to them."

Sam looked up at the other figure that had followed her father out of the jungle. "Dad, who's this?"

"His name is George. He's an engineer, Dumond was holding him hostage. He says his company built satellites for Dumond and then they kidnapped him. He claims he knows what Dumond is really up to and can help us."

"Can we trust him? How do we know he's not lying?"

"Mike trusted him. He told him all about our family." Randall's head once again sank into his hands.

Sam left her father's side and walked straight over to George, her eyes never leaving his face. George shifted uncomfortably. She stopped a foot short of him.

"Who are you and what do you want?"

"I … I'm George Walker. I work for Gemini Orbital Services. Mr. Dumond hired my company to build four satellites for him. He said he was going to use them to test a new technology he was developing. He said he wanted to meet me to look at the last satellite and then his men kidnapped me. They took me to this jungle compound and have been forcing me to help them with their plan."

"How do I know that any of this is true? For all we know, you could be working for Dumond. He could have hired you to befriend us and then signal him when he's ready to jump us again." Sam tilted her head to catch George's gaze again. He was clearly nervous.

"No, I swear I'm not working for him. Geez, I'm just an engineer! He was going to kill me if I didn't get away. Please, I'll help you and your dad, just don't send me back to that crazy man."

"So what's his plan, George? What is Dumond trying to do?"

"Like I said, he hired my company to build four satellites for him. We already launched three of them into orbit. The fourth one is going up next week. He told us he was going to use the satellites as relay stations to test a new technology his company had developed."

"Go on."

"He was going to bounce a large, ground-based laser off the satellites to ground stations and use it to power machines. He said his company was testing the technology to see if it was feasible to deliver energy to any spot in the world without having to build a nearby power plant. If it worked, his company would be the only one that could offer to send power to anyone, anywhere in the world."

"But that's not what he's really planning to do?" Sam asked.

George shifted uncomfortably again. "Sort of. The problem is that a laser that powerful would need huge amounts of energy. It's just not feasible with current technology..."

"And..."

"Then I found out about the generating facility he's building. It's huge. Larger than anything I've ever seen. He and his men said they had found a power source to operate it. The scale of energy they talked about was off the charts!"

"So what's the plan, George? What's Dumond going to do?"

"A focused beam from a strong laser is pure energy. The problem so far has been the impossibility of building a laser powerful enough to overcome the dispersion caused by atmospheric interference. The other problem has been that we haven't had a strong enough power source to make it work. But, now, Dumond has built the laser, and if he gets his power source working, he can use it. Once the system is working, he can deliver a huge energy pulse anywhere on earth, or in space. The pulse we're talking about would be more than the energy needed to power a few simple machines. The energy delivered would exceed the energy produced by both atomic bombs dropped on Hiroshima and Nagasaki during World War II."

"He's created a super weapon!"

"Exactly. He can destroy entire cities from space or use his system to take down satellites."

"What was your role in this, George? What does Dumond want you to do?"

"I'm an electrical engineer, and I design systems to integrate the power systems and the machinery they drive. Dumond wants me to look at this power system and figure out how to use it to power his laser."

"What do you know about the power system?"

"Not much. Just that it's some sort of new technology that no one seems to understand, and for some reason, it was developed out in the middle of nowhere. Dumond needs to relocate it to his power facility and figure out how to hook it up to his laser. If he can't, his whole plan goes up in smoke."

Sam softened somewhat. She felt he was telling the truth. She took a deep breath, realizing that the information she was about to share with George was going to sound crazy, but she had no choice.

"George, I need to explain something to you."

Sam told George how her father believed he had found the ancient underground city. She also explained how Dumond had funded her father's field research, so he could

185

step in to take the power source as soon as they found it. George listened intently, if somewhat incredulously, to some of the details that Sam imparted.

"So you're saying that there's an ancient civilization that's thousands of years old, made up of creatures which are possibly from another world, and that they decided to set up camp in the middle of the Amazon rainforest?"

Sam nodded.

"They built a huge underground city and have been monitoring human activity from there, using a secret power source that they developed. That's the power source that Dumond wants to use to power his laser, the one that I'm supposed to figure out how to operate. Is that about right?"

She could see that he wasn't buying the story.

"I know it sounds kind of crazy, but yes, that's it."

George looked into Sam's eyes. She could see the wheels turning in his head.

He's trying to figure out if I'm lying or crazy. Can't say I blame him.

George sighed and nodded. "There's something else you should know, Sam. He believes in aliens, too."

"Who believes in aliens?" Sam asked.

"Dumond. I overheard a conversation he was having with one of his men. He claims that he was abducted by aliens when he was young, and they did terrible things to him. Sam, he's a psychopath, and his experience with these aliens, real or imagined, warped the hell out of him. He was talking about how they had the power to control his mind and body. He said that after being abducted, he vowed he'd find a way to get back at them and use their power for himself. When he said it, he looked possessed! He's scary as hell!" George said, his eyes growing wider.

"It's okay, George, you're safe now," Sam said, taking his hand.

"Okay, but what are we going to do?"

"Get to the underground city first and stop them."

George's mouth fell open. He had the look of a small child who had just been told that Santa Claus and the Easter Bunny weren't real. "You can't be serious?"

"I am, and you're coming with us."

Sam walked over to her father. He was still sitting on the ground, his head between his knees. She put a hand on his shoulder.

"What do I do now?" Randall asked.

"You have to finish this, Dad. That's what they would have wanted you to do."

"I don't know if I can."

"We'll do it together."

She glanced at George, who looked back without saying a word.

Randall slowly rose to his feet, wiping the tears from his eyes.

"Before we try to find Vilcabamba, there's something we need to do, first. When Kristoph was holding me captive, I met another scientist who knew about the medallion and its backstory."

Randall explained the trip to the tomb with Richter and how Kristoph's men had executed him. He also told her about the book in the sarcophagus.

"The purpose of the medallion must be explained in that book and we need to understand what the medallion is for."

"I found the secret note in your journal explaining that the medallion is 'THE KEYSTONE' but to what?" Sam asked.

"The answer to that question must be in that book," Randall replied.

"So now we're going into the jungle to find a book in a tomb?" George asked.

"No. Sam and I are going George. You need to wait here for us," Randall answered.

George shifted, nervously, "How far away is it?"

"It's not far. We should be back before nightfall."

Chapter Twenty-Seven

Randall and Sam walked through the shrouded pathway on their journey back to find the tomb that Richter had shown him. Still in a state of shock over losing Mike, he found his mind wandering between the past and the present. Once again, Randall felt the humidity beating him down as he trudged through the jungle. The path was relatively clear but hiking through the undergrowth was still exhausting. Pushing aside his current predicament for a moment, Randall found himself wondering how much longer he could realistically keep up with the physical demands of field work. While these were not typical circumstances, the simple fact was that Randall was getting older and working in these conditions wasn't as easy as it had been when he was a young man.

When Richter had said the path led to a compound in the middle of the jungle, Randall had known it was Dumond's base Richter had seen. Despite this knowledge, finding the path hadn't been easy. The compound was large, and he and Sam had to be careful while they searched for the opening to the trail. On several occasions, they had had to hide as guards protecting the perimeter of the camp made their rounds. Finally, after a great deal of searching, Sam found the entrance to the trail connecting Dumond's base with the tomb. What Randall hadn't known was how far the compound would be from the tomb.

"So the burial mound is along this route?" Sam asked hoping to break the silence.

"Yes. According to Dr. Richter, he had traveled along this path from Dumond's base, all the way to the coast where Kristoph's men had dropped us off. We started from a clearing on that end of the path and walked for about an hour until we came to the tomb. The problem is, I'm not sure how far away we are on this end. I'm hoping it won't take us too long to find it again."

"Why didn't Kristoph's men take the book when you were in the tomb?"

"They're trained killers, not scientists. Kristoph wanted them to get the medallion and hadn't said anything about a book. When they saw that the medallion was gone, they didn't search the coffin. They just murdered Richter," Randall stopped for a moment to consider the loss of Richter as well. He quickly realized he didn't have time to reflect on the grief of losing others with so much hanging on their success. He had to keep moving. "To be honest Sam, they knocked me unconscious. For all I know, they may have taken the book, but we need to see if it's still there. I'm hoping there might be some information in it that can shed light on the purpose of the medallion."

"If the medallion is so important, how did the tribe lose it?"

Randall smiled, he could imagine the wheels turning in his daughter's head. "The legend tells about a woman tricking the Chief and stealing the medallion for herself, thinking it would grant her great power. She took the medallion and went back to her people but when they found out what she had done, they killed her, and buried her in the tomb with the medallion around her neck as punishment."

"How did you get it? I remember Mom getting the call and driving out to pick it up for you, but she never made it back."

Randall felt a twinge of pain, even after so many years, the memory of that day was still painful. So much loss. He sighed.

"After your mother died, I didn't go back to the University for several weeks. When I finally came back, there was a small package on my desk, wrapped in brown paper. I opened it and found the medallion inside. There was no message with it. In fact, there was no writing on the paper except my name. Given my mental state at the time, I didn't ask questions. I just put it in my desk drawer and forgot about it. The package sat there for months. By the time I found it again and asked around, no one remembered how it had gotten to my office."

"Maybe I can help explain," a voice called out from the trail behind them.

Randall spun and found himself facing a man who looked vaguely familiar. He was a little shorter than Randall, with a slighter build. His face was humorless, and his long, dark black hair framed his face. He was holding a gun at his waist, pointing it at Randall.

"Who are you?" Sam said, turning to face him as well.

"Your dad knows me, or should I say, he should know. Remember me Nick?"

"Charles. What in the hell are you doing here?" Randall said, his memory finally clicking in.

"I'm here for the medallion. That's why I orchestrated all of this."

"Dad, who is this guy?" Sam asked.

"My name is Charles Young, and I worked with your dad a long time ago. He and I didn't really get along did we, Nick?"

Randall watched Charles carefully. "He and I were graduate students in Georgetown together. When I was going through my rough patch, he caused me more grief than anyone at the college."

Charles walked closer to Randall and Sam, keeping a careful aim on them as he did. "You forgot to mention that you cost me my job."

"No, you cost yourself your job. You were so busy trying to score points with Dr. Adele and the rest of the tenured faculty by making my life a living hell that you forgot your purpose as a student. If you had focused on your research, you'd be a tenured Professor by now," Randall replied.

"I guess we'll just have to agree to disagree. The important thing now is getting my medallion back. Do you have it?"

"What do you mean your medallion, and how did you know we would be here on this trail?" Randall asked.

"I've been planning this for some time. I'm the one who sent you the medallion, but of course, I didn't let you know it was from me. If I had, you never would have accepted it. Once the University fired me, I struggled to find work. I finally landed at Bates, a small Liberal Arts school in Maine. Perhaps you've heard of it?"

"You knew Richter."

A sickening smile spread across Charles' face. "I met him when I was working at the college. It was easy to manipulate him. He was so desperate for a friend that when I showed a little interest, he jumped on it like a starving dog that hadn't eaten in weeks."

Sam shook her head in disgust.

"So, you knew about his research?" Randall asked.

"Of course. He helped me piece together the location of this tomb, and I retrieved the medallion without his knowledge. Of course, as you can imagine, it cost me a pretty penny to get it. I had to sell everything I owned, and leverage myself to the hilt, to get the money to find that damn thing. It wasn't cheap to hire locals to hack through this horrible jungle."

"Why Charles, why would you go through all of this trouble? You can't possibly expect to get something out of this?"

"The legend says that the one who possesses the medallion can control an advanced technology unlike anything else. Do you know what that means? Fame, fortune and best of all, revenge on everyone who has ever crossed me, starting with you. Now, if you don't mind, we're losing daylight. We need to find the tomb, so you can unravel the mystery of the medallion and explain how I can use it."

The group moved forward through the canopied path, stopping occasionally to drink from their canteens. Randall tried to strike up a conversation with Charles to dissuade him from his quest.

"You don't need to do this. If you still have your job at the college, you can still become a tenured professor."

"Do you know how long that would take? I like my plan better," Charles responded.

"You're willing to murder innocent people for money?"

Charles shifted uncomfortably, his face becoming serious. "If you do what I say, you and your daughter might live."

Nick turned to face Charles. "You know I wasn't responsible for what happened to you."

Charles shoulders sagged, but he quickly recovered. "I want that medallion, and you're going to help me get it."

They kept walking. After some time, they arrived at a familiar spot. Having walked from the opposite direction, the opening was now on the south of the trail. After exchanging a glance, Randall and Sam walked into the circular clearing and to the entrance in the side of the hill.

"Stop there," Charles said. "Ms. Randall, you're coming in with me."

"The hell she is. She has nothing to do..."

"I think you're forgetting your place here. I'm the one with the gun, not you. If you didn't want your daughter to be a part of this, then you shouldn't have brought her."

Randall began to move toward Charles when Sam stepped in front of him. She placed her arm on his shoulder.

"I'll be all right, Dad, he won't hurt me. Will I know what I'm looking for when I check the coffin?"

Randall's anger subsided as he looked into his daughter's eyes. He then turned to face Charles.

"You wanted me to come here to help you understand the purpose of the medallion. If I don't go in with you and there are symbols to interpret, how are you going to know what they say? Let Sam stay here, and I promise I won't try anything. I'll do as you say, and I will interpret anything we find."

Randall watched Charles face as he mulled the situation.

"Fine, but I'm warning you, Nick, if you try anything, I'll shoot you…and then her," Charles stated, pointing his gun at Sam.

"I understand."

The two men entered the earthen mound, Randall in front with his flashlight and Charles close behind, his gun pressed into Randall's back. Randall stopped for a moment as his eyes adjusted to the darkness. He felt the hard steel of the gun barrel dig into the small of his back.

"No tricks!"

"I'm just letting my eyes adjust to the darkness before moving in."

They resumed walking and soon covered the distance to the first chamber. Randall stopped for a moment and shone his light around the room. He then shuffled the remaining way into the rear chamber, where the coffin lay in the same state as before. Richter's lifeless body lay slumped on the floor, the blood pooled under the gaping gunshot wound in his chest.

"My God…" Charles said.

"You're responsible for his death."

Charles breathing was fast and shallow.

He's realizing this isn't a game.

After a long pause, Charles spoke, "Get on with it, Nick."

Randall moved gingerly around Richter's body and stood by the side of the coffin. Shining his light in, he once again looked to the feet of the skeleton and saw the wrapped package. He reached in with his free hand, slowly guiding it

195

through the beam of light. He grabbed the book. It wouldn't move. He grabbed it more tightly and pulled harder, but again, failed to pull it out. He leaned into the casket, looking more carefully at the bundle. It was wedged under a small rectangular section of rock protruding from the side wall of the box and a small raised triangular piece of rock on the base of the box.

"What in the world is taking you so long?"

"It's wedged under some sort of ledge in the coffin. I can't seem to get it free."

"Move," Charles motioned for Randall to get out of his way. He nearly tripped over Richter's body. Randall caught himself, then shined his light at Charles, who reached in and pressed against the rectangular ledge with his gun hand, while grabbing the package with the other. The stone moved under Charles' pressure, receding into the side of the coffin. Charles wrenched the parcel free and turned to face Randall.

"See, Nick, sometimes you just need to be a little more aggressive."

As Charles spoke, Randall detected a faint rumbling sound. It became louder and the earthen tomb began to shake. A look of confusion came over Charles's face.

"It was a trip lever! We need to get out of here," Randall grabbed Charles' arm, and yanked him toward the entrance of the tomb.

The ceiling collapses on them as they ran. Dust rained down through the beam of Randall's light as he towed Charles behind him. Large chunks of rock fell from the earthen roof and the whole chamber shook violently. Randall nearly stumbled over a large stone, releasing

Charles' arm in the process. Catching himself he spun back, shining his light towards Charles' face, which was ashen.

Randall grabbed his arm again and pulled him back toward the entrance. Earth rained down on them as they pushed forward. The opening to the outside loomed brightly in front of them, but debris was beginning to build up in the path. Another vicious jolt rocked the chamber, sending both men careening to the floor.

Randall struggled to his feet. Having lost his light, he groped for it on the floor.

"Nick! Help me!"

Randall found the light and turned to search for Charles as dust choked his lungs.

"Keep talking, I'll follow your voice!"

Charles spoke rapidly, fear ringing in his voice. Randall located him quickly. He shined his light over Charles body, inspecting for damage. Charles face was contorted in fear and pain.

"My leg," he whimpered.

Randall pointed the light down his body. Large rocks covered Charles left leg from the thigh downward. Randall knelt beside him and moved a large stone causing Charles to moan in pain. He worked quickly, heaving the heavy stones as dust and debris continued to rain down around him.

The earth shook again. More rocks broke free.

Randall used his body to shield Charles.

"Dad! You've got to get out of there!"

"I can't, Charles is trapped!" Randall said, casting a glance at the ever-dwindling opening back to his daughter.

Randall dug at the jagged rocks pinning Charles' leg. The coarse stones tore his skin. His fingers bled. The dust choked him so badly he could hardly breathe. There were too many boulders. He couldn't move them all.

"Nick," Charles gasped.

Randall stopped digging and turned his flashlight to the injured man's face.

Charles was holding his gun, the barrel pointing directly at Randall's head.

"There's no way I'm getting out of here alive," Charles said.

Randall froze, staring directly into his eyes.

Charles smiled, "Sorry, Nick." He turned the gun to his own head and pulled the trigger.

Randall recoiled at the sudden gunshot blast. Opening his eyes, he stared in shock at Charles' now lifeless body. The tomb had claimed its second victim in as many days.

"Dad! Are you okay? I'm coming in!"

The sound of Sam's voice pulled Randall back to reality. "I'm okay! I'm coming out!"

Randall picked up the package lying near Charles' body and cast a final glance at his former adversary.

"Goodbye Charles."

Randall scrambled towards the entrance, trying desperately to keep his balance as the world around him rocked wildly. The dirt continued to pile up on the other fallen debris. The opening grew tinier by the second.

Randall struggled the final few feet and reached the opening. It was too small to walk out. Randall flung the package out of the tomb and into the clearing beyond. He began climbing up the debris pile on his stomach, digging his fingers into the dirt and pulling his body up a few inches at a time.

Dirt poured down on him, getting into his eyes, clothes, mouth and any other exposed body part. He spit it out, wiping his eyes clean with one hand while climbing with the other. The best he could do was squint as he dragged his injured body up the dirt hill toward daylight.

He was close. With one final pull, his torso shot out of the hole and into the sunshine. Sam, grabbed his arm, yanking him the rest of the way out of the earthen grave.

Randall rolled on the ground, coughing and spitting up dirt as he tried to clear his lungs. His eyes burned with sweat and dirt, and he was unable to catch a good breath of air.

Sam raced to his side, offering him her water bottle. Randall gulped the water and immediately began to gag. He spit out a muddy handful of water and coughed extensively while his lungs burned from a lack of oxygen. Sam propped him up on a backpack and tried to give him more water. Randall pushed the liquid aside and continued coughing.

After several minutes, the coughing subsided, and an exhausted Randall looked up at his daughter, his face covered with dark dirt except for small, circular bands of clean skin, outlining his eyes.

"What happened in there? I heard the gunshot and thought the worst."

Randall explained how Charles had unwittingly set off the trap and became pinned under the debris.

"I tried getting him free, but the rocks were too heavy and there were too many of them..."

"...and you couldn't move them all."

"In the end, Charles knew there was no way I could free him. He took his own life, so I wouldn't stay behind to try and save him."

Randall sat for a moment, staring off into space. He glanced back at the tomb and shook his head. He closed his eyes and sighed deeply. Several minutes passed as he gathered his thoughts. He rubbed his temples, trying to find reason in the violence he had experienced since he had started this journey. There was none. All he could do was finish the job and stop Dumond.

More time passed, and he finally spoke.

"Where's the package?"

Sam left Randall's side and searched for the bundle he had thrown from the tomb. After some time, she returned holding a leather-bound book. She stared at it intently, flipping through the first few pages as she walked. "What is this?"

"I'm not really sure, but it's definitely the same writing we found on the tablets at Paititi and on the medallion."

"How are you able to decipher this writing?" Sam asked.

"Back when we weren't speaking, I didn't really have much to do in my spare time, so I concentrated on learning their language. I'm not going to lie, it was rough going at first, but with a lot of practice, I came to understand the flow of the language. Now, reading it is second nature to me."

Randall sat up and took the book from Sam. He studied it, intently, flipping from page to page, as if searching for something.

"Well?" Sam asked.

"Grab a seat, this is going to take a while."

Chapter Twenty-Eight

Randall found a large, flat stone, and decided it was as good a place as any to read. As he sat down with the book, while Sam left to scout the area. He flipped open the cover and began reading with great interest. The book was the story of the woman who had stolen the medallion. It was also a history lesson on the tribe that had broken away from the main group living in Vilcabamba.

This is the tomb of Luna Quispe, daughter of Matias Quispe, and this is her story. Let this tale serve as a warning to all who would disturb the great power of Ayar Cachi and the ancestors. After being forced from the sacred city, Ayar Manco and our ancestors settled along the sacred river and built the jungle city, Paititi, with the help of men sent by Ayar Cachi. There, our people flourished as the mother jungle and river provided us with ample food and water. We lived there peacefully for many generations, and contact with our brethren in Vilcabamba became less frequent as we were able to live off the bountiful land without their assistance. As such, the younger generations began to believe that Ayar Cachi and the great sacred city were simply fables created by the elders.

One such disbeliever was Luna Quispe. Luna practiced the dark magic, which was forbidden by the elders and believed the stories of Ayar Cachi were attempts by the elders to control her power. One day, she tricked one of the elders, Huayna Capac, into believing she was sorry for her evil ways and asked to learn about the ancestors.

201

Happy to help the wayward girl back onto the right path, Capac spent a great deal of time with her, teaching her the old ways and telling her stories passed down by our people. She learned quickly, grasping the ancient teachings and becoming an expert on our people's lore. Capac was satisfied with the progress of his pupil but continued to withhold the one story which she sought most. The story of the Ayar Cachi's staff.

Finally, after many moons of training and studying, Luna approached Capac and asked, "Teacher, you have taught me many great things, and I am forever in your debt."

Capac replied, "You have been a true and faithful student Luna. I am happy that you have changed your ways and have decided to serve your people. The ancestors smile down upon you, now."

"Thank you master. There is one last thing I would like to learn; something I have asked many times."

"You seek the meaning of Ayar Cachi's staff. As you have completed the prescribed training, I will share this secret with you now."

Capac related the story of the staff and its ability to control the great power bestowed upon the ancestors by our founders. He explained how the staff worked. The staff and headpiece are to be placed, as one, into the great power source to awaken the ancient gods from their slumber, when the time of the reunification is at hand. Only a descendent of Ayar Cachi can operate the great power source, once again uniting the people of Paititi with their brethren in Vilcabamba, returning them to the land of the ancestors. Capac also told Luna where the staff was kept and who watched over it in the sacred city. Little did he know the deceit in Luna's heart and the great sorrow her actions would bring upon our people.

Luna devised a plan, and, with the help of her closest followers, she used the knowledge learned from Capac to find the Sacred Cave and discover the location of Vilcabamba. But her treachery was discovered. The keepers of the staff killed her followers and confronted Luna. She battled with them and during the struggle, the sacred staff was broken, and Luna escaped with the headpiece.

Angry with the treachery wrought by the evil one, the keepers of the staff followed Luna, eager to find the headpiece. Realizing she was a member of the jungle tribe, they attacked Paititi, killing many, until Capac was able to explain what Luna had done. Capac apologized for sharing the sacred secrets with Luna, explaining that she had fulfilled the necessary training to learn them. The keepers of the staff returned to Vilcabamba to protect the remaining piece of the shaft and warned our elders to punish Luna.

The elders chose our greatest warriors to seek the evildoer and exact our revenge. They tracked her for many days, but Luna, treacherous as ever, eluded them. Finally, one of their scouts, located the evil she-witch and Topa Pachacuti, our greatest warrior, led his troops and captured Luna, bringing her back to Paititi to pay for her crimes.

The charges brought against her included stealing and damaging the sacred staff and causing the death and injury of many of her tribes-people at the hands of the staff keepers. It was decided that her punishment would be entombment at the site where Topa Pachacuti finally captured her. She was placed, alive, into a stone sarcophagus, bound and gagged with the medallion around her neck and this book was placed at her feet. The tomb was sealed, and a warning was inscribed on the door, as a reminder for all who would consider trying to steal the medallion, again. A trap was also set for anyone who would dare disturb this book; a trap causing them to be eternally entombed with Luna for their evilness.

Only the one ordained by our ancestors can return the headpiece to our brothers in Vilcabamba and restore the staff to its former greatness, allowing for the great unification to take place. Until that time, we are charged with protecting the headpiece and keeping it from falling into the hands of our enemies. It is our sworn duty to protect it, and we are willing to pay with our lives to keep it safe. Woe to those who would seek to claim the headpiece. Suffering and death surely await them.

Randall closed the book, a new sense of dread filling him. Surely the protectors of the headpiece had learned it was taken and that Luna's tomb had been disturbed. If that was the case, then Sam and he were in grave danger. He looked around nervously, and not seeing Sam, stood quickly and began looking for her.

"Sam, where are you?"

Panic seized Randall. He had to find Sam.

He called to her repeatedly. No answer.

Randall backtracked over the path they had covered, but found no trace of Sam. He sprinted back by the tomb, paused to look for her outside, but not seeing her, he continued running in the opposite direction along the trail.

He called out again and again but got no reply. It was as if the jungle had swallowed her alive. Defeated, he stopped. He bent over, placing his forearms on his knees, trying to catch his breath. His breathing slowed once more, and he heard a faint noise.

"Dad?"

His heart raced, "Sam, tell me where you are!"

"I'm to your left and behind where you were sitting."

"Where?"

Randall burst through the tree line and into a small clearing. He spotted Sam sitting on the stump of a fallen tree. As he approached, he noticed how still she was, almost as if she was trying not to move. He called to her softly, but she didn't turn to look at him.

Randall finally closed the last few yards and approached his daughter, not breaking eye contact with her.

"Are you okay?"

"Turn around."

He did. Randall was confronted with a small army of natives, armed to the teeth with spears, clubs and blow guns. He assumed they were the protectors of the headpiece. They didn't look happy.

Chapter Twenty-Nine

Randall was engulfed by a sea of green and was hopelessly lost, unable to tell what direction they were traveling. His guides, however, seemed quite sure of their surroundings. Despite his concern, Randall was thankful he had found Sam who walked directly in front of him. The trail they were following, if that was an appropriate description of their path, was faint at best, but as they walked, Randall saw distinct markings on some of the plants and trees suggesting they were cut at some time in the past. This suggested it had previously been used as a route, further supporting the notion that these natives were the guardians of the headpiece as implied in the book. Randall also noted that they bore a striking resemblance to the Capanhuaco and were clearly related to them.

The presence of this new group added a new wrinkle to an already complicated situation. There were now two different tribal groups descended from the original inhabitants of Vilcabamba, and Randall couldn't help but wonder what this group wanted from Sam and him. Were they a bigger part of the reunification plan or would they be excluded from the party? If the latter was true, how would they respond to the notion that he was trying to help the Capanhuaco? The questions hung heavy on his mind, but he sensed he would soon have his answer. Randall hurried to catch up with Sam.

"How are you doing, kiddo?"

"I'm fine, but I'm wondering who these people are and what they want from us."

"I think I know."

"Why did I think you were going to say that," Sam said, with a sarcastic look, eliciting a chuckle from her father.

"They're the guardians of the medallion or headpiece as they refer to it. As the descendants of the woman in the tomb, it's their job to protect the medallion from intruders. When we pulled the book out of the sarcophagus, we set off a booby-trap they designed to seal thieves inside."

"So this tribe is related to the Capanhuaco? Then they should want to help us get the medallion back to their relatives."

"Maybe, but I'm not sure they're part of the reunification plan. According to the book, this woman, Luna Quispe, wasn't very popular with the Capanhuaco. After she stole the medallion, the guardians of the staff figured out that she was from the Paititi tribe, and they took out their anger on the Capanhuaco. In the process, they killed many of the tribespeople, until one of the elders was able to explain that Luna and her team were acting on their own."

"So the two tribes might not be on speaking terms."

"Exactly."

"If you're right, then we're in trouble."

The heavy vegetation finally parted as Sam and Randall found themselves in a small clearing filled with natives going about their daily lives. Unlike the great stone structures, they had observed in Paititi, this village consisted of more traditional thatched huts and simple fire pits. They walked among the tribespeople who were busy carrying water and grinding grain to prepare their meals. The contrast between the living conditions of this tribe and the Capanhuaco was remarkable. Paititi was a thriving metropolis with relatively modern luxuries compared to this village. Sam and Randall shared a glance.

One of the warriors who had captured them motioned for the two Archeologists to move toward the largest hut in the village. Sam and Randall obliged, slowly making their way to the simple structure. The warrior motioned for them to sit near the entrance while he entered the shelter. After a short time, he reappeared with another man who looked nothing like the other villagers. The new stranger was far taller than the inhabitants, Randall judged him to be nearly six feet tall. He had sandy brown hair and hazel eyes in stark contrast to the dark manes and brown eyes sported by his companions. The new stranger eyed Sam and Randall with suspicion and then re-entered his hut as the warrior motioned for the two scientists to follow him in.

Upon entering, Randall was shocked by another surprise. The interior of the structure held artifacts entirely out of place for a jungle tribe. An ancient desk with faded and weathered books sat in one corner of the hut. An old globe sat on the ground next to the desk, along with several small steamer trunks, the likes of which were popular with ocean-going travelers in the heyday of luxury liners. Resting on one of the trunks was a picture of distinguished looking gentleman, wearing trousers with suspenders, over a clean button shirt. He was carefully studying a ceramic pot, his glasses perched on the edge of his long, slender nose.

Randall walked over to the trunk and knelt by the picture. Somewhere in the deep recesses of his mind, a small spark of recognition flashed in Randall's memory. It took a few moments, but the name eventually came to him.

"Dr. James Shields," he said absentmindedly.

"So you know my father," the tall stranger said with a hint of surprise in his voice, his British accent remarkably out of place.

Randall turned to face him. "Dr. Shields was your father?"

"Who's Dr. Shields?" Sam asked, feeling left out.

"Dr. James Shields was the reason I went into archeology. He studied the tribes of the Sacred Valley in depth; embedding himself with them for years at a time. He was the first archeologist to directly confront the notion that the local inhabitants were simple savages completely devoid of any social structure and culture. He demonstrated that the tribes were highly organized with a clear distribution of duties. He also proved that they possessed a rich cultural heritage, based on both spoken and written stories passed down by generations."

"What happened to him?" Sam asked.

"Some of his contemporaries didn't appreciate him challenging accepted theory, but he had already established himself as one of the foremost experts in ancient Peruvian cultures, so no one dared to confront him. The last time he was seen, he was leaving his base camp with a small contingent of staff."

"Where were they going?"

"They were trying to map out a path through the sacred valley. Their goal was to confirm reports of a previously undiscovered tribe that lived somewhere deep in the jungle, but they never returned."

"Did anyone look for them?"

Randall nodded. "Several search parties looked for them, but no one found a trace." Randall turned back to the picture, then looked at the tall stranger by his side. "I had no idea he had a son. What's your name?"

"My English name is Liam, but this is the first time I have spoken it to someone from the outside world. Your account of my father's disappearance is accurate but incomplete."

"Please, I'd like to know what happened to him."

"My father's party encountered trouble from the moment they broke camp. Two members of his team died when they lost their footing along an ancient crumbling path that ran along the ridge of a small mountain peak. Unfortunately, they were carrying a great deal of the supplies when they fell. The path they had crossed became unusable, so my father had no choice but to press on. The main trail they were following lead them directly into the heart of the jungle. Within a few days, they were hopelessly lost. Out of supplies, and exposed to the elements, they began to starve. Two members of the party contracted malaria and needed medicine."

"What did they do?"

"My father set out to search for food, as the remaining healthy member of the party stayed behind to watch over their sick comrades. My father stumbled upon a stream with a small net with fish trapped in it. He took the net and filled a canteen he was carrying with water and went back to his friends. When he got there, the other men were dead. Murdered."

Randall sat motionless, listening intently to Liam, mesmerized by the story of what had happened to his archeological role model.

"My father was overcome with grief and set out to find his friends' killers. He wandered for some time, unable to find anyone. Cold, tired and starving, he became delirious. He passed out, sure he was about to die, but woke up inside of a thatched hut. He was lying on animal skins, the wounds on his body cleaned and dressed. Still very sick, he was unable to stand. He lay there for some time until a native woman came and fed him. Eventually, one of the elders of the tribe visited him. He spoke a native dialect my father understood and explained they had found him unconscious. The elder invited my father to stay as long as he needed."

"So, your father went native?" Sam asked.

"Yes," Liam replied. "With time he recovered. Overwhelmed with the kindness shown by the tribe he asked if he could stay and try to repay them. The tribe welcomed him with open arms. Their way of life was simple and appealed to my father. He grew accustomed to life in the bush, eventually becoming a full member of the tribe. He used his experience to help them, becoming a trusted member of the group. As his reputation grew, so did his stature in the tribe. The chief asked him to be a shaman for their people. My father proudly accepted. He married a native woman, and she gave birth to me."

"That's amazing. But how did learn to speak English so well?" Randall asked.

"The one thing my father didn't abandon was his love for his native tongue. As I grew older, he taught it to me. Until now, I haven't had much use for it."

Randall shook his head in disbelief. "What an extraordinary story. My God, your father was a legend in the archeology community. If they knew about this, he would be even more revered!"

"No one will learn of my father's tale," Liam said, flatly.

"You mean my daughter and I can't tell anyone?"

"You and your daughter will not be permitted to leave. We are entrusted with guarding the headpiece and the sacred book. One without the other is useless. Someone has taken the sacred headpiece, but we still possess the book, and we will not allow it to fall into the wrong hands."

"So what are you going to do to us?" Sam asked.

Liam spoke several words in his tribal language, and the warrior guarding the door of the hut exited and returned with three additional warriors.

"You will be my prisoners until we can find the headpiece," the stranger motioned for his warriors to surround Sam and Randall.

"Take them to their cell."

Chapter Thirty

Sam and Randall sat on large stones in the cave that served as their make-shift prison cell. The setting sun provided little light from the front entrance as the afternoon faded into the early evening. Randall contemplated their next steps but couldn't see an obvious escape. The wooden poles serving as the "bars" of their cell door were thick, and the construction of the entrance was sturdy. Even if they were able to jimmy the cell door, there was the matter of two rather fierce-looking warriors posted outside the entrance to prevent their escape.

Randall glanced over at Sam, who was deep in thought. No doubt she was assessing the situation, trying to find a way out of their predicament. Randall smiled. One thing was certain with his daughter; no matter how bad things became, she was determined to find a solution.

"Any ideas?" Randall asked.

"None."

"The gate looks pretty sturdy," Randall said, grabbing a pole and trying to move it. It didn't budge.

"There's no way out the back, either. The cave extends for about 25 feet, but there are no openings or even cracks in the earth," Sam said, wrinkling her nose.

"The only way out is through the front door, and that doesn't seem likely."

"I was thinking our best bet may be to distract the guards. I could pretend to be sick, and when they come in to check on me, we could overpower them."

Randall shook his head, "Too dangerous, if it doesn't work, they might hurt you."

"We have to try something."

The words had scarcely left Sam's lips, when one of the guards fell to the ground in a heap, a huge lump forming on his temple above his left eye. The second guard turned in surprise and rushed to his friend to help him. As he did, a small figure appeared from the brush, making a beeline for the distracted warrior.

The attack was quick. Over in a few seconds. The second guard fell to the ground next to his comrade, both men unconscious, but alive. Randall stood in awed shock at the ferocity of the assault and the sheer efficiency of the attacker who moved with feline-like precision.

After confirming the guards were unconscious, the assailant moved toward the entrance of the cell. Randall instinctively stepped in front of Sam, his body tensing for a fight. His eyes struggled with the poor lighting for a glimpse of attacker's face. He suddenly realized who it was, and his body went slack.

"Amaro, how in the world did you find us?"

The cell door swung open.

"Come my friends, we cannot remain here. I must get you back to my tribe where we can protect you."

"I take it you know each other," Sam said smiling.

"This is the guide who led our expedition to the temple. I thought he had been killed when we were attacked at the entrance," Randall gripped Amaro's hand and shook.

"Thank you for saving us, but we can't go back with you yet. This tribe has the sacred book and we need it."

"Then we will wait for darkness and take it back."

Chapter Thirty-One

Randall, Sam and Amaro waited patiently on the edge of brush as the sun slowly set and the horizon turned to black. Having bound and gagged the guards and locked them in the cage, they focused their attention on the happenings in the main part of the village.

Amaro explained the customs of his people and correctly predicted that there would be a ceremony celebrating the return of the sacred book where the entire tribe would be present. While this would help them retrieve the book, Randall realized they were still in grave danger until they put some distance between themselves from the tribe. It was forbidden for Amaro to touch the sacred text, so the task of retrieving it fell to Randall and Sam who had quietly crept to the edge of the clearing behind Liam's hut. This placed them opposite where the tribe was gathering.

The plan was simple but required perfect timing and a bit of luck. The only entrance into the hut was at a nearly 90-degree angle to the main gathering place. Sam and Randall would traverse the outside of the hut, taking the route that placed the hut between themselves and the tribespeople. Amaro, who was standing guard, would give the signal when the tribe was distracted, allowing Sam and Randall to slip into the hut unnoticed. Once inside, they would have several minutes to locate the book, at which time, they would wait for Amaro's signal that the coast was clear. Then they'd exit and come back the same way they had come in.

Sam and Randall made their way to the entrance and waited for what seemed an eternity for the signal. Upon hearing the call of the Blue Fronted Amazon, Amaro's rendition of the native bird was perfect, they crept into the hut.

Inside, the darkness was so complete that Randall couldn't even see his hand in front of his face, and they had to wait a full minute for their eyes to adjust. Sam headed for the desk and quickly scanned the top shelf. The book wasn't there. She began rummaging through the drawers, using her phone light to cut the darkness.

While Sam focused on the desk, Randall stood guard by the entrance, peeking out from a small sliver of an opening in the cloth covered door. He could hear the tribal leaders speaking, their voices so clear, it seemed like he was sitting next to them. They were no more than 20-yards away, and he realized that if he and Sam needed to make a quick getaway, it was likely they would be spotted.

Let's just get it and leave.

Randall wiped his sweaty palms on his pant legs then peeked over at Sam, who moved quickly and quietly searching for the book. The hands on his watch ticked loudly, a deadly reminder that time was short. They had to find the book before Amaro gave the second notice. Randall's leg twitched nervously. There was nothing he could do but wait and rely on Sam to find the book.

After several minutes, Sam came back to the opening.

"Got it!"

Even in the darkness, Randall could sense the mile-long smile on his daughter's face. He glanced at the illuminated dial on his watch; they had been inside the hut for four and one-half minutes. Amaro would give the signal as soon as the coast was clear.

Randall glanced out at the tribe again. They were fully entranced by one of their leaders, whose animated face shown in the light of the fire. Five minutes passed, and they waited anxiously for the all clear signal. Five and half minutes. Still no signal. At six minutes Randall's concern bordered on panic. There was no telling how much longer the ceremony would last, and if it ended before he and Sam could exit the hut, there would be no chance of escaping.

At seven minutes, the familiar bird call came.

Finally!

Randall pushed the cloth door open for Sam who silently slipped through the opening. Randall followed close behind. His foot caught on a small jar near the entrance. He watched in horror as he sent it hurtling into the midst of the gathered tribe. Randall froze, staring at the now silent group.

All eyes of the tribe were locked on him as he sprinted from the hut under the brightly lit moon. As he turned the corner the screams from the tribespeople exploded behind him in a loud cacophony.

Randall raced for the tree line, watching as Sam disappeared into the brush. He didn't need to look back; he heard and sensed hundreds of feet beating the earth behind him.

Small projectiles crashed around him as he covered the final few feet to the edge of the jungle. Amaro and Sam were already moving through the dense foliage as Randall finally cleared the edges of the village.

"Hurry, Dad!"

Randall pushed aside large palm fronds, vines and branches, struggling to make headway through the dense vegetation. He stumbled over a fallen tree branch in his path and tumbled to the ground, coming to rest on the forest floor, facing the village.

The quiet of the jungle was shattered as the villagers burst through the edge of the bush, pursuing Randall as if they were famished, and he was their favored meal.

Randall scrambled to his feet, lurching forward through the darkness. He almost fell again. The natives gained on him, their nimble bodies moving swiftly through the brush. One pursuer was nearly upon him. Randall heard his rhythmic breathing and saw him as he glanced over his shoulder. The villager was within several feet of Randall when he dropped abruptly to the ground. Shocked, Randall looked ahead on the trail and saw Amaro lowering his weapon and resuming his trot.

Randall caught sight of Sam who led momentarily before Amaro caught and passed her. The three ran parallel to a river which fed into the jungle where the keepers' village lay. The bank of the river offered a smoother, easier surface for running, but also presented much less cover to protect them. Amaro led them to a small boat he had hidden along the shoreline, but Randall had no idea how close they were.

Again, projectiles struck the brush and ground around Randall as the natives gain on him. He was in a footrace for his life and was losing to the diminutive natives, who were much more accustomed to the physical demands of pursuit.

Without warning, a villager popped out of the bushes, no more than two feet away from Amaro. The warrior parried him with a large stick, knocked him unconscious and backwards into the river.

Samantha shot her dad an incredulous look, then turned and continue running.

The hill sloped upward as the land climbed away from the river, making the trek more demanding. Randall pumped his legs the best he could, but he soon realized he was running out of steam. Despite his continued fitness regimen, instilled in him by his time in Special Forces, age was catching up with him. Meanwhile, his pursuers were undeterred by the uphill incline.

I have to keep running, played on a loop in his mind as his legs slowly turned to rubber beneath him. He was slowing down and realized that if they didn't reach the boat soon, the keepers would catch him. The only redeeming thought was that Sam had the book. As long as she and Amaro made it back to the Capanhuaco, they still had a chance of stopping Dumond and making the reunification a reality.

Randall glanced at the river which was now about 15 feet down and to the right of the trail. They were still climbing, but the incline became more gradual. Sam and Amaro had put distance between themselves and Randall, who called out to his daughter.

"Sam, I'm not going to make it. Take the book back to the Capanhuaco!"

As if a wall suddenly appeared on the trail, Sam stopped and turned.

Randall slowed to a jog and motioned for her to keep running, "Don't stop! You need to get that book away from here!"

"I'm not leaving you!"

Amaro appeared at Sam's side and spoke to her briefly, pulling her along. She ran with him, looking back at her father as she moved down the trail. After a couple of minutes, Sam and Amaro crested a hill and disappeared from his sight.

Exhausted now, Randall turned again to look at his pursuers. They continued their relentless pace, closing to within twenty yards of him.

Every fiber of his being cried out for him to surrender, but he willed himself forward. If he could make it to the crest of the hill, he could gain speed going down the other side.

He pressed on, reaching the peak, then glanced over his shoulder. They were within ten yards now and not showing signs of slowing. He could see the determination in their faces. The lead warriors carried large sharpened spears. There would be no surrendering this time. He knew in his heart that they would make him pay for stealing their sacred text.

Randall crested the peak and began running downhill. With gravity on his side, he was able to temporarily outrun his pursuers and increase his lead on them. His good fortune was short lived, however, as the tribal people soon crested the hill as well and began closing the gap again.

His weary legs hurt with each stride, and his chest burned with fatigue. Realizing he was only minutes away from being caught, Randall took one final breath, making a push for the boat, hoping it was only a short distance away.

His final burst of energy soon faded, and Randall decelerated to a slow jog. He glanced over his shoulder and saw the wide-eyed warriors closing in on him. It was no use, he couldn't go on. He slowed even further, resigned to his fate. At least Sam would be safe.

"Dad, down here!"

Randall flinched at the unexpected sound of Sam's voice. He glanced over the edge of the hill and down to the river. Sam and Amaro were in the boat, making their way toward him. The current was carrying the boat quickly, and they would soon be directly under him.

"You'll have to jump!"

Randall backed from the edge. The light from the moon was bright enough for him to judge clearly that he was about twenty feet above the water. If it wasn't deep enough, he would likely be crushed from the impact or paralyzed.

He glanced at the quickly approaching warriors, then back down at the water.

"Hurry, you need to jump in front of us! I don't think we can steer back for you!"

The warriors were only ten feet from him now, and the boat was almost under him.

Hope this is deep enough.

Randall sighed, closed his eyes, opened them, then dashed toward the edge and then off. It seemed like he was freefalling in slow motion. He could feel his stomach rise inside his body which tingled with the feeling of temporary weightlessness. After what seemed like minutes of floating, the water finally reached his feet, and Randall pierced the surface keeping his legs as straight as possible to ensure a relatively clean entry.

He sank and sank, the momentum of the jump carrying him deep into the river. The buoyancy finally arrested his fall, and he kicked his feet and pushed his way toward the surface. As he breached, the boat came careening right at him. He pushed away as hard as he could, and narrowly avoided having his head crushed by the bow of the vessel. As the boat skidded by, he felt two strong hands grasp him under the arms and haul him into the boat like he was light as a feather pillow.

Amaro laid Randall's weary body in the bottom of the hull while Sam steered the small craft. Arrows, spears and rocks splashed around the boat but mostly fell behind them as the current carried them quickly downstream.

Randall felt like his body was made of lead. He couldn't move or talk. It took his every effort to just breathe in and out. He turned his head toward his smiling daughter.

"We thought we might lose you back there. When Amaro told me the boat was just over the hill, I knew our best chance was for me to help him get the boat and bring it back to you."

"That's my girl," Randall said weakly. Every part of his body ached, and he closed his eyes trying to recover from the long run and jump. They were safe now and could focus on returning to find the medallion.

"Amaro, how long until we get back?"

"About an hour. Rest now my friend for we will soon need to move again."

Randall didn't need to be told twice. He closed his eyes, happy that the day's events were finally over.

Chapter Thirty-Two

Amaro led Randall and Sam back to the clearing and to George, who was sitting on a fallen log only several feet from where they had left him. Upon seeing them, George jumped to his feet and raced towards them, clearly happy to see their faces again.

"What happened? I thought you were only going to be gone for a couple of hours? I was getting worried that I was going to have to spend the night alone in this creepy jungle."

"Sorry George, we ran into a little trouble," Randall said, taking a seat on the stump.

"That's okay, I was just worried about you. I'm really glad you're both back," he said, patting Randall on the back.

"My friends, I must go back to my tribe and tell my leaders what has happened. Good luck," Amaro said, walking to the edge of the clearing. Randall watched as he left and after a few moments, Amaro disappeared into the dark underbrush.

After a short rest, the three made their way back through the jungle, moving in the direction of the ruins. Conversation was sparse as they made their way in the moonlight.

"Dr. Randall?" George asked sheepishly.

"Yes?"

"I heard Dumond talking about something called the Drake Equation with one of his men, a huge soldier with a mustache," George said.

"That must have been Ackers," Sam added.

"Anyway, he said he heard you give a lecture about it. What was he talking about?" George asked.

"He was referring to an astronomer who developed an equation for estimating the number of intelligent civilizations in the galaxy. He showed that, mathematically speaking, the universe should be teeming with intelligent life."

George wrinkled his nose. "If that's true, then why haven't any alien species contacted us?"

"That's a good question, and there are several theories that might explain it. First, if a civilization is much more advanced than we are, they might not bother trying to communicate with us. Relatively speaking, we're cavemen compared to them. Think about it this way. If there was an anthill on the side of a road, no human is going to stop and try to communicate with the ants because they're too simplistic to understand what we are trying say," Randall replied.

"I can see your point."

"Then there's another theory that advanced civilizations might have some sort of rule about not interfering with the development of more primitive species. They might worry that if they did, it might cause some sort of cosmic imbalance or problem for the simpler life forms."

"Like the prime directive in Star Trek!" George exclaimed.

Randall smiled. "Right. But I tend to believe in another explanation. I think that we have contacted alien species, but in very limited capacities."

"How do you mean?" George asked.

"If you look at history, there are hints about extraterrestrial visitations scattered throughout the world."

"Such as?"

"Well, there are the ancient petroglyphs around the world that seem to portray humanoid figures sporting unusual headgear like Apollo-era astronaut helmets," Randall said.

"What? You're kidding, right?"

"Not at all, in fact, there's one Mayan carving that looks like a man sitting in a space capsule with knobs and buttons. After seeing it, you have to wonder how the ancient Maya could have created an image like that, unless they had actually seen one."

"I had no idea," George said, shaking his head in disbelief.

"You're not alone. Most people aren't aware of these things and mainstream science doesn't want to address the possibility that our ancestors may have interacted with advanced species."

"Sorry to break up your conversation boys, but we need to get going," Sam said, surveying their surroundings. Her mood darkened, and Randall noticed that she had a strange expression on her face.

"Is something wrong?" Randall asked.

"Doesn't it seem odd to you that none of the soldiers followed you when you ran out of the compound? Someone must have heard the gunshots and noticed that the medallion was missing," Sam said.

Randall shrugged, "Maybe they thought some of Kristoph's men had survived the attack, stole the medallion and returned to their ship."

"Maybe, but I feel like something's not right. Dumond isn't the sort of man who would just give up on finding the city and the power source, especially after building the power station and the satellites."

"I guess they just haven't figured out what's going on yet, so we'd better hurry before they do," Randall said.

As they re-entered the ruins, Sam once again marveled at the craftsmanship of the tunnel. Despite the terrible turn of events, she was still filled with awe at the discovery. "This could change the way we view human history," she said to herself. She stopped and stared. "It *will* change the way we view human history."

The trio soon reached the inner chamber, then traversed down the ropes that Ackers's men had left. The path was becoming more familiar for Sam and her father due to the previous trips, but from the expression on George's face, the experience was otherworldly. Walking through an elaborately carved rock structure, far under the surface of the Earth, must have been a far cry from the clean rooms at Gemini Orbital. He smiled broadly, but it quickly vanished as they approached the crevasse.

"Why is it so hot in here?" George asked.

"It is a lot warmer than before," Sam said.

Slowly inching his way to the edge of the crevasse, Randall discovered the source of the heat.

"Magma."

Sam joined her father, shining her light down into the depths of the crevasse. The formerly bottomless pit now had

227

a termination point. One that ended in hot molten rock. George inched his way to the ledge to see for himself.

"That doesn't look good."

"How far down would you say that is?" Sam asked.

"Maybe fifty to eighty feet. I don't like this. Between the more frequent earthquakes and now this magma, this place is giving all the signs that it's going to blow. We need to get you as far away from here as possible," Randall said.

"Wait a minute, what do you mean this place is getting ready to blow? What's going on here?" George asked.

For the moment, Sam ignored George. She was worried about her father. "We're too close now. Besides, we still need to find out what happened to Phil."

"Sam, I already lost him and Mike, I can't handle the idea of losing you. I-"

"That's why we need to move quickly," Sam said, cutting her father off in mid-sentence and jerking her flashlight upward. "Look at this!"

Randall's eyes shot upward and across to the other side of the crevasse. Once more, disbelief gripped him. What had been a solid wall of rock when Kristoph's men had found him was now a tunnel. "It's an open path again. What in the hell is happening here?"

"That's a good question. Can someone please fill me in on what you're talking about? I'm starting to feel like a fifth wheel." George said impatiently.

"The first time I came down this cavern I was alone, the path was open, and I went across. The next time I was here with Sam, Dumond, and his men, and there was a sheer rock face on the other side. Now it's open again," Randall said.

"That makes absolutely no sense. How could it be open, then solid rock, and then open again? You must have come down different tunnels."

Randall shined his light directly into George's face and shot him a withering look, the kind that only a parent or teacher can muster.

George backed down and resumed his quiet disposition. Sam just smiled, watching George and her father from a distance. She readied herself for the jump.

Sam's flashlight danced about the cavern crazily, cutting a zigzag pattern through the darkness. Before they could stand, Randall and George watched as the light, and Sam, leapt across to the other side. She landed gracefully, pulling to a stop in a crouched position.

"Come on guys, we've got to get moving!" She called.

Without debate and with a small smile returning to his face, Randall backed several feet away from the crevasse. His hands once again became cold and clammy as he thought about his last and nearly fatal attempt to make the leap across. Heart racing wildly, Randall ran, full speed, and leapt with all his might at the last possible moment. As he arced through the air, he could see Sam slowly step to the side to make way for his landing. He landed cleanly, but hit the ground hard, his left leg buckling under him. Tumbling to a stop, Randall forced himself to his feet, his left leg pulsing with pain.

"Dad, are you alright? It looks like you hurt your leg."

"It's fine," he said, rubbing the injury. "I'm just getting way too old for this shit!"

"You always used to tell me, you're only as old as you feel."

"Yeah, and right now, I feel pretty damn old," he said, smiling at Sam and limping in pain.

George stood on the other side of the crevasse, looking at Sam and Randall, his eyes blinking in disbelief.

"Come on George, you're next!" Sam called out.

George was shaking now. Randall could read his mind. Nothing about being an electrical engineer had prepared him for this moment.

I bet he'll never complains about being bored again at work.

"You'll be okay George. I know you can do it," Sam said.

George looked over at Sam, who stood with her hands on her hips, smiling in support. He took several steps backward and swallowed hard. Giving out a small whimper and running at full speed, George launched himself. He traversed the crevasse, then came crashing down on the other side, a heap of humanity crumpled upon the floor of the cavern.

Sam ran over to him. His eyes were shut tight and he was covered from head to toe in fine gray dust. She couldn't help but smile.

"Are you hurt?"

George opened his eyes and did a mental inspection of his body. Everything seemed to be intact. "I don't think so," he replied.

Sam smiled and reached down to help him up.

The three peered down the now open cavern; more darkness lay ahead. Time passed slowly as they made their way down the winding path, but their effort was soon rewarded. A short distance ahead, a faint glow appeared.

"What is that? Is that ... light?" Sam asked.

Even in the darkness, Randall could sense his daughter's disbelief at what lay ahead of them. He felt a great sense of relief knowing that the earlier episode had not been a hallucination. Suddenly he was struck by a realization.

"Do you know what this means? They're real Sam, they're real!"

"Who's real?" The light was becoming brighter and larger as they walked closer.

"The creatures that live in Vilcabamba." Randall replied. "They did communicate with me, and they're not like anything you've ever seen."

It was the way her father said it that caused Sam to stop. During the journey back, it had never occurred to her that she would come face to face with incontrovertible proof that humanity was not alone in the cosmos. The thought caused her to shudder involuntarily. As a scientist, it was one thing to theorize about such things, but it was something altogether different to confirm it. Sam wasn't sure if she was exhilarated, afraid, or a combination of the two.

"Creatures?" George asked. No one responded.

"Sam, are you okay?" Randall asked.

Sam hadn't realized that she had stopped walking, but her father's voice jerked her back to reality. "Uh huh."

Randall walked back and put his arm around his daughter's shoulders. "It's alright, sweetheart, I'm here with you. They're friendly and they want to help us."

George joined them. "What do you mean by creatures?"

Randall explained his earlier encounter to the newest member of their team. George's knees almost buckled, but Randall caught him.

"Whoa there, it's okay George."

"Next time you ask me to come along on one of your adventures, remind me to just say no."

They covered the last hundred yards quickly, and Sam was rewarded with an amazing sight. The size and sheer scope of the underground city was overwhelming. Vilcabamba was much larger than Paititi and as beautiful as the jungle city was, Vilcabamba was even more exquisite. Suddenly gripped by the inquisitive nature that only a scientist could have, she began to categorize the sights she was experiencing, grasping the magnitude of the moment. She moved forward into the opening of the cavern that held the city. It was magnificent, an archaeologist's dream!

A short distance ahead, there were steps leading down into the city. Sam turned to look at George and her father, who followed closely behind. Randall smiled and nodded for her to keep going. George, on the other hand, looked overwhelmed.

The stonework was incredible. The fine level of detail rivaled the artistry of Michelangelo himself. The stone animals and shapes that adorned the walls, as she descended the steps into the city, surpassed any artifacts she had ever seen. Intricate carvings of chinchillas, llamas, and vicuña – sort of a combination of an alpaca and a camel – seemed almost lifelike. But these weren't the only wildlife depicted. Exotic animals she had never seen before were also carved out of the stone. In the past, Sam would have dismissed finding such depictions to a simplistic culture trying to explain the unseen forces of nature at work. Now, she wasn't so sure. These weren't relics covered by earth for hundreds or thousands of years; these were functioning structures still in use today. She reached out to touch one. The surface of the stone was perfectly smooth.

"The detail is absolutely exquisite," she said quietly.

Her father nodded his agreement just as George caught up with them.

Sam stooped and peered under one of the sculptures, finding herself in the shadow of the magnificent piece of art. She was immediately struck with the realization that the cavern was exceptionally bright. Slowly, she slid out from under the statue and gazed up at the ceiling. Just as her father had described, a large, orb shaped light hung, suspended in mid-air, directly in the center of the ceiling which arched majestically over the city.

"This is unbelievable," Sam said. "At first, I didn't know what to make of your stories, but now ... this is just amazing. How could this have been here so long, without anyone in the world knowing that it exists?"

"Actually, a few others did know about this place," Randall said. "The Capanhuaco for one, and other indigenous tribes as well. There've been stories told about the existence of lost cities for generations. The problem is, since we didn't grow up listening to these stories, we had no idea that places like this exist. We just assumed that no one else knew about them either."

Sam moved forward and found herself at the bottom of the steps. Vilcabamba stretched out before her. From this vantage point, Sam came to appreciate just how large the structures were and just how small she was. It was as if an unknown light had suddenly illuminated her mind. All of a sudden, petty, worldly squabbles seemed insignificant.

"Where are they?"

"I'm not sure."

"When you were here last time, where did you see them?"

"I wasn't here for very long before they came," Randall said. "I made it about this far and then they appeared."

Sam looked around them and then scanned the higher portions of the cavern. "I don't see anyone. Maybe they're waiting for us to make the next move?"

"Dr. Randall," George said, "these creatures you saw, what did they look like?"

Randall didn't have to think long before conjuring the image in his mind. "They were very small, had no body hair whatsoever, their skin was milky-colored, and they had no discernable mouths."

George recoiled at the description. Once again, the incredulous look appeared on his face, only this time, it vanished rather quickly. Apparently, his mind was adjusting to this new reality.

"Wait a minute, you said earlier that you had a conversation with them, but how's that possible if they didn't have mouths?" George asked.

"I didn't say I had a conversation with them. I said I communicated with them or, to be more accurate, they communicated with me."

"How?"

Randall felt a sense of frustration growing, but he quickly realized just how foreign this must be for George. He settled himself and then explained his theory. "George, we're talking about a much more advanced species than humans. If you accept that fact, then the next part is easier."

George nodded in agreement.

"My theory is that these creatures come from a civilization much older than our own. As a result, they have been evolving for much longer than humans. At one point, they may have communicated the same way we do, with the spoken word. Over the course of time, as their intellect increased, certain parts of their brains also evolved, and they developed the ability to communicate without speaking."

"So you're saying they communicated telepathically?"

"Right. At some point in their evolution, their species simply developed or discovered how to communicate without the need to speak."

"But they communicated with you, so does that mean that humans possess the same ability?"

Randall stopped for a moment, looking perplexed. "I hadn't thought about it that way, but yes, you're right. I guess humans do have the ability." Again more thought. "They might be more physiologically like us than I had originally thought. They clearly have a similar anatomical structure: a head, torso, arms, and legs. Since I was able to communicate with them, their brains must be like ours as well."

"Do you realize what this means?" Sam asked.

"Yes, we could be seeing what the human species will evolve into some day. I wonder if their physical size also decreased as their mental powers grew. That would be a big advantage to a growing civilization. Smaller physical size means fewer resources are needed to sustain life."

"Can you imagine the things they could teach us? I would love to talk with them about engineering!" George said.

Sam could see that the fear and doubt that George had once held had been replaced by excitement. He looked like a kid staring at a big stack of presents on Christmas morning. It reminded her of how her father looked when he developed a new theory and found supporting evidence. She smiled. George and her father seemed to be really hitting it off now.

"Uh guys, sorry to interrupt, but we're running out of time."

"You're right. Sorry, I got a little carried away," Randall said.

Surveying Vilcabamba, Randall spoke again. "I think this city is laid out in the same manner as Paititi. It's just much bigger."

"That explains why it feels so familiar. But the artwork looks different, it's more intricate. What do we do next?"

"If the layout is the same as the jungle city, then we need to go over there," Randall said, pointing to a large structure sitting atop a huge staircase.

"Right, the map room! Dad, there was a missing tablet in Paititi, was it there when you went?"

"No, it was gone, but the Chief told me that it was the tablet that spoke of the key."

"And now we have the key and understand what it's for. If the tablet tells us where to use it, we should be able to stop Dumond."

Sam was excited now. She began sprinting; George and her father followed behind. Soon they were at the base of the stairs leading to the map room.

"Holy smokes! This thing is a lot bigger up close. That's a lot of steps!" George commented.

"Yep, and they're not going anywhere, so let's keep moving," Sam replied.

The three walked up the steps and stopped near the middle. Sam once again turned to take in the view of the city. "Amazing," she said under her breath. From their vantage, the city swept away in all directions in gentle curving circles. The symmetry of the layout of the buildings and streets that populated the city was perfect. Even more surprising was that from their high perch, they could see shapes inlaid in the streets and structures that couldn't be seen from the ground. There were animals and even humanoid shapes that the builders had surreptitiously incorporated into the city's design. Shapes that could only be seen from an elevated platform.

Randall soon caught up with his daughter and was happy for the short respite. Despite his exercise regimen, he felt his age finally creeping up on him. George was also winded, his engineer body not accustomed to this much physical exertion. Sam, not wanting to hurt either of their feelings, waited a few extra minutes, pretending to look around at the scenery.

"It feels hot in here, even hotter than it was in the tunnel," Sam commented.

"The magma's getting closer to the surface. This volcano is getting ready to erupt," Randall replied.

"That's a happy thought." George had finally caught up to them.

Sam smiled. "We better keep going."

The view from the map room was unlike anything they had ever seen. As the highest point in the city, the entire kingdom came into view. Beautiful structures filled the vista in every direction. Enormous stone monuments, intricately carved, adorned the city and balanced carefully upon smaller structures that lifted them skyward. What had appeared as grids from lower could now be seen as concentric circles, radiating outward from the middle of the city. At the center of the town was a smaller, non-descript domed structure, which glowed with a strange bluish-gray color. The symmetry was perfect.

Sam strained her eyes, staring toward the dome.

Randall arrived by her side. "Admiring the view?"

Sam pointed her finger at the dome. "Look over there."

Randall squinted in the direction Sam pointed. He wasn't sure if the light was playing tricks with his eyes, but a fine bright beam seemed to emanate from the center of the dome, spanning to the very top of the cavern. "Is that a light?"

"I know, right? I'm not sure. This is incredible! I know I keep saying that, but I don't know how else to describe it."

"Just imagine, this is a window into a different species. Their culture and history are laid out in front of us. Best of all, we don't have to theorize about how they lived. We're seeing it first-hand. Just think of everything they can teach us. This could be the end of war, disease, and poverty. Things will never be the same for humanity."

"Yes, it is quite impressive, but I didn't come here for the view," said a familiar voice.

Sam and Randall turned to see Dumond and his men, weapons drawn.

"You son of a bitch!" Randall said, taking a few steps in Dumond's direction.

"It's good to see you too, Dr. Randall," Dumond replied as Colonel Ackers stepped forward, pointing his gun directly at the approaching professor.

"Just give me a reason," Ackers sneered.

"How in the Hell did you find us?" Sam asked.

"You didn't really think you could just sneak into my compound without me knowing and make off with my prized possession, did you? Speaking of which, who has my medallion?"

"You bastard, you killed Mike and Phil!" Randall said, fists clenched in rage.

"They just got in my way, Professor, it was nothing personal."

Taking the box containing the medallion from Sam, Dumond opened a compartment and removed a small item, not much larger than a grain of rice.

"RFID device, goddamn it," Randall said. "Okay, Dumond, you have the medallion, you know where the map room is. If you let Sam go, I'll help you figure out how the key works."

"Professor, do you really think I'm that stupid? I can't take a chance on leaving any loose ends. Besides, you're in no position to bargain with me." Dumond nodded his head in Sam's direction as one of the soldiers came forward and grabbed her by the arm, poking his gun into her side.

Randall realized that his options were limited. "Okay, Dumond, what do you want from me?"

"It's very simple. I need you to tell me how to use this key."

Randall nodded his agreement.

Turning to George, Dumond said, "Mr. Walker, glad you could join us as well. Looks like you can finally help us finish our little project."

The group marched forward between the giant columns that guarded the entrance to the map room structure. There were no doors in sight. Randall searched the wall and found what he was looking for: strange symbols, arranged in neat rows, glowing with a blue light.

"Sam, do you have my book?"

Dumond nodded to his guard, who released Sam.

"Here you go."

Randall opened his book searching for the correct section. He fanned through many pages, scanning as he flipped.

"We're waiting, Dr. Randall."

He finally found the page he was looking for, then began tapping the symbols on the wall. Without a sound, a door opened in the wall, exposing the room hidden within.

"That's a neat trick," George said.

In the outer chamber, there were large, rectangular panels with smaller grids filled with text and symbols inlaid into the wall. The panels were arranged in linear fashion, almost like a comic strip in the Sunday paper. Randall walked to the panel on the far left and stopped.

After a few moments, Randall began mentally translating the inscription, without divulging any information to the group. The countdown to the event horizon was almost up. The eruption or whatever cataclysmic event that was going to take place would happen in about an hour. Randall also discovered they were missing part of the key and without it, the system wouldn't work. In fact, using the medallion alone would cause harm to the user. A safety feature installed by the designers of the system to prevent outsiders from accessing the engine.

After a few moments, Dumond spoke. "Dr. Randall, in case you've forgotten, I want this power source and I believe you're stalling. If you are, your daughter will pay with her life."

Without looking at him, Randall said, "This isn't like reading a magazine. This is a previously unknown language. Besides, there are new symbols that I've never seen. These things take time." Randall continued reading.

A few minutes later, Randall said, "I know where we need to go."

They walked further into the main building. At first, something seemed odd to Sam, but then she realized what it was. "These rooms are lighted, but I don't see any wires or switches."

"Dr. Randall, I'm disappointed in you. As a woman of science, I thought it would be clear to you that this energy source doesn't follow the constraints of our own simple technology," Dumond said.

"What do you mean?" Sam asked.

"The energy is projected through the air, through a transfer of electrons vibrating at the proper harmonious frequency. Haven't you noticed that your phone hasn't lost its charge since you've been here? And what about your flashlights? Still as bright as they were when you first arrived, I imagine?" Dumond said.

"Of course! Why hadn't I thought of that?" George said.

"You see, Dr. Randall," Dumond said, "I've been looking for this place almost as long as you have, except I needed your medallion to confirm the theory. Now, I'm happy to say that we understand how to interface the power source with our own technology, to utilize it in a matter that will make me a rich and powerful man. All thanks to you and your daughter."

"That could explain why Paititi hadn't been discovered. The power source must have created some sort of electronic interference that blocked the city's view from the air," Sam said.

"I've heard about research the military is doing into cloaking tanks and other equipment on the battlefield. From what I understand, they've been able to electronically bend light around objects to create the illusion that they aren't there for extremely short periods of time. But the energy needed to do it, even for less than a second, is tremendous," George added. "This energy source must be incredibly powerful."

The thought of Dumond harnessing and using the energy source sent a shiver down Randall's spine. There was no way he could let that happen.

The group moved through the building into a room in the center of the structure. The tablet room. Sam moved forward examining the stone slabs.

"The tablets are all here, Dad, none of them are missing."

Randall once again moved to the far-left tablet and began to read. It was an instruction manual for the operation of the power system.

"Well, Professor?"

"It's not here."

"What do you mean?"

"This isn't the control panel where we use the key. The control panel is at the center of the city inside the dome structure. That's the actual power plant for this place, this is just a side terminal."

Dumond walked over to Sam, grabbed her forcefully by the arm, and placed a pistol to her head. "Dr. Randall, I'm losing my patience." He cocked the trigger.

"This isn't the control panel! Look, do you see any openings for the medallion? It's the key to the system, but we have to use it at the power plant. Listen to me Dumond, this room is an informational depository. A library if you will. Did you see the other panels in the wall as we walked in here? Those are like computer banks with keys that operate systems within the city. This is like the server room for a fully interconnected, citywide system. But they realized that their relatives out in the jungle city might be the ones to have to operate this system. They're a group that split off from the main community more than a thousand years ago, and they don't have the same technology. The tablets and wall inscriptions are here to explain to them how to operate the power system."

"For what?"

Randall hesitated, realizing that the genie was out of the bottle now. "For the great reunification. The moment when the Paititi tribe and the Vilcabamba tribe are reunited."

For the briefest moment, Dumond flinched, but quickly regained his composure. Ackers on the other hand fumed.

"I knew they were withholding information. I say we kill them now. I don't trust this piece of shit for a minute," Ackers said.

George stepped forward. "He's telling the truth, Mr. Dumond, this doesn't look like a power panel. Think about the control room of one of your nuclear reactors. There's no monitoring system to keep track of critical systems. This is a workstation tied into the mainframe. We need to go where

Dr. Randall says. That's where we'll find the main panel," he said.

Dumond thought for a moment and released Sam's arm. "Colonel, while I appreciate your enthusiasm, I'm going to allow Dr. Randall one final indulgence. If you are wrong, Professor, or if I find that you are lying to me, your daughter will pay with her life."

Dumond holstered his pistol. "After you, Dr. Randall and Mr. Walker."

The group began the long walk to the center of the city. Again, they walked in silence.

"Are you okay?" Randall asked his daughter.

"Been better, but yeah, I'm alright."

Almost as if experiencing a sixth sense, Randall felt that the group was not alone in the cavern. He tried casually looking about the cavern for signs of life but saw none. His actions didn't go unnoticed.

"Is something bothering you, Dr. Randall?"

"Well, Dumond, if you must know, being held prisoner and having my daughter held at gunpoint tends to make a father tense. I don't suppose you would have any idea what that feels like, though."

"In my experience, fathers are overrated. The best thing my father ever did for me was to force me to grow up and become both physically and mentally strong," Dumond replied.

It was the first sign of weakness Dumond had shown. Sensing that he had finally hit a nerve with their captor, Randall decided to press further. "Sounds like you and your dad didn't get along. That's a shame. My experience has been that kids who don't have a positive father figure in

244

their lives usually grow up to be nervous and insecure. Some hide it better than others by acting like tough guys and intimidating people. But under the surface, they're just scared little kids. I see it all the time at school."

It appeared to work. Dumond lunged at Randall, taking his pistol from its holster and placing it at his throat. "Careful, Professor, my generosity has its limits. I don't think you're in a position to be lecturing me about who has the power right now."

"Mr. Dumond!" one of the soldiers yelled.

Dumond removed the gun from Randall's throat and resumed his normal demeanor. "Well, Professor, I guess we'll soon see if you were right or if you die." Dumond walked away from Randall joining the soldier who had called him.

"Bright move, pissing off a guy who's got a gun to your kid's head," Ackers said.

Without missing a beat and without looking him in the eye, Randall replied, "What's it like being a lackey for a complete psychopath?"

In a quick movement, Ackers raised his gun and struck the professor between the shoulder blades, knocking him to the ground. Then he grabbed him by his collar and jerked him to his feet.

"I'm going to enjoy offing you, you piece of shit," Ackers said.

"I can see why you enjoy working for him. You're a complete psychopath, too," Randall replied.

Another blow, this time to the stomach.

"Stop it! Why are you doing that to him?" Sam ran to her father's side.

Catching his breath, Randall said, "It's alright Sam, he didn't hurt me."

Before he could strike another blow to Randall, Ackers's radio crackled: "We're here."

Chapter Thirty-Three

Volcano Disaster Assistance Program Director Tom Reinsdorf stared intently at the map before him. By all indications, El Misti was ready to erupt at any moment. Evacuation routes had been established and local authorities were in the process of evacuating residents in anticipation of the eruption. Decisions were based on computer simulations of which areas would be most impacted. The problem with the process was twofold. First, computer simulations of eruption patterns were useful, but there was no way of knowing how and where the eruption would occur. Second, no matter how hard they tried, there was never any way to reach everyone who would be impacted by the eruption. These facts tugged at Tom's mind and left him feeling like he needed to do more.

"Tom, the helicopter's here," Keith Peterson said.

"Thanks, Keith. I want you and Theresa to continue coordinating the evacuation and monitoring from here."

"Are you sure it's a good idea to take that bird up around the mountain in these conditions?"

"We've been through this before. There are several small villages near the base of Misti and I want to do a sweep of the area to make sure we've gotten folks out of the main blast area. The best way to do that is by air."

Keith sighed.

"I appreciate your concern, buddy, but I'll be fine. I'll have my radio with me if you need to reach me," Tom said.

"Be careful up there, boss."

"Will do."

Tom ducked under the rotating helicopter blades and entered the passenger side of the craft. Strapping himself in, he turned to the pilot.

"I'm Tom Reinsdorf, nice to meet you."

"Jesse Jones. Have you been near a volcano this close to eruption before?"

"Yes, twice before, but I appreciate you taking me up there," Tom said, pointing in the direction of Misti.

Jesse nodded and increased the throttle causing the Sikorsky to lurch into the sky. Tom sat back and contemplated the situation, hoping Misti would hold off her eruption long enough for them to get back safely.

Chapter Thirty-Four

The dome that housed the power station was larger than Randall had anticipated. From their view at the Tablet Room, it had appeared small in relation to the other structures in the city, but up close, it was massive. The dome was perfectly smooth and was made from a single piece of metal alloy. There were no perceptible seams or rivets anywhere and it glowed with a familiar bluish-gray hue.

"Well, Dr. Randall?" Dumond asked.

Randall walked around the structure until he found the control panel. He recognized several of the symbols and realized that he was becoming more familiar with the strange language. Pressing several buttons in sequence, Randall read a small display embedded in the wall that confirmed his worst fear. Fifty-two minutes until the event horizon swept over them. Making matters worse, he wasn't exactly sure what would happen. Without realizing it, Randall muttered under his breath, "Shit."

"What was that, Dr. Randall?"

Randall quickly recovered. "There are a few new symbols here that I need to decipher, but I'll figure them out."

Randall punched several more keys and a panel slid open silently in front of them. The group flinched at the sudden movement. The open space now revealed what Randall had been looking for: the ignition switch into which the medallion key would fit to operate system. He stepped to the side, "Here you go, Dumond."

Dumond pushed his way past Randall, who took several steps back and moved next to Sam.

"Very good, Dr. Randall. Colonel, bring me the medallion."

Taking the medallion from the container, Dumond turned it over in his hand and smiled. Randall could sense Dumond's distrust as his gaze shifted between the medallion and Randall's eyes.

"Why don't you do the honors, Professor?" Dumond asked.

Randall was startled by the offer. "No, Dumond, you've won the day, you should do it."

Dumond's smile broadened at Randall's response. "Did you really think I wouldn't figure it out?"

"Figure out what?"

"I know there's a reason you want me to use the key instead of you, and I don't think it has anything to do with allowing me the glory of the moment. There's a failsafe built into this system, isn't there? If this isn't done correctly, the person using the key is injured or killed. Isn't that the case, Professor?"

"I don't know what you're talking about."

"Ackers, bring her to me," Dumond said, motioning to Sam.

Ackers grabbed her by the wrist and violently pulled her toward the control panel. Dumond handed her the medallion. "Take it!" Sam grudgingly complied. "Now use it to engage the system!" Sam's hand shook as she inched the medallion closer to panel.

Randall raised a hand. "Wait! Yes, you're right, there's a fail-safe, and we don't have the entire key. There's a shaft that fits into the back of the medallion that operates the system."

"Where's the rest of the key?"

Randall hesitated.

"Tell me or I'll kill your daughter."

"Chief Yupanqui from the jungle tribe has it. When I met him, he had what I thought was a walking stick, but based on what I've read here, it must be the rest of the key that's needed to operate the system."

"Colonel, get the Professor's notes."

Dumond reviewed the notes and compared them to the symbols on the screen of the control center. For a moment he seemed confused. Then a grin slowly snaked across his face.

"So, you were keeping secrets from me. And to think I spared your daughter's life. Dr. Randall, your services are no longer required." Dumond turned to Ackers and nodded.

The Colonel released Sam's arm and swung his weapon up to shoot her. Instead, his left arm jerked back as an arrow struck. A moment later he grunted in pain. Instinctively looking down at his wounded arm, he saw the arrow projecting through his forearm, the head leaving a ragged, torn flap of skin on the exterior. He looked up just in time to see another arrow arcing through the air. He sidestepped it right before impact, watching it harmlessly strike the side of the power dome.

Randall turned to look in the direction from which the arrow had come. Silhouettes of small warriors dotted the courtyard of the Tablet Room above, and arrows rained down on Dumond's men, striking like venomous serpents protecting their den from intruders. The mercenaries turned to face their attackers.

In the ensuing commotion, Randall grabbed the medallion, and Sam's arm, yanking her away from the mercenaries. "Run, George!"

The three ran around the large dome-shaped building, seeking to put as much distance between the raging battle and themselves as they could. Realizing time was short, Randall knew that they needed to make it to Yupanqui and his men. The only hope of stopping Dumond was to get the medallion to the tribe. Yupanqui already had the shaft. If they could get the medallion to him, he could start the system and complete the reunification before the volcano erupted.

"We need to get the medallion to the Chief," Randall said.

"But we're running the wrong way!" Sam responded

"First, we need to put some distance between us and Dumond. This way!"

Randall made a sharp right turn at the first intersection they reached. His plan was simple. Lose Dumond and his men in the maze of streets, then zigzag their way back to the Chief at the Tablet room. With a little luck, they could make it to the tribe in time and get their help to escape before the volcano killed them all.

∞

Ackers ducked for cover inside the open control panel, his left arm throbbing in pain. He cut the arrowhead off with his knife and pushed the shaft out the other side of his arm, letting out a groan of pain. Taking off his shirt and tearing a strip from it, he wrapped the wound tightly to slow the flow of blood. His eyes were wild with rage. His only concern now was finding Randall and killing him painfully and slowly.

Dumond ducked into the control panel opening. "Ackers, what are you doing, you fool! Get out there with your men and get that medallion!"

Ackers regarded Dumond with disdain, grabbed his throat, and lifted him several inches off the ground. For the first time, he saw fear in his employer's eyes. "Shut the fuck up, you little pissant." Ackers tossed Dumond aside like a rag doll, the smaller man landing in a heap by the control panel. Ackers coolly picked up his assault rifle and walked back out of the niche.

Grabbing the first man he saw, he screamed into his ear, "Where did Randall go!"

The mercenary blinked in surprise and pointed in the direction the professor and his group had run. Ackers released the man from his iron grip and ran off in pursuit.

C380

Another quake rocked the cavern, shaking the city violently and causing rocks to plummet from the cavern above.

"This place is getting more and more unstable. We're running out of time!" Randall shouted.

"How much time are we talking about?" George asked.

253

Randall glanced down at his watch while he ran. "Forty-eight minutes." There was a slight pause. "How did you know that the control panel showed the remaining time?"

"Your response when you accessed the control panel. That's the first thing I would have checked and, judging by your reaction, I knew we were pushing it."

"Dad, what happens in forty-eight minutes?"

"I'm not exactly sure, but in forty-eight minutes I think this volcano is going to blow!"

"Forty-eight minutes! We'll never get out of here in time!" George yelled.

"How could they predict the eruption time of a volcano? That's impossible!" Sam said.

"I don't know. Their technology is thousands of years ahead of ours," Randall said, almost out of breath.

So far, his plan was working. The group had zigzagged several times through the streets and eluded Ackers and his men. Of course, Randall thought, Yupanqui's tribe was playing a large role in keeping them occupied. Stopping for a moment to get his bearings, Randall paused at the end of a row of buildings and motioned for Sam and George to be silent and stay put. He walked gingerly to the edge of the last structure on the street and slowly peered around the corner.

Just as he suspected, the Tablet room was directly to their right and about 300 yards from their current location. Unfortunately, there would be little cover for this last dash. He had unknowingly led them to what appeared to be a public square, beautifully landscaped, but with very few structures.

"This looks like a plaza. It must be where they all get together," Sam said, sneaking up behind her father. "Look over there." She pointed to a small feature that looked like a fountain, but instead of water, there was smoke.

"The magma is leaching into the water system. It's finding its way up through fissures in the rock."

"What are we doing?" George asked, joining them. Seeing the large open space, he commented, "This doesn't look good."

"George, on my mark, we run full speed, no stopping! Sam, you're the fastest, you take the medallion. George and I will draw the attention of Ackers's men. George, you run diagonally across the square toward that small building in the middle. That will offer you some protection. I'll run at Ackers's men to draw their fire."

"Are you crazy? You'll be killed!" Sam yelled.

"It's our only chance. Sam, count to ten after George takes off, and then make a beeline for Yupanqui. If something happens to George or me, you keep going. We need to get that medallion to the tribe. If we don't, they'll never get out of here and return home. Hundreds or even thousands of lives are counting on you, Sam. Promise me you won't stop if something happens to one of us."

"I can't leave you!"

Randall held his daughter by the shoulders and looked into her eyes. "Sam, I've already cost Phil and Mike their lives, I wouldn't be able to live with myself if thousands of other innocent people died as well. I need you to do this. Promise me."

Tears welling in her eyes, she couldn't speak. Instead, Sam just shook her head. "I can't. I just found you again."

Randall took a deep breath. She was stubborn, but he couldn't blame her, after all, she was his daughter. Finally, he spoke calmly and quietly. "Sam, you know I love you and I don't want to be separated from you ever again. But we need to get the medallion to Yupanqui and his people. If there was any other way, I would do it, but this is our only chance."

Sam stood, tears streaming down her face. She nodded in agreement.

"George are you ready? Go!"

George sprinted like an Olympic runner out of the starting blocks. At the same time, Randall ran in a zigzagging pattern toward the armed mercenaries, waving his arm to draw their attention. His plan worked a little too well. Those not directly engaged in the firefight with the natives turned their attention to him. Small bursts of dust kicked up near his feet as the soldiers fired round after round at him. Less attention was paid to George, but at least one mercenary spotted him and began firing. Sam, waiting and watching from the relative safety of her hiding spot slowly counted to ten. Upon reaching the magic number, she clenched the medallion firmly in her palm and made a mad dash directly toward Yupanqui.

The scene in the cavern was utter chaos. Natives firing arrows at the soldiers. The soldiers returning fire at the natives. Sam, George, and Randall running in three different directions with mercenaries trying to shoot them as well. The sight reminiscent of a *Mad Magazine* interpretation of army tactics gone awry. All the while, the clock ticked down toward Armageddon.

Of the three, Sam was the first to reach her destination. She hoofed it up the steps to Yupanqui, holding the medallion out to him as she doubled over in exhaustion, unable to speak. The chief smiled, took the medallion, and thanked her. She collapsed on the ground, her body thoroughly expended with physical and emotional exhaustion. Yupanqui's men surrounded her, creating a human shield.

George arrived at the small structure in the plaza and dove for cover from the gunfire. He landed awkwardly, tweaking his wrist in the process. Despite the imminent danger to himself, his thoughts turned to Sam and her safety. He looked up at the tablet room and did not see her. In a panic, he stood to search again for her and saw someone lying on the ground at the chief's feet. His heartbeat quickened, worried that she might be injured or worse. His fear was quickly allayed as he saw her rise to her feet, protected by the chief's men.

Randall was taking the worst of it. Running toward the soldiers seemed to have an unnerving effect on them. Seeing him as a possible direct threat to their safety, the mercenaries rewarded him with a hail of gunfire. To his amazement, he had not been hit. Yet. His muscles screamed with pain as his endorphin-fueled zigzagging pushed his body to its very limits.

Keeping count as he ran, Randall determined that Sam should have had time to reach the tribe and George should have made it to the shelter by now. He had pushed his luck as far as it could go, and he had no desire to see his journey end in this manner. But he was tiring and there was no cover to be found. The spray of bullets was becoming more intense

– the soldiers only had one target to concentrate on now, and unfortunately for Randall, it was him. It was only a matter of time before they adjusted fire and hit him. Randall needed a plan. Now.

Cൠൠ

Sam watched from up high as her father tried changing course away from the mercenaries. He made a final zigzagging turn, a hornet's nest of dust balls kicking up all about him. Then it happened. He fell to the ground and lay motionless. They had finally gotten him. The soldiers ceased their fire at the Professor and resumed full engagement with the tribesmen.

"Come on, Dad, get up, get up!"

George, oblivious to Randall's predicament, came huffing and puffing up to the tablet room, no worse for the wear. He sidled up next to Sam and put a hand on her shoulder. "Thank God you're alright. I thought you were hurt when I saw you lying on the ground up here." Sam was unresponsive, her attention fully rapt on something happening in the plaza below. Turning to look, George discovered what she was focused on.

Randall was still motionless. From a distance, it was impossible to see the extent of his wounds. Sam was overcome with a sense of helplessness. It couldn't end this way. It wasn't fair.

"I'm going to get him," George said, starting down the steps to the open plaza.

Sam grabbed his arm. "No, you'll be killed, too!"

"I can't just leave him there! I have to do something."

The cavern began shaking violently again. The ground heaved as if a giant fist had punched the earth from beneath their feet, sending Sam and George sprawling to the ground. The shooting stopped, and dust filled the air, obscuring Sam's view of her father. It also obscured the view of Ackers and his men.

CRÆO

Randall realized it was now or never. As soon as the shaking subsided, he was up and running. Playing possum had given him a chance to rest and he was determined to use every ounce of energy left in him to make it to the tablet room. This time, he didn't zigzag, he ran straight and fast. The mercenaries, shaken by the latest jolt from the earth, at first failed to realize that their target wasn't dead. The break in the shooting didn't last long, as several resumed their deadly sniping at him.

"Look, look George! He's on his feet and running toward us! Come on, Dad, go!"

From their vantage point, it almost looked like he was running in slow motion, his small body flitting across the open ground. Yupanqui, seeing the situation unfolding, directed his best archers to concentrate fire on the soldiers who were firing on Randall. They watched as the muzzle flashes went off and used them to mark their targets. Several of their arrows connected and soldiers fell to the earth.

Randall was nearing the end of the plaza. There was one block remaining between him and the steps leading up to the tablet room and safety. He reached the intersection of the last street, turning the corner by the nearest building. He was greeted with a vicious full body blow. He dropped to the ground, writhing in pain. Ackers had found him.

"Thought you were going to make it? Well, you were wrong. Get up!" Ackers gritted through clenched teeth, picking up Randall like he was a bag of feathers. Bracing his feet, Ackers flipped Randall over his shoulder and slammed him back into the ground. Randall couldn't breathe, the wind knocked from his chest.

Ackers grabbed Randall and flung him against a nearby wall, his hand clenched in rage around his throat. He squeezed harder. The professor's eyes were as large as saucers, bugging out of his eye sockets from the pressure. Randall kicked his feet in futility, trying to find Ackers's abdomen, but had no luck. No amount of hand to hand combat training would help him now. He dug his fingernails into the mercenary's arm, and warm red blood trickled down his forearm. The grip only grew stronger. Randall could feel the asphyxiation now, his oxygen-deprived brain beginning to shut down. Ackers released his grip and Randall fell to the ground, choking for breath.

Ackers staggered backward. An arrow had dug deeply into his back causing him to release his grip. Randall watched in disbelief as Ackers reached over his shoulder, grabbed hold of the arrow, and wrenched it from his back with nothing more than a slight grimace of pain. He lurched toward Randall and once again stopped in his tracks. This time an arrow had gone straight through his left bicep. Randall didn't wait to see the response this time, he struggled to his feet and began running again for the stairs. Upon reaching them, he leapt up two at a time, never turning to see if Ackers was pursuing him. He didn't stop until he reached the top and collapsed at Sam's feet.

"Ackers … where is … he?"

"He ran back down the street, holding his arm. Are you alright?" Sam asked as she and George helped him back to his feet.

"Never better." Randall managed a smile. He glanced at his watch: twenty-six minutes left.

Yupanqui came over, knelt by Randall, and placed a hand on his shoulder. "Thank you, my friend, for helping my people."

Randall smiled. "Thank you for helping us out of that mess!"

Yupanqui nodded. "Come, there isn't much time, we must get you all to safety."

Chapter Thirty-Five

Dumond picked himself up and checked for injuries. Shaken, but uninjured, he checked the control panel: twenty-five minutes until eruption. Thanks to Randall's notes, he had discovered the escape pod rising directly from the center of the power dome and how to operate it. Randall had undoubtedly been keeping this piece of information from him, but once again, he had outsmarted his opponent. Realizing that he had lost his chance to gain the power source, he would have to be satisfied with his opponents being blown to bits when the volcano erupted.

Dumond entered the escape pod. In a matter of minutes, he was safely on the surface above the volcano, calling for his helicopter to pick him up. Oddly enough, another helicopter appeared from the distance, one he did not recognize.

☙☙

"Tom, you've got to see this!" the pilot shouted over the helicopter engine's roar.

"What is it, Jesse?"

"This guy just appeared out of nowhere on the slope of the hill. I don't know where the hell he came from."

"Well if he doesn't get out of there soon, he's going to be in some serious deep-fried trouble. Take us closer, we've got to get him out of there."

"You sure about that, Tom? This thing looks like it's ready to blow."

"I know, but we can't just leave him there."

Jesse banked the Sikorsky toward the lone figure.

The helicopter pilot made a beeline for the person on the mountainside. No one was sure how much time they had before the volcano erupted, but it was safe to assume that it would be sooner rather than later. When he had closed to within several hundred yards of the mystery man, he caught a strange sight out of his peripheral vision. Another helicopter appeared out of nowhere. "Tom, are you aware of any other birds that are supposed to be in the area right now?"

"No, we're the only ones cleared to be in this airspace, why?"

"Take a look at ten o'clock."

Tom glanced up and to the left.

"What the hell? This airspace has been shut down, does that guy realize how close Misti is to going off?"

Gunfire raked the airspace around the chopper. "Whoa! What's that guy doing?"

"We're not sticking around to find out." Jesse banked the Sikorsky hard to right, bringing it around one hundred and eighty degrees in a matter of seconds. The g-forces brought on by the sharp turn pushed Tom into his seat like a large stone had just been tossed onto his lap. The gunfire abated, and Reinsdorf looked back at the lone figure on the ground.

He didn't stand a chance against the helicopter that had just shot at them.

"Jesse, we need to get on the horn to the local air traffic controllers and let them know what's going on."

"Will do, I just want to put a little more distance between us and that nut job in the other chopper."

CApart

The fighting had ended as Yupanqui's men dispatched Dumond's remaining mercenaries. Still lying on the ground by the tablet room, Randall looked up to see the smiling faces of his daughter and George. He rose to his feet as Sam put an arm around him. "I thought I'd lost you, Dad."

George came forward and grabbed Randall's hand, shaking it vigorously. "Glad you're okay. We were worried about you."

"Thanks guys, I'm okay, but I think it's time for us to get out of this mountain." Randall looked at Yupanqui. "We'll follow you, Chief." The leader of the tribe stood motionless for a moment, which seemed strange to Randall. He then noticed several figures a few feet in the distance, walking toward them. Most of them were Yupanqui's tribespeople, but one was significantly taller. Randall judged the height of the bigger one to be about six feet.

Obviously, he's not one of them. Or, if he is, he's someone important. Randall kept his eyes locked on the taller figure. The smaller ones stopped walking, but the last one continued toward them, his pace quickening.

"Dad, who is that? Why is one of them so much bigger than the rest?" Sam asked, unsure of what she was seeing.

"I'm not sure," Randall replied as he stared at the tall figure slowly moving in his direction. As the stranger approached, a distant glow of recognition struggled to the surface of Randall's subconscious, fighting its way through the murky depths of his memories. He had seen the tall one before, but where?

Sam was the first to recognize him. "Oh my God, it's him! Dad, it's him!"

Suddenly, as if a searchlight had snapped on inside the darkness of his mind, Randall saw the stranger and realized who it was. "Phil!"

Rarely was Randall at a loss for words, but this was one of those occasions. The young graduate student ran up to his mentor and gave him a monstrous hug, lifting him up off the ground. "How are you, Dr. R?" Phil said, grinning like a Cheshire cat.

"How ... what ... you're okay!" Randall stammered.

"I'm okay, these nice folks helped me out."

"But what happened to you? We set you down on the floor and then the earthquake hit, and you disappeared! We looked all over and couldn't find you!"

"To be honest, it's a bit foggy to me, too. I remember I was fading fast, slipping into and out of consciousness. The last thing I remember, the earth was moving and then things went black. When I woke up, I was in a bright room, lying on a table. At first, I thought you had gotten me to a hospital ... but it didn't look like any hospital I'd ever seen. The funny thing is, I wasn't scared. I guess I was in bad shape because I just passed out again, but then someone patched me up. Look, I barely even have a scar!" Phil lifted his bloody shirt to reveal only the faintest trace of where the bullet had pierced his chest. "Next thing I know, I wake up with some of Yupanqui's people staring down at me. Then they brought me back to the cavern. Pretty weird, huh?"

"After what we've been through, it just seems like par for the course, but it sure is great to see you, son." Randall squeezed his shoulder, thankful for a chance to see his friend again. Wiping his eyes, he said, "We'd better get going; we don't have much time. Chief, which way is out?"

The group followed Yupanqui, who led them down a previously unseen tunnel. They walked in relative silence for a short distance.

"By the way, Dr. R, where's Mike?"

Randall stopped immediately, the lump returning to his throat. Unable to look into his graduate student's eyes, he said, "Mike didn't make it, Phil."

Phil blinked and hesitated before speaking again. "What do you mean?"

Randall steadied himself. "I found him in Dumond's compound. He must have been brought there when Dumond found you two in the tunnel. I was able to sneak into the compound and into the room where he was being held, but a guard heard us talking and burst into the room ready to shoot. I fought with him and his gun went off. The bullet hit Mike … I couldn't do anything to help him … he died in my arms."

Phil remained motionless.

"Phil," Sam said softly, touching his arm, "I'm really sorry. I know you two were close."

Phil fought back tears. Only an occasional sniffling noise broke the deafening silence. Finally, he spoke. "I can't believe he's gone. He was like a brother to me." Now the tears began falling. Phil tried mopping them up with the sleeve of his bloody shirt. "It's not fair, I could have been the one who died, but they saved me. Why did it have to be Mike?" Phil's head began shaking back in forth as if he was trying to get the image of his dying friend out of his mind.

"I'm sorry Phil, I ..." was all Randall could say.

The group stood in the same spot for some time while Yupanqui patiently waited.

Finally, George spoke. "Guys, I got to know Mike while we were in that room together and I know this is hard, but we still need to find our way out of here. Mike thought of you as his family and he would have wanted all of you to get home safely."

Phil was the first to respond. "You're right. It's bad enough losing Mike, I don't know what I would do if I lost you guys, too." They walked along in silence, following Chief Yupanqui to a fork in the tunnel.

"My friends, follow this to the surface. I must return to my people; our time is at hand." Randall stared up the shaft that led to the surface. A faint but persistent glow shimmered in the distance. Daylight.

"Thank you, Chief, we'll never forget you." Randall shook his hand.

Yupanqui looked squarely into Randall's eyes. "You will always be remembered by my people for what you have done for us." Looking at Sam now, he added, "You and your father are heroes to my tribe." With that, Yupanqui departed from the group.

Randall started up the angular tunnel, anxious to get Sam, Phil, and George to safety. He took two steps and stopped. Something seemed to be calling him back into the main cavern. Not quite a voice as much a sense of unfinished business. "You all go on without me, I'll be a few minutes behind you."

"Is everything okay?" Sam asked.

"Everything's fine, I'll only be a couple of minutes. You three get to the surface." Randall turned away from them and walked back into the cavern to end the possibility of discussion. Phil and George looked at Sam, who hesitated momentarily but began walking up the tunnel. They followed her.

Randall entered the cavern and was greeted with an eerie silence. He sensed a presence but never actually saw anyone or anything.

"I have so many questions for you and there is so much my people could learn from you. But you haven't returned to offer explanations, have you?"

Although no words were uttered, Randall understood that the answer was an emphatic no.

"Then why did you call me back?"

"When you accessed our database, you learned about my people. Our history and our purpose on your planet. You also discovered some troubling information."

"They're real, aren't they? Who are they? Where are they from and why are they here?"

"Our understanding of them is limited, but their purpose here isn't peaceful."

"Can you help us? What can I do if I encounter them?"

"When the time comes, you will know."

268

Randall stood in the middle of the tunnel, somewhat uneasy about the conversation taking place inside of his mind, but his confusion was soon replaced by a brief sense of profound serenity.

"Can you tell me what they're called?"

"We simply call them The Others. More than this, I cannot tell you."

Randall was overwhelmed with a sense of wonderment and uncertainty.

"What should I do next?"

There was no reply. Randall stared into the shadows and caught a slight movement out of the corner of his eye. Someone or something was walking toward him. He braced himself for what would happen next.

The figure moved slowly and deliberately, staying in the shadows. When it was finally within arms distance of Randall, it stepped into the light.

Shock gripped Randall as he stared into the face of Chief Yupanqui.

"It's you," he said, a sense of bewilderment washing over him. "I just imagined the whole experience of meeting your brethren," Randall said, unsure what to think.

"In time, all things will make sense to you," Yupanqui said, a warm smile on his face. He reached up and grasped Randall's shoulder. "You are a good man Randall. Watch over your family and appreciate each day with them."

Yupanqui turned and disappeared back into the shadows as Randall stood motionless, once again dumbfounded by the turn of events.

After a few moments, Randall started up the gently sloping shaft, suddenly feeling exceptionally fatigued. His muscles ached, and his every movement was a struggle. His body was finally experiencing a let-down after many days of operating on sheer adrenaline. Suddenly, all Randall could think about was a warm shower and a long nap.

His thoughts were abruptly interrupted by a new thought: *They are in danger.* Randall stopped dead in his tracks. *Who is in danger?* But before the words had finished, he realized the answer. He ignored the fatigue and picked up his pace. Three words suddenly flashed brightly in his mind: *Ackers is here!* His slow jog morphed into a sprint, the beam of his flashlight bouncing madly as the words repeated in his mind, *Ackers is here, Ackers is here!* A new thought flashed through his mind: *Duck.* He did, just in time for the shiny metal blade to pass narrowly over the top of his head.

Ackers let out an animalistic grunt. "I'm going to kill you, mother fucker!" Even in the dim lighting, Randall could see the madness in his eyes. "No one fucks with me and gets away with it."

Randall sensed immediately that there would be no reasoning with Ackers. He was too far-gone. Instead, he employed the opposite tact, hoping to throw him off. "It's going to be pretty pathetic when you get your ass kicked by a guy who makes a living lecturing to college students."

Ackers responded by swinging his knife in violent uncontrolled arcs, each closer than the last. As Ackers swung again, Randall parried the blow with his forearm, knocking the mercenary into the wall. Ackers was fuming. Not aware of Randall's previous Special Forces training, he was bewildered that the academic was able to match him in hand-to-hand combat. He stood facing Randall, his knife shifting from hand to hand. Randall, for his part, marveled that his combat skills were still sharp.

Ackers breathed in short, snorting noises, his eyes wild with rage. This time, the attack was well disciplined. Ackers drove Randall back against the rock face, cutting off his line of retreat at each attempt. Randall, his back literally against the wall, searched desperately for a weapon. He found none. His prey now cornered, Ackers made his move at Randall, pinning him against the wall with his open hand, while driving his blade in an upward arc at Randall's chest. Randall grabbed Acker's knife wielding arm with both of his hands, using all his force to slow the impending impact of knife to chest. Ackers grunted against the opposing force, willing the knife closer to his target. The knife slowly pierced Randall's stomach – he let out yelp of pain. With all his force, he pushed the knifed hand sideways, the blade tearing a ragged wound in his stomach. Ackers staggered against the sideways force, the knife moving past Randall and becoming embedded in the cavern wall. The pain in Randall's stomach was at first a searing heat, then a throbbing ache.

Randall backpedaled away from Ackers, but the mercenary regained his footing and drove his elbow into Randall's injured stomach. Randall staggered backward, holding his stomach. Ackers gripped the knife handle, wrenching it from the wall. Ribbons of light from the surface created a surreal view of the crazed mercenary lurching closer to Randall. Ackers lunged, the knife blade leading the charge. Randall dodged to the side. The blade swung again, catching Randall in his left thigh. He spun away from Ackers, his stomach and thigh oozing blood. The stench of

271

sweat and blood filled his lungs, causing Randall to wretch. He wiped his mouth, watching Ackers circle him like a wild beast moving in for the kill.

Another attack, this one up high. The blade of the knife narrowly missed Randall's right cheek as he pulled away. Ackers countered with a kick to Randall's stomach, which sent him careening into the wall. He bounced off, falling to the ground, gasping for air. Despair gripped him. If Ackers beat him, he would surely kill Sam and Phil as well. Randall dragged himself to his feet, knowing that if he didn't he was dead. An evil smile crawled across Acker's face. "It will all be over soon."

"Come on, you psychopath, come and get me!" Randall goaded.

The crazed mercenary's eyes narrowed, the look on his face a mixture of confusion and sheer hatred.

Ackers grunted. "Get ready to die, asshole." He moved toward Randall, who matched each movement forward with a step back. "You talk tough for a man who keeps backing up," Ackers said, savoring the moment.

Randall watched the mercenary, his eyes locked on his every move.

Ackers moved forward, breathing heavily, switching the knife from one hand to the other. "Where are you going, Professor? There's nowhere to hide."

Ackers bull-rushed him, trying to tackle him to the ground. Randall rolled onto his back, placing his booted foot into Ackers's stomach. Using the mercenary's own weight against him, Randall launched Ackers into the air and sent him flying into the tunnel wall. Ackers hit the wall hard, letting out a scream as he did, his body making a loud cracking sound as it impacted. Randall watched as the now lifeless body dropped the floor, the mercenary's contorted face coming to rest looking at Randall. It was over now, Ackers would never harm his family again.

Randall grabbed his flashlight and sprinted up the tunnel, which grew hotter by the minute. He shined the light up and down the shaft, moving back toward Vilcabamba where Ackers had first attacked him. "There has to be an exit here somewhere!" The increasing heat within the tunnel made it more difficult for Randall to move. Finally, he found what he was looking for: a side tunnel. Randall turned the corner and saw Sam, Phil and George bound and gagged on the ground.

"Thank God, are you all okay?"

Randall removed Sam's gag first.

"Dad, you have to watch out, he's crazy! Ackers caught us, tied us up and said he was going to kill you!"

"It's okay Sam, he's gone now. He can't hurt anyone else. We've got to hurry; this volcano is going to erupt any moment now."

Randall glanced at his watch. Eleven minutes remained until the event horizon.

Once again, the earth shook violently. Chunks of rock fell from the roof of the cavern. The air became choked with dust. George was the only one still tied up.

"Sam, Phil, get out of here, I'll get George."

"We can't leave you!"

"Phil, get her out of here! Now!"

Phil grabbed Sam and forced her into the shaft, pushing her toward daylight. Another earthquake shook as they stumbled up the cavern.

The small side cavern was filled with dust, obscuring anything farther than an arm's length away. Randall felt his way along the side of the cavern until he found George, still bound and gagged, and not moving.

"George!" Randall removed the gag first and put his ear against his friend's mouth. He was rewarded with a string of coughs. He struggled to find the knot in the rope Ackers had used to tie George up. The cavern shook again. Randall shielded George from falling debris. Once the shaking stopped, he was finally able to untie him.

"Come on, we need to get out of here."

George screamed in pain as Randall pulled him to his feet. "My leg, I think it's broken. Goddam it, it hurts like Hell!"

Randall waved away the dirty air, revealing a nasty gash and a purple-black lump the size of a baseball on George's leg.

"It's broken, but we've got to move. I'll get you out, but you're going to have to help me. You've got to use your good leg to walk." Randall grabbed George under the armpit and hoisted him onto his shoulder, bracing the young engineer by placing his arm over his own shoulder. "Okay, we move on three. One, two ..." Another violent shake, worse than the previous two. Debris was everywhere, and the two men were thrown to the cavern floor.

George screamed in pain. "Dr. Randall, you've got to get out of here, just leave me."

Randall struggled to his feet, grabbing George once again and moving toward the main tunnel. As they reached the shaft, they immediately felt the heat. Randall glanced down to where Vilcabamba had once been. There was only superheated, glowing magma slowly forcing its way up the main shaft. As they moved into the main tunnel, a wall of heat hit them. The main exit had become a blast furnace. Randall struggled forward; the ragged wound in his stomach felt like someone had shoved hot coals into him. The air was thick with dust, which coated his throat and the inside of his lungs. The combination of the intense heat along with the choking, dusty air was a deadly elixir, one that promised to make the last hundred yards a nightmare for Randall and George.

They pressed forward, Randall telling himself, *Just a little farther*. Another earthquake struck. More debris and dust choked the shaft. The pair lost their balance and crashed against the hard, rocky floor. George moaned in pain, Randall coughed up brown mucus. The movement of earth created a curtain of dust, which temporarily blocked out all light from the surface. Randall picked himself up, his thigh pulsing with pain. He grabbed George and they continued their slow crab-like crawl out of the mountain.

Minutes passed like hours, the heat increasing with each step forward. The light was becoming brighter now; they were getting closer. The shaft of light beckoned them forward, and Randall responded with a surge of energy. "Just a little bit farther George."

Randall could hear Phil's voice and he knew they were close now, maybe fifty feet. The added strain of carrying George through the dust-choked chamber had drained him of his energy.

"Phil, Sam, can you hear me! Hey guys, we need help."

"Dr. Randall, we're here!" Phil entered the shaft, Sam close behind.

"Grab George and help him out."

Phil and Sam grabbed their injured friend and carried him to the surface. Randall leaned against the side of the cavern, needing the rocky wall to hold himself up.

"Come on, Dad, you've got to keep moving!"

Randall pulled himself to his feet and continued the march forward toward daylight, moving slowly with exhaustion. His muscles burned like never before, but the thought of exiting that hell on earth drove him forward.

Sam and Phil gently set George down on the ground outside the cavern. "I wasn't sure if I'd ever see daylight again." He smiled weakly.

Sam kissed him gently on the cheek. "We never would have left you behind." Under his dusty mask, George's cheeks blushed from the unsolicited affection.

Just another twenty feet, Randall told himself. Then the earth moved again, this time more violently than the other times. Randall was knocked off balance, tumbling sideways into the side of the tunnel and then to the ground. His flashlight, no longer under his control, danced crazily in the air. Randall slowly got to his feet and surveyed the darkness. Seeing the beam of light, he bent down and grabbed it. Large chunks of rock had fallen from the roof of the cavern, sealing his path out. He was trapped, only a few feet away from Sam and Phil.

Randall sank to his knees, exhausted and beaten. His entire body ached, and he was light-headed. He slowly lowered himself to the ground and sat, feeling the extreme heat radiating from the oncoming magma. He glanced wearily down the cavern toward the molten rock, seeing that it had progressed slowly but steadily in his direction. From the other side of the rocks, he could hear Sam and Phil's voices, distant dismembered sounds floating off into the distance.

He assessed his options, quickly concluding that there weren't many. He could try digging his way out through the fallen rocks, though getting through was not likely, given their size and weight. His only other option was to head back toward the magma and hope he could reach the side tunnel before it was engulfed and hope that it led to another way out. Once again, this wasn't much of an option. He wasn't even sure if the opening to the side tunnel was still there and, if it was, there was no guarantee it would lead to the outside world. Randall rubbed his eyes. The only thought that crossed his mind was that he hadn't come this far just to trip at the finish line. Randall willed himself not to quit. He had to make it to the side tunnel.

Pulling himself to his feet, Randall made his best attempt at running back down the tunnel toward where he had left Ackers's body. As he drew nearer to the magma, its heat increased dramatically. Using his light, Randall tried to see if the side tunnel was exposed. He couldn't tell from this distance, so he kept running, the heat getting more and more unbearable. Another earthquake struck and again he was thrown about like a rag doll.

The dust was palpable, covering the inside of his mouth with a fine layer each time he inhaled. If there were a hell, this was surely it. Randall fumbled for his light, which had tumbled to the ground when he had fallen. He stopped looking; no time for that. He felt his way in the darkness, the soft glow of the magma producing the only light in the tunnel.

Blind and fumbling in the dark, Randall could not tell if the side tunnel was there. Only that the magma was getting closer and he was quickly running out of real estate. He estimated that the magma was a mere twenty to thirty feet away now; his face felt like it was burning, and his clothes seemed ready to ignite. Still no side tunnel. He groped onward, feeling both sides of the tunnel for any sign of an opening. He could no longer take the heat. He had to go back.

Randall slid his hand one last time where he thought the opening should be. At first, he wasn't sure, but then he felt a gap in the stony wall. It wasn't as big as before. The falling rocks must have partially sealed it, but the opening was big enough to allow him to pass through. With the remaining strength in his body, Randall pulled himself up and through the opening. Once on the other side, he realized that he was not as hot anymore. The fallen rock, acting as an insulator, had kept this side of the tunnel cooler for now. Rising to his feet, Randall's arms felt ragged and burned from rubbing against the rocky surface.

He continued to feel his way through the dark and move onward through the tunnel. He had gone several feet when he tripped and fell to the ground. He had fallen over Ackers's body. Suddenly, a thought gripped him: Ackers might have something useful to help him get out. Overcoming his instinct to move away from the corpse, Randall searched through his pockets. He found a small cylindrical item in his cargo pocket. "Please let it be a light." It was. Randall rummaged through the other pockets and found a knife, a compass, a canteen, and a final item that produced a sense of both hope and foreboding. An explosive device. At least that's what it appeared to be.

Randall's thoughts raced wildly. If he could get back down the main tunnel, he might be able to blast his way through the fallen rocks. Moving quickly, he ran back to the opening that he had gone through only minutes before. The magma was almost directly below him. He had about eight feet before it covered the opening. The heat was devastating, and Randall had to pull back before being overwhelmed. It was too hot, he couldn't go back over. He breathed deeply and realized what he had to do.

Moving quickly, he returned to Ackers's side and removed the soldier's shirt. Dousing it with water, Randall cut it into three pieces. He then made two holes in the largest piece, wrapping it around his face. The two remaining pieces were used to make coverings for both hands. Rising to his feet, he quickly climbed back to the opening. He closed his eyes, took a deep breath, and pushed himself over and through the rocky opening. Randall landed upside-down, his hands on the ground holding him like he was trying to do military-style pushups against the rocky wall. His left hand closest to the magma felt like fire. He quickly pushed off and fell sideways away from the magma. Tearing the shirt from his face, he raced back toward the blocked opening.

"Sam, Phil, can you hear me!"

"Dad, is that you? We can hear you. Are you okay? What happened?"

"I'm going to blow an opening in the tunnel. Move away from the entrance and let me know when you're back!"

Phil yelled. "Go, Dr. Randall, go!"

Randall, holding the device in his hand, depressed a small button that read *Arm Device*. A small green light immediately began blinking, first slowly, then more quickly. Randall realized that it was time delayed, but had no idea how long. He raced as close to the magma as he dared, dropped to the ground, and covered his head and neck as best he could.

The explosion rocked the cavern, sending rocks flying wildly through the air. Randall looked up and saw the most wonderful sight he could have imagined. Daylight! Jumping up, he ran as quickly as his damaged body could manage, exiting the tunnel to safety. Exhausted, he fell to the ground.

Chapter Thirty-Six

"**D**ad, you made it!" Sam ran over to her father, kneeling to see if he was all right. Slowly, Randall opened his eyes and looked at his daughter.

He grinned broadly. "Good to see you, kiddo. Wasn't completely sure if I ever would again. Phil, good to see you, too. Where's George?"

"He's okay, he's right over there," Phil said, pointing in George's direction. Clearly in pain, George waved back to Randall. Randall lifted a tired hand in acknowledgement.

"Well, we're still not out of the proverbial frying pan. This volcano is going to blow its top and we need to find a way to get out of here," Randall said, looking at his watch. There were only a few minutes left in the countdown to Misti's eruption.

"Dad, what happened with you and Ackers?"

"Let's just say that Ackers won't be bothering us again and leave it at that."

"Did you kill him, Dr. R?"

Randall looked his graduate student in the eye and nodded. Phil stuck out is hand to help his professor back to his feet. Randall grasped hold and pulled himself up.

"What do we do now?" Phil asked.

As Randall pondered the question, a strange noise appeared in the distance. They all turned to look. Sam was the first to spot the source of the noise.

"Is that a helicopter?" Sam asked.

"It looks like it's coming our way. Phil, help me get George. If this is one of Ackers's men, we're in big trouble. I hate to say it, but if the bullets start flying we'll need to go back into the tunnel." Randall winced internally at the thought of going back in, but it was the only shelter they had. He and Phil hoisted George to his feet, supporting him one under each shoulder.

The helicopter approached like a large sullen bird, arcing slowly over the earth toward them. Within a minute it was hovering yards away from them, hanging menacingly in the sky.

"Get ready to run," Randall warned the group.

"This is Dr. Tom Reinsdorf from the United States Geological Survey. This is an active volcano site and we expect eruption at any moment. Are you in need of assistance?" The voice rang out like the voice of God from above. The group nodded and waived them down. "We're unable to land here. Stand by." Tom looked around the cabin of the helicopter and had an idea. "Jesse, what's the capacity of that cable we use to haul the sonar unit?"

"It's rated to 2,000 pounds, why? You're not thinking of pulling those folks up on that, are you?"

"Do you have a better idea?"

Jesse thought for a moment and glanced at the ticking time bomb beneath them. Reluctantly, he shook his head. "Okay, there's a safety harness in the side of the bay. You need to detach the sonar unit and hook the safety harness on the carabineer instead. We can lower the harness and haul them up one at a time. There's a toggle in the bay that operates the hoist. You got all that?"

"What about the injured guy?" Tom asked.

"Sorry, he's going to have to deal with it if he wants to get out of here."

Tom keyed the mike again. "We're going to lower a cable and safety harness to you on the ground. You'll have to strap in and we'll haul you up one at a time. If you understand that, give me a thumbs up." Four thumbs quickly popped into the air.

Tom maneuvered his way to the cargo bay of the helicopter. Just as Jesse had instructed, he found the harness and swapped it in place of the towed sonar unit. Opening the side bay door, he released the harness and cable, then lowered them slowly to the ground.

"Sam, you first!" Randall yelled above the din of the helicopter.

"No, we have to get George up first, he's hurt," Sam protested.

"No, Sam, you need to go first. I'll be fine," George answered.

Sam decided it would be a waste of time to argue. Grasping the hanging harness, she strapped herself in and gave a thumbs-up to the figure standing in the helicopter bay. In a moment, she was slowly moving up and into the sky, her feet dangling toward the earth. The ascent was slow but steady, and Sam slowly rotated as the splayed cable fed back onto the spool. For a moment, she marveled at the incredible view, but her thoughts quickly turned to the others. She was concerned about getting everyone else safely into the helicopter and wished the winch would retrieve her more quickly. Finally, she arrived at the opening of the bay. An enormous man was standing there waiting for her.

Before she could even think to speak, he reached out with a huge hand and grabbed the harness, hauling her into the helicopter.

"Are you okay?"

"I'm fine. We need to hurry and get the rest of them in," Sam said, removing the harness as she spoke so as not to waste precious time.

The harness began its second journey down. This time, Phil and Randall strapped George in. He protested, saying it wasn't fair and that Phil or Randall should go, but they ignored his pleas. Once safely attached, Randall gave the thumbs-up sign again and George was whisked into the waiting chopper.

Randall and Phil looked at each other. "You next, Dr. Randall."

Randall shook his head. "No way, Phil, you're going next. I got you into this mess so it's my responsibility to get you out."

"But …"

"There's no discussion. Here, I'll help you get the harness on." Randall swung the harness around the back of his graduate student, who stood helplessly as his professor strapped him in first. A sudden jolt came from the ground as the earth heaved once more, knocking Randall and Phil off balance. Phil, partially strapped into the harness, was flung to the side, half of his body in the harness, the other half dangling out. Tom didn't wait, hitting the toggle switch; he pulled Phil up to the chopper, while the student hung on for dear life. Once he was safely aboard, Tom began lowering the harness a final time. As he did, he heard Jesse yelling.

"They're back, Tom, we need to get the hell out of here!"

Gunfire once again raked the air around the Sikorsky. The group looked out the back of the helicopter to see the combat helicopter barreling down out of the sky toward them. Time was short.

"The harness hasn't reached the ground yet."

"Well you better hurry, that guy's coming fast! If he hits us with that Gatling gun, we're dead meat!"

Randall glanced at his watch, the eruption was less than a minute away. He stared up at the cable which crawled toward the ground, seeming to move in slow motion. Finally, the harness reached him.

The combat helicopter had closed half the remaining distance to the Sikorsky. Tom picked up the speaker again. "On the ground, grab the harness now!" Randall complied, climbing as best he could into the harness.

"Hang on everyone."

Before he could fully strap in, the helicopter lifted into the sky, with Randall dangling helplessly from the end of the cable. The helicopter skimmed the uneven and now collapsing surface of Misti as the timer on Randall's watch began to beep. A loud rumbling sound came from deep within the mountain as lava spewed forth from the tunnel and other fissures which had developed in the side of Misti. Randall took a deep breath, relieved that there was no large explosion from the volcano, theorizing that the huge opening in which Vilcabamba resided must have provided space for most of the force of the volcano to disperse.

His relief was short lived. The pursuing combat chopper was quickly closing the gap, its pilot seemed hell bent on using them for target practice. Jesse banked their chopper hard to the right to try and evade their pursuers. The force of the turn sent the passengers summersaulting across the cabin of the Sikorsky, only stopping when they reached a hard surface. The force of the turn knocked Tom away from the cable toggle, causing Randall's upward motion to stop. Struggling to his feet, Tom lurched back to the controls, trying desperately to get his final passenger into the relative safety of the helicopter cabin. More bullets sprayed the air around them, several striking the tail section of the Sikorsky. Sheet metal tore away as the bullets ripped through the rear of the helicopter like a heated knife through butter.

A veteran military pilot with multiple tours of duty in both Iraq and Afghanistan, Jesse was no stranger to being shot at and his response was immediate: a hard banking move to the left. Once again, the passengers were thrown about the open back of the helicopter, each one experiencing the nauseating sensation of seeing at one moment the side of the helicopter, then the floor, followed by the ceiling.

"Grab something!" Tom yelled, clinging to the handrail as he fought gravity trying to pull him out of the open door of the chopper.

George, nearly delirious from the pain, grasped the edge of the seat he had been placed into. Sam managed to grab a section of webbing used to secure items to the side of the chopper. Phil wasn't so fortunate. Grasping wildly at any secure item within reach, he tumbled toward the open helicopter door.

"Jesse!" was the only word Tom could manage to get out. The pilot, realizing the situation, banked again to the right as Phil continued his death tumble. Reaching the opening, Phil's legs were the first to make their exit from the Sikorsky, his body dropping like a lead weight tossed from the side of a building. Tom grasped desperately at him as he floated helplessly by him and out the door.

"Phil! Sam screamed.

Phil was shocked at how quiet his mind had become. Falling out the door, he was consumed by the raucous noise of both the thumping of the helicopter blades and the sudden rush of wind by his ears. He had the sensation of moving very slowly, like a person trying to run away from some unforeseen danger in a dream. He tumbled downward with nothing to arrest his fall. He felt a tug, an impact with something hard and his fall suddenly stopped. In a stunned state, he turned his head to the side and was greeted by a familiar sight. Professor Randall had caught him.

During the helicopter's aerial acrobatics, Randall had swung back and forth under the Sikorsky like a pendulum. Fortunately for Phil, his final arc had placed him directly under the open door when Phil fell out. Randall simply hooked the falling graduate student as he fell past him, each of them suffering little more than a few bumps and bruises.

"I've got you!" was all Phil could make out over the din of wind and helicopter propeller noise.

Tom scrambled to his feet, regaining his balance. Jamming himself between a wall-mounted seat and the frame of the aircraft, he steadied himself and hit the toggle switch for the cable. The winch slowly returned to life, steadily retrieving the precious cargo at the end of the cable. The wind played havoc with Randall and his now added cargo. The two were tossed about as the cable slowly wound its way back into the dipping and diving helicopter. Randall looked up to find the helicopter slowly growing in size as they drew nearer.

With the cable spinning, Randall eventually faced the rear of the Sikorsky. He immediately regretted the view that greeted him. There in the sky behind them was the imposing silhouette of another helicopter. Randall suddenly realized why their helicopter was zigzagging so madly.

"Dumond," he said out loud, realizing that they had not seen the last of the crazed industrialist. As he watched helplessly, he witnessed small bursts of flame jetting out from a gun mounted under the belly of Dumond's helicopter. He needed no help realizing that they were being shot at, and he and Phil were as exposed as newborns on the day they arrived on this earth. He heard whizzing sounds like angry hornets pass within inches of his lower extremities. "Come on, hurry and get us up!"

"That maniac in the other chopper is still there. Were you ever able to reach the control tower to report what happened?" Tom asked over the intercom, still holding the toggle to retrieve Randall and Phil.

"Negative. I sent several messages, but I don't know if they were ever received. Whatever's going on is really interfering with our communication system. I think we're on our own here."

Sam struggled forward to the front of the helicopter. "How far are we from a safe landing spot? The guy who's flying that helicopter behind us is crazy. If he has his way, he'll turn your helicopter into Swiss cheese."

"We still have a way to go and that bird back there is faster than us. Factoring in the added weight only makes us that much slower."

"Can you call for help?"

"Tried that already, but something is jamming our communication system."

"When did you try?"

"Right before we picked you up. We saw some guy standing all alone on the mountain and were going to help him out when this thing showed up." Jesse gestured toward the combat chopper behind them. "We tried calling air traffic control but all I got was static."

"Try it now, I have a feeling it will work."

Jesse gave Sam a long, hard stare. H didn't know who she was but doubted that she knew anything about electronic communication systems on aircraft. Sam sensed his doubt. "What's your name?"

"Jesse."

"Jesse, I know you don't know me from Adam, but you have to trust me here. I'm pretty sure I know why your radio wasn't working. The underground facility we escaped from was jamming your signal, but the cause of the interference is gone now." She placed a hand on Jesse's shoulder. "Please."

Jesse keyed the mike. "Control tower, this is November 2115, over."

"November 2115, this is Air Traffic Control Arequipa." Jesse shot a glance in Sam's direction. She had a smile plastered on her face and gave a small "I don't know" shrug.

"Tower, this is November 2115, we have a situation. We are under fire from hostile aircraft, I repeat, we are under fire from aggressive aircraft."

"November 2115, are you near Misti?

"Affirmative, tower, hostile aircraft is an EC-665 Tiger Combat helicopter, I repeat an Echo Charlie Six, Six, Five Combat Chopper!"

Bullets once again whizzed by the Sikorsky, several finding their mark. Glass exploded from the rear of the injured helicopter, causing everyone dropped to the ground for protection.

"Goddam it! Tower, this is November 2115, we are hit and continue to take fire from aggressive aircraft. Do you read?"

"November 2115, we read you. You are on a four-mile final for 9R. What are you doing by the volcano? The Directorate of Air Transportation has closed all air traffic to that region. You are in restricted airspace."

"Roger that, tower, I am operating under the authority of the United States Geological Survey. We were monitoring Misti and picked up four civilians stranded on the mountain. We are now being pursued and attacked by unknown aircraft. We have suffered damage."

Jesse heard only silence on his radio.

"We got them!" Tom announced, pulling Randall and Phil into the bay of the Sikorsky and closing the door.

More gunfire and more hits to the Sikorsky; the engine was now smoking. "Strap yourselves in!" Jesse put the Sikorsky into a steep dive, heading for the craggy, rocky surface of Misti.

"What are you doing, Jesse?" Tom asked, his face white as a sheet.

"Trying to save our collective asses!"

The helicopter fell straight toward the earth at frightening speed. As the earth drew nearer, Tom's concern grew that they would not be able to pull out of the death dive. Finally, the pressure was too much.

"Jesse, pull up this damn helicopter! There's no point trying to save us if you kill us in the process!"

At the last possible moment, Jesse pulled back on the stick. It fought back tremendously, inertia not wanting their path to change. With great effort, he leveled out the Sikorsky and immediately looked back to see the other helicopter following closely behind. He wasn't finished. He began to fly very low, hugging the contour of the ground below him and trying to use the natural features to evade the other helicopter. This technique, Nap-of-the-Earth, while unsettling to others, was second-nature to Jesse, given the number of times he had used the strategy during his military service.

Tom looked on wearily. "Have you done this before?" Jesse nodded and then he saw what he wanted: a tree-lined stream. He aimed the Sikorsky straight for it. Flying below the tree line, Jesse skillfully guided the injured helicopter along, the other helicopter still in pursuit but unable to get a clear enough view to take a shot.

"So what's the plan?"

"Arequipa Airport is on the other side of this mountain. We're going to fly like this as long as we can, and when we get to the other side of the mountain, we're going to make a beeline straight for the airport. Hopefully by then we'll have radio access again and can get some help to get this guy off our tail."

Not much of a plan, Tom thought to himself, but he didn't have any better ideas. Instead, he walked to the back of the helicopter to check on their new guests.

"You folks okay?" They responded with a round of nods. "Good, now can you tell me what the hell is going on here?

We caught the light show from Misti, saw people popping out of the side of a goddam volcano, and now we have another helicopter trying to kill us."

Sam and Randall exchanged glances, and then looked back at Tom. No one said anything. Tom sighed. "Are you serious? We just pulled your assess out of the fire, and you're going to give me the silent treatment?"

More blank stares.

"Fine, I'll tell you my friend's theory." He pointed to Jesse in the cockpit. "He thinks there's a secret testing facility of some sort under that mountain, and something went terribly wrong. Is it a government facility? What are they testing, and what were you folks doing there?"

Randall saw the opening and jumped in. "He's right, it is a secret facility, but we don't have anything to do with it. We were researching archeological ruins inside the mountain and stumbled onto the facility."

"There's an archeological site in Misti?"

"Yes, and while we were there, we ran across these unsavory characters who weren't happy about us being near their facility. They took us prisoner and we had to escape."

"You were taken prisoner?"

"That's right. We escaped through the tunnel you saw," Randall answered.

"Jesse and I heard and saw an explosion. What happened?"

"An earthquake closed the opening before my dad could get out. He had to use an explosive charge to blow a hole in the side of the mountain to escape," Sam said.

Tom cocked his head to the side and, looking unsure about the story, nodded for them to continue.

"The guy you saw pop out of the mountain before us, is the head of the facility. He wasn't very happy that we got away. That's his helicopter and he doesn't want us sharing what we saw with the outside world," Randall said.

"What did you see?"

"Just a lot of fancy electronic equipment and soldiers toting weapons. That's the thing, the place looked like a state-of-the-art research facility, but we have no idea what they're testing. We were just in the wrong place at the wrong time. To tell you the truth, we were lucky to get out alive."

Randall searched Tom's reaction to see if he was buying his story. He knew that when, or if, they made it back to civilization safely, he would have to explain what had happened to the authorities, as well. He viewed Tom as a test case. If he could convince him, he might have a chance to convince the authorities. Of course, it would help that the University could confirm his research story. The only loose end would be George, and they would undoubtedly check to confirm each of their identities before letting anyone go.

"So you're all archaeologists?" Tom asked.

"All of us except George, there." Randall pointed at his injured friend. "He's an engineer, and we asked him to join us because of alleged electromagnetic interference associated with the site. None of us has the expertise in that field, and I have a colleague, Dr. Francisco Andrade, who has worked with George before. He recommended we contact him. Of course we found that the cause of the electromagnetic interference was the facility and whatever they're doing there."

Tom rubbed the back of his neck, "I guess I'll just have to take you at your word. The electromagnetic interference part makes sense. We tried calling the control tower on several occasions and couldn't get through until after we saw the light show and explosions."

Tom stared at Randall, then turned to look at Sam and the others.

"We barely got out of that tunnel before some major volcanic activity started. I could be wrong, but I think parts of the mountain started to collapse. There was magma coming up the tube we escaped through. My guess is that the geothermal activity down there destroyed most of the facility and whatever was generating the electromagnetic field. That would have been right around when you picked us up."

Randall watched as Tom studied him, still unsure if he believed the explanation. Small details aside, his story was mostly true and would explain most of what Tom and Jesse had seen and experienced.

Tom scratched his head and had a thoughtful look on his face. Randall could see him weighing the facts in his head.

"We've been through a lot, and I just want to get us all home," Randall said, placing a hand on Sam's shoulder.

Tom's posture softened. "What are your names?"

"That's my daughter, Samantha; this is Phil, he's a graduate student who works for me; and I'm Nick Randall. And your name is?" Randall stuck out his hand.

"I'm Tom Reinsdorf, with the United Stated Geological Survey. We're here helping the locals deal with this volcano. Jesse and I were taking one more pass over Misti when we saw you all. Good thing we happened along when we did." Tom extended his hand and the two men shook.

"Well, Tom, I'm grateful that you did come by and even more grateful that you were willing to stop and help us out. You guys really put yourselves in some serious danger to help out a bunch of strangers."

"Thanks, but we should probably hold off on any appreciation until we actually get you all back to safety."

"Tom, I need you up here!" Jesse called.

"Excuse me, folks." Tom walked up to the cockpit, leaving the group alone. "What's going on, Jesse?"

"We're almost to the other side of the mountain, and I've got some bad news. Looks like one of those shots we took must have hit a hydraulic line. We've been losing pressure, and I'm having a hard time keeping this bird under control."

"Are you saying we're not going to make it?"

"I'm not sure if we'll be able to fly all the way back to the airport, and even if we do, there's no way we'll be able to take any kind of evasive maneuvers. It'll take all I've got just to keep this thing in the air."

"So once we clear the mountain, we'll be sitting ducks for those guys to cut to pieces. Is that about right?" Tom asked. Jesse nodded. "How far are we from the airport?"

"About three miles out. You'd better tell them to strap in tight, we might have to make an emergency landing and hope for the best." Tom nodded and disappeared back into the main cabin of the helicopter.

The injured Sikorsky struggled forward, smoke pluming from the damaged hydraulic line in the rear tail structure. Not a light craft to begin with, it now handled like a brick with wings. Jesse struggled to keep control, but the added weight of the extra passengers only made flying that much more difficult. And to make things worse, they were quickly approaching the end of the curving, tree-covered path he had used to keep the other helicopter from getting a clear shot at them.

Tom addressed his passengers: "Everyone, if I give you the signal that we're going down, I need you all to hold onto something solid and brace yourselves for impact. Jesse will try his best to keep the helicopter under control, but he can only do so much." With this piece of news, glances were exchanged in the main cabin as grips tightened around anything that appeared solid.

As the Sikorsky cleared the tree line, Jesse glanced back to see how close his pursuers were. He immediately regretted looking, as the combat chopper popped immediately into view. Although Jesse couldn't see his face, he felt certain that the gunner in the opposing chopper had a wide grin on his face seeing the ailing Sikorsky in wide-open skies. The now familiar sound of fifty-millimeter rounds ripped the air around them and, once again, some found their mark. Jesse could hear screams from the back as another window exploded inward. The stick became heavier in his hands, and his worst fears were soon realized.

"We're going down!"

A wide ribbon of smoke trailed the Sikorsky as it plummeted from the sky. Barely able to control the descent, Jesse wrestled with the heavy stick, using both hands. As best he could, he aimed the flying block of metal for a soft piece of earth with tall grass, hoping the brush would cushion the impact of landing.

Bullets continued raining down on them; the combat helicopter gunman was having a field day with his wounded prey. Within minutes, the Sikorsky had lost almost all altitude.

"Brace for impact!" Jesse pulled up on the stick with all his might as the helicopter approached the ground. The effort paid off as the helicopter became buoyant for a fraction of a second before hitting the ground with a loud thud.

The Sikorsky had managed to maintain its structural integrity despite the hard landing, but it was damaged beyond repair. Jesse glanced back at the hovering combat helicopter, a ribbon of blood trickling down his face partially obscuring his view. "Is everyone alright?" Groans came first from the back, then slowly, responses from each passenger.

"We're okay," Phil answered.

Jesse wiped his forehead and removed his safety harness. Reaching under his seat, he removed his .45 caliber handgun. Glancing to the side, he saw a groggy Tom trying to shake off the effects of the crash landing. Turning his head in Jesse's direction, Tom's eyes grew wide at the site of the gun.

"I know it's not much, but it's something. Stay here with the rest of them." With that, Jesse popped the door hatch and moved outside the smoldering chopper.

Slowly making his way toward the back of the Sikorsky and using the fuselage as a shield between the other chopper and himself, Jesse took careful aim and fired several rounds at the hovering chopper. Almost instantly, the combat chopper pulled up and to the right and flew out of sight. Dumbfounded, Jesse lowered his weapon, looking at the smoking barrel. Tom's voice called him back to reality.

"Jesse, we're getting a call on the radio." Jesse opened the side door to hear the good news.

"November 2115, this is air traffic control, I repeat, has assistance arrived? Are you still with us?"

"Tower, this is November 2115, we're alright. Hostile aircraft has left the area." Glancing through the cracked windshield, for the first time Jesse noticed the three hovering helicopters, emblazoned with the Coat of Arms of the Fuerza Aérea del Perú.

"November 2115, good to hear your voice. We lost your transponder, are you on the ground?"

"Roger, tower, I don't think we'll be flying this thing back anytime soon. The help you sent is here, we'll see if we can reach them on the radio and hitch a ride home. Do you have a frequency for me?"

Jesse contacted the hovering military craft, one of which landed in a small clearing near the damaged Sikorsky. As he watched it land, he felt a large, strong hand land on his shoulder. Jesse turned to see Tom's grinning face.

"Nice job Jesse."

"Thanks Tom."

Chapter Thirty-Seven

Upon arriving at the airport, Randall and company were greeted by armed military personnel. Word of the strange occurrences at Misti had reached the upper levels of government, and the Peruvian army had been sent to speak to the Americans who were plucked from the side of the volcano only moments before the eruption. Along with the military contingency were several emergency medical personnel waiting to take George to the hospital and to treat the others for their various injuries.

"Where are you taking him?" Sam demanded.

"Your friend will be taken to Clinica Arequipa for treatment of his wounds," the soldier in charge responded.

"I'd like to go with him," Sam said.

"That will not be possible. All of you, this way," the soldier responded.

Sam looked over his shoulder at George as he was loaded onto the stretcher. He seemed out of it, the result of the pain medication.

"George, don't worry, we'll get over to see you as soon as we can," Sam said.

George raised his head slightly and cocked it to one side as if trying to catch her voice in his ear. Then he slumped back into the stretcher, disappearing through the sliding doors.

299

Sam, Phil and Randall slowly walked down the long corridor, flanked on all sides by armed and serious young men with short-cropped hair and large black weapons.

"Dr. R, I'm not so sure if I want to go on your next field assignment," Phil said, eliciting a chuckle from Randall.

"It's good to see you smile, Dad," Sam said, squeezing his hand.

"We'll be okay, Sweetheart."

They sat in the gray, non-descript room for close to an hour, the door guarded on the outside by the same soldiers who had escorted them in. Finally, the door swung in on its squeaky hinges, and a distinguished looking man with tinges of gray in his hair entered. He was tall and thin with a chiseled, worn face and he carried himself with an air of importance.

"I am Colonel Fernando Acarapi of the Ministerio de Defensa. I have some questions for you."

One by one, the Colonel questioned them, taking them separately into a smaller interrogation room. Their stories all matched, and upon returning them to the larger room, the Colonel left them once again, instructing the guards not to let them out of the room until he returned. Alone in the room, Sam looked at her father, who was standing off to the side, deep in thought. She recognized the look as the one her father wore whenever a difficult problem arose that required intense concentration on his part. Puzzled, she walked over to him.

"Penny for your thoughts?"

"Hey kiddo, just thinking about things."

"Like what?"

300

"We've all told Colonel Acarapi the same thing, but we left out the part about Vilcabamba. I think he bought it, largely because most of what we've said is true."

"But?"

"But the part of the story that he might be able to punch holes in is the part that involves George. I'm sure they're trying to reach Francisco, and he's not going to know anything about him. I should have thought about that before I told Tom that Francisco knows him. If I just had some way to contact him before they do, I'd feel a lot better about our chances of getting out of here instead of facing more interrogations with government officials."

The door to the interrogation room swung open once again and Colonel Acarapi strode in with a serious look on his face. Randall's heart immediately sank.

"Dr. Randall, I have news for you. I spoke with your friend Dr. Andrade at the University, a very friendly man, I must say. He confirmed that you and your friends were conducting fieldwork in the area as you explained. He also said that they lost contact with you many days ago and that he was very worried about you and asked me to tell you that he is very happy that you are alive."

Randall nodded, waiting breathlessly for the rest of the news.

"I also asked Dr. Andrade about your friend, Mr. Walker." Acarapi turned to look at Sam and then back again at Randall. "He spoke very highly of him and his fieldwork experience. Dr. Andrade asked how Mr. Walker was doing and was concerned for his well-being as well. I explained to him that Mr. Walker's injuries were not serious and that he is out of surgery. The doctors expect a full recovery in several weeks."

Randall exhaled slowly and felt a great weight lifted from his shoulders. Somehow Francisco had pulled it off.

"We're preparing to take you all back to the University. You must be exhausted and happy to have this ordeal behind you."

"We are, Colonel, and I appreciate you arranging transportation for us," Randall said, rubbing his tired eyes.

"Dr. Randall, you mentioned that this Dumond fellow oversaw this facility you stumbled upon. You mentioned that he was French. Is that correct?"

"Yes, that's right. I believe he's in the energy business, nuclear energy to be specific."

"Do you have any other information on him? Any proof to support your claims of what happened in this underground facility?"

Randall shook his head. "No, I don't."

"But he had mercenaries working for him and a base located in our jungles, not far from the mountain?" Acarapi asked.

"Yes. We were all at his base at one time. It's located somewhere in the area I showed you earlier. A rather large base in fact, with a helipad and multiple buildings. I'm sure if you sent a helicopter or airplanes to the area they would be able to spot it from the air."

A disdainful smile crept across Colonel Acarapi's face. "We did, Mr. Randall, and we could locate no such base."

Randall realized that he had to contain his emotions and curtail any response to the Colonel if they wanted to go home. Instead of speaking, he simply nodded his head while holding the Colonel's gaze.

"Wait here and I will have my men escort you to the vehicles that will take you back to your College."

"Colonel, what about George? Will we be able to see him soon?"

He nodded. "He should be released in a day or two, according to the doctors. Here is how you can contact him." The Colonel reached into his shirt pocket and produced a small note with the name and phone number of the hospital and room where George was recuperating.

Acarapi was good to his word. Several unmarked SUVs sat waiting outside the building, ready to take them back to the college.

The ride to the University was uneventful, and Randall was grateful for this small bit of fortune. Phil slept while Randall looked out the window, once again contemplating all that had happened. Sam asked quietly, "Are you okay, Dad?"

Randall looked away from the window, smiled, and took his daughter's hand. "I am now. How are you?"

"I'm good, glad we're heading back home soon."

"Me, too."

"But?"

"I'm just wondering how Francisco was able to convince the army that he knew George and had worked with him before. I always knew he was sharp, but this one takes the cake." Randall glanced over to see a crooked smile on his daughter's face. "What?"

"Remember when you were spinning your yarn for Tom in the helicopter?" Sam asked.

Randall's brow furrowed.

"I texted Francisco about George and told him to be ready for a call."

Randall smiled and kissed his daughter on the forehead. "That's my girl."

Chapter Thirty-Eight

At the University, Francisco was waiting for them as the Escalade pulled up in front of the administration building. Randall could see him standing with his hands folded behind his back, the top button of his shirt undone, and his tie loose. Randall waived as they pulled up; Francisco smiled back. As the door of the SUV opened and Randall exited, Francisco walked up to him.

"Good to see you back safely, old friend."

"Glad to be back. Did you hear about Mike?"

Francisco nodded slowly, closing his eyes as he did. "I was very sorry to hear about him. He was a fine young man."

Randall nodded in agreement, "Did you contact his mother?"

"I did."

"How is she?"

"My friend, she has taken the news as well as she could. As well as any of us could take such news." Francisco put his hand on his friend's shoulder. "I am very sorry for your loss, but you cannot blame yourself. These men who accosted you were trained killers, and I'm shocked that Monica was working with them." Randall could hear the sincerity in his friend's voice, and it offered him some comfort.

"I'll call Mike's mother myself as soon as I can and make arrangements to pay my respects."

As the two men spoke, Sam slipped out of the SUV and Phil followed closely behind her. They slowly came up by Randall's side, not wanting to interrupt the two of them.

"Sam, I'm so happy that you're alright!" Francisco said, giving her a big squeeze. "You too, Phil," this time extending his hand to Randall's helper.

"I'm sure you're all exhausted, why don't we go into the lounge? We'll find something for you to eat and drink. Come!" Francisco put his arm around Sam and led her and the others into the college's administration building. It was Saturday, and the campus was relatively quiet.

The faculty lounge was beautifully appointed. Large, overstuffed chairs and couches were arranged to create intimate meeting spaces. Beautiful local art hung from the walls, and several flat screen televisions were hung strategically to allow resting faculty to watch while they ate or sat in the comfortable seating. Upon entering the lounge, Phil spied the couches and made a beeline for them.

Seeing Phil speed for a sofa, Sam followed, taking the couch opposite him. Falling into the soft padding she closed her eyes. The exhaustion was finally hitting her hard, and as she sat, it was clear that she wouldn't be able to get back up without some assistance. Randall and Francisco walked over to two overstuffed chairs set at ninety-degree angles to each other. Francisco waited until Randall sat before sitting himself.

"Tell me everything. What did you find?"

Francisco was sitting on the edge of his seat, leaning forward in anticipation. Randall could see the excitement in his eyes. He looked like a small child waiting to see what kind of goodies his parents had gotten him for his birthday.

"It was real, Francisco. Vilcabamba was enormous, and the intricate artwork was incredible."

Randall went on to tell his friend about the details of the underground city, and their incessant battles with Dumond, who, Randall explained, managed to escape from the volcano before it erupted. This fact seemed to unsettle Francisco, who withdrew into his thoughts after Randall revealed it. However, his mood quickly brightened.

"And the inhabitants of Vilcabamba, did you meet them?"

Randall sat back into his chair, a pensive look on his face.

"I'm not sure. I think I did, but it might have just been a dream." Randall went on to explain his meeting with the creatures but how he woke up in the cavern with a lump on his head and no proof in hand.

Francisco waived his hand in disregard, "It doesn't matter, the discovery of Vilcabamba will still change the way the world looks at human history. You encountered an ancient underground city with technology beyond anything we would expect from the period. You now have concrete proof to support your ideas and challenge prevailing theories! Once we publish our findings, everyone will want to fund our research!" Francisco was on a roll now, his exuberance overflowing his bucket of containment. Randall hated to burst his balloon, but he had no choice. He had to bring his dear friend back to earth.

"There's just one problem, old buddy. We don't have a shred of evidence."

The expression on Francisco's face morphed once again, this time into a frown. Deflated, he plopped back down into the chair.

"No proof at all? How could this have happened?" Francisco stood up and began pacing the room. "I realize the eruption probably destroyed or concealed most of the city, but surely some artifacts have survived. Once the magma cools we can launch another expedition, this time with armed escorts. We can uncover the remains of the ruins and bring back proof!" Francisco thrust a finger into the air to emphasize the point. Glancing down at Randall, he noticed his friend shaking his head from side to side.

"It's gone, Francisco. There's no way anything survived the eruption and the lava flow. Besides, without any proof, who's going to support us?"

Randall watched as Francisco sat back into his chair, mouth hanging open for a few seconds. For a moment, he seemed ready to say something, but then caught himself and sat back once again. His eyes were locked on a section of floor directly in front of him, his shoulders sagging under the unseen burden that was suddenly thrust upon them. Randall stole a quick glance in the direction of Sam and Phil. Sam was now laying on the couch, while Phil lay motionless on the sofa next to her. Both were fast asleep. It was the first peaceful moment they had had in some time and Randall had no desire to disturb either of them. He turned back to face his friend.

"Francisco, I know this must come as a blow, but I'm okay with it. I now know that my theories aren't crazy and, more importantly, I got Sam back.

Randall could tell his old friend was still in shock, "Are you alright?"

With a slow determination, Francisco pushed himself back into his seat, sitting upright. His eyes brightened, and he nodded, appearing to be having a silent conversation with himself. He finally looked back to Randall.

"Whatever happens from here, we will confront it together, my friend. We have been through rough times before, yes?"

Randall smiled and nodded to Francisco. "We certainly have."

Francisco sat back in his chair and propped his chin on his right hand. Randall could see that he was deep in thought. Finally he turned to Randall. "We still have unspent funding from your benefactor. His most recent donation was deposited about a week ago, and it was substantial. Perhaps your research should turn in another direction."

"Maybe, but I'm not sure I want to use any more funding that came from Francis Dumond."

"Well, this is a matter for us to discuss later. In the meantime, I'm sure you must be hungry. I see Sam and Phil have decided that sleep is more important than food at this time, but would you like something? Maybe a strong drink?" His mouth drew into a big smile as he finished the sentence.

"Yes to both, especially the drink. Do you have a blanket for Sam and Phil?"

"Of course! I will retrieve them, along with that drink. While I'm at it, I think I'll fetch something for myself!" Francisco shot out of the chair theatrically and walked briskly to the door. As it closed slowly on its hinges, Randall stood and walked over to his sleeping daughter. Seeing her asleep on the couch brought back warm memories from a time long ago. Sitting down gently next to her, he brushed her hair back from her face and gave her a small kiss on the head, just as he had done when she was small. As he stood back up, he felt a rush of blood to his head and became dizzy. The lack of sleep and physical exhaustion had finally caught up with him.

His body tired and battered, Randall walked slowly and carefully back to the chair he had occupied and sat down heavily on the cushion. It was a very soft and comfortable chair, he thought as he slowly found himself losing consciousness. "Very comfortable indeed." The words seemed to float into space as Dr. Nicholas Randall drifted off to sleep.

Did you enjoy the story?

Please consider leaving a review: Click Here

The Nick Randall Series by Robert Rapoza In Order

By Robert Rapoza

The Lost Tribe

The Bermuda Connection

(The Bermuda Connection excerpt starts on next page)

The Devil's Heart

Coming Spring 2022

Washington's Ghost

THE BERMUDA CONNECTION

ROBERT RAPOZA

THE LOST TRIBE

Chapter One

August 17, 3:02 A.M.
Hamilton, Bermuda

Jamie Edmunds knew something wasn't right. The sensation of a million microscopic feet traversing her skin was an omen of something terrible about to happen.

She lay in her bed, staring at the ceiling of her second story apartment. The sound of her heart beating in her chest echoed through her mind like a jackhammer. The darkness of her room interrupted only by the bright glow from her bedside alarm clock. She stole a glance. 3:02 a.m. The coming day would be hell.

She brushed her long brown hair behind her ears and rolled onto her side, hoping a new sleeping position would help. It didn't. Everyone she knew was asleep at this late hour. Except her. She was completely alone. Isolated in her bedroom away from the rest of the world.

She forced her eyes closed, and laid there in her nightshirt, willing herself to sleep. Her body shivered, and she pulled the flower-patterned sheets and blanket up to her chin. But it wasn't the cold causing her body to tremble. It was fear. Memories came flooding back of past nights when she couldn't sleep, and she remembered what happened next. Dread washed over Jamie like a wave smothering her in darkness.

The trembling grew worse. Her breathing fast and shallow.

There's something in my room.

The words popped into Jamie's mind. She tried to dismiss the thought as an overactive imagination.

I'm alone in my bedroom, I'm alone in my bedroom.

No matter how many times she repeated it, the words rang empty. The sense that someone, or something, was nearby overwhelmed her. She didn't want to look but had to know. She tilted her head to the side and saw ... nothing. Her eyes drooped shut and she breathed a sigh of relief.

A soft clicking noise rose from the corner. Jamie's eyes popped open. Her muscles tensed as terror ripped through her. Sheets of perspiration trickled down her face and chest, her nightshirt clinging to her wet body. She slowly turned her head toward the sound. A figure lurked by her dresser, masked by the darkness that enveloped the room. It moved slowly, as if studying her from a distance. She sobbed.

No, please. Not again!

More movement, this time steady, calculated. The being moved from the shadows until it stood over her, its translucent skin gleaming in the moonlight. It peered at her with cold, dead eyes. She tried to scream but couldn't. The being controlled her now, her body under its influence. It moved closer, its bald, mouthless head tilted to one side as it examined her.

It drew back the sheets in a slow, mechanical fashion, exposing her nightshirt-clad body. It reached for her with long, slender, fingers. She wanted to cry, but tears wouldn't come. The creature wouldn't allow them. The fingers inched menacingly closer to her.

❦

Nick Randall sat upright in his bed, torrents of sweat cascaded down his body. Disoriented, he grabbed the bat he kept propped against the wall. His trembling hands bumped the nightstand. The bedside light nearly crashed to the ground, wobbling before settling again. He gripped the bat tightly, and scanned the room, ready to strike the creature.

He looked toward the corner where he had first seen it. Nothing there. His eyes darted around, adrenaline coursing through his body. He twitched at every sound. Slowly, sanity returned, and he realized it had only been a nightmare. He set the bat across his lap.

Why do I keep having this dream and why am I always the same woman?

His pulse quickened at the thought of being alone in the apartment with the creature. In the dream, he had felt completely powerless and isolated, unable to keep the being at bay. He shivered at the thought of being violated by it. A mixture of despair and anger welled inside of him as he balled his fists.

He glanced at the clock: 3:05 a.m. He fell backward onto his bed, gulping large breaths. His heart pounded so hard it felt like it would rip free of him. There would be no more sleeping tonight. Fear would keep him from returning to the land of dreams.

Randall thought back to when these episodes had begun. The nightmares had started a couple of weeks after his trip to the jungles of Peru, searching for the lost city of

Vilcabamba. The odd physical attributes of the tribe that led him to the ruins—enlarged heads with bulging eyes—was a minor footnote compared to the discovery of Vilcabamba … and its otherworldly inhabitants.

The discovery of the lost city had changed the way he viewed archaeology. Sadly, the eruption of El Misti, the volcano that powered Vilcabamba, had destroyed any proof of his discovery, and brought the entire episode to an end. Or so he had thought. The experience was now influencing his dreams.

Can this really be happening?

Randall shook his head. They were only nightmares. He sat on the edge of his king-size bed and glanced at the side where his wife Ann used to sleep. He wished she was with him, by his side, her warmth comforting him. His fear was suddenly replaced with deep sadness and longing. He turned to face the window and dropped his head into his hands.

What the hell is happening to me? Am I losing it?

He forced himself to his feet, feeling the hard wood floor beneath him. Shivering, he slid on his lamb-wool slippers and reached for his robe. He didn't dare look at the thermometer; he knew that it wasn't the temperature causing him to tremble.

He stumbled over to his desk, plopped down in his black leather chair, and flicked on his desk lamp. The sudden brightness caused him to wince. He sat motionless while his eyes adjusted, unsure of what to do next. Pressing the power button of his computer, he heard the hard drive whine to life. Research. That was the solution to his problem. He needed to learn why he was having these terrible dreams and needed coffee. Lots of it.

Chapter Two

August 17, 3:32 A.M.
Arlington, Virginia

Dr. Jacob Taylor swiped the hijacked keycard through the reader. The red denied button glowed.

Just relax and do it again. Slowly this time.

He wiped the sweat from his temple using the back of his hand and took a deep breath. This time the green access button lit, and the electronic lock popped open, allowing him access to his company's restricted archives. He grimaced at the sound of the lock disengaging. It might as well have been a gunshot. He glanced over his shoulder. No one there.

He didn't have clearance to be in this section of the archives. If he was caught here, he'd never see the light day again, but he needed to know what his company was planning to do with his research. He and his research partner, John Randall, had worked too hard and for too long to be shut out now.

The problems had started months ago. First, there were unannounced visits by military personnel to their lab at Alpha Genetics. They had questioned Jacob and John about the memory blocking serum they were creating. Then came the unexplained removal of clearance to certain areas within the lab. Finally, they lost oversight of their research, the supervising scientist, Dr. Monroe, assuming full control over the project.

It had become clear to Jacob that the company had plans for their serum, but those plans didn't include him. He couldn't let that happen. He had to find out why he had been blackballed and what role the military had played in these developments.

The company had spent hundreds of thousands of dollars to maintain secrecy, installing multiple layers of security to protect this information. As a result, Jacob had been forced to liberate Dr. Monroe's security badge to access the archives.

He had chosen the evening shift, hoping that whoever monitored the security cameras was either dozing off, or simply didn't realize who was allowed there. From his brief encounters with the muscle-headed security guards, they considered each scientist to be just another lab coat. If he didn't look directly into the cameras, there was an excellent chance, no one would be able to identify him. He hoped.

He skulked over to the main workstation, taking a seat in front of the monitor. He slid Dr. Monroe's badge into the computer's card reader. The monitor blinked to life, a single green box on the screen asking for a password.

A creaking sound came from the door. Jacob popped up from the seat, and dove behind the desk, which partially shielded him from view. He held his breath, pressing his body against the metal file drawers to minimize his exposed profile.

He waited. Nothing.

Slowly, he slid along the side of the desk and peeked around the corner toward the door. No one was there. His body fell slack, his head pounding with each heartbeat.

He returned to the monitor and typed Dr. Monroe's password into the system. He had attained it from Julie, one of the technicians, telling her he was in hot water with Monroe. He had lied, saying he couldn't find a file on his computer and needed to pull it from the lead researcher's system. At first, she had been hesitant, so Jacob had turned on the charm. The rumor had been that Julie had a thing for Jacob. The rumor had been true. A combination of Monroe's legendary temper and Jacob's good looks had done the trick.

She had even told Jacob about Monroe's secondary password, explaining that the security system employed a dual layer of encryption.

Jacob hit enter and a message blinked on the screen.

Password does not match profile. Security protocol engaged.

To his horror, a timer appeared on the monitor. It was counting down from fifteen seconds.

What did I do?

His mind went blank.

The timer counted down, *14, 13, 12…*

Jacob pulled a strip of paper from his pocket, re-reading the password. It matched what he had entered.

10, 9, 8…

He stared at the paper, then the screen.

It's case sensitive!

Jacob re-typed the password, one button at a time.

5, 4, 3…

He hit enter. The timer froze at 2.

He nearly cried when the screen blinked, granting him access to the archives.

He scanned the folders on the hard drive, finally finding the encrypted file for his research.

He clicked on it.

Another password request.

He carefully typed Monroe's secondary password, this time making certain he made no errors.

I hope this is right.

He said a silent prayer and hit enter.

The system went quiet, a string of repeating dots filling the center of the screen.

Oh crap, what now?

The file popped open, revealing multiple documents.

Jacob searched the list of files, carefully choosing which to open and read. After twenty panic filled minutes of reviewing documents — his heart stopped each time he heard a sound — he found what he was looking for.

Jacob pulled a flash drive from his coat pocket and inserted it into the USB port, copying the files he wanted. Finished, he unplugged the drive and stashed it back into his pocket. Next, he removed Monroe's card from the computer.

I've got to get the hell out of here!

He crept toward the door. His footsteps sounded like thunderclaps.

Jesus, someone's going to hear me!

He pressed his ear to the door, straining to hear if there was noise on the other side. The only sound was his deep and shallow breathing. He cracked open the door and looked through.

All clear.

He pushed it open, wincing as it creaked on its hinges. Finally satisfied that no one was in the hallway, he slid out of the archives.

Both terrified and exhilarated, Jacob allowed his imagination to run wild knowing that what he had done here today was worthy of a Robert Ludlum novel. But he wasn't home free yet. He still needed to escape the building and get somewhere safe to read the contents of the flash drive. He took the stairs down to the parking level, occasionally glancing upward to make sure he wasn't being followed.

Finally reaching level P4, he paused, placing his hand on the metal handle. It was icy in his grip, his fear amplifying every sensation. He pushed the door open and strode into the garage, trying his best to appear natural.

Jacob walked briskly through the gray concrete parking structure, the sound of his footfalls the only thing to keep him company.

Just a little farther and I'm home free.

He reached into his pocket and fumbled his keys, nearly dropping them. His hands shook violently, his legs like jelly. It was hard to walk, but he willed himself forward.

"Working late today, Dr. Taylor?"

Jacob froze a moment, then spun on his heel to face the voice that had addressed him. Three men in suits stood several feet from him. The one in the middle wore a sickening grin. He was flanked by two larger men. They were all armed.

"Um, yes … just wrapping up a project," Jacob's voice cracked.

"I believe you have something that doesn't belong to you."

"What do you mean?"

"We can do this the easy way or the hard way. Either way, you're not leaving with that drive."

"Wait, I can explain…"

Buy the Bermuda Connection

Made in United States
Troutdale, OR
08/09/2023

11942030R00184